A Cribbean Summer

Tricia Lee

A Wings ePress, Inc.
Contemporary Romance Novel

Wings ePress, Inc.

Edited by: Lorraine Stephens
Copy Edited by: Karen Babcock
Senior Editor: Anita York
Executive Editor: Lorraine Stephens
Cover Artist: Christine Poe

Wings ePress Books
www.wingsepress.com

Copyright © 2007 by Patricia C. Hernández
ISBN-13: 978-1-59705-814-8
ISBN-10: 1-59709-814-9-

Published In the United States Of America

Wings ePress Inc.
3000 N. Rock Road
Newton, KS 67114

What They Are Saying About
A Caribbean Summer

"That was the fastest I ever read a book. I like how you keep the reader trying to figure out what is really going on with everyone."

—Sandi Braudrick,
a firefighter who loves to read

"*A Caribbean Summer* was a very entertaining book to read. I got caught up in the story, and found it hard to put down."

—Cheri Smith,
columnist for Caney/Soldier Creek Community,
The Madill Record

Dedication

For Jackie C. H. and Katherine C. T. Many thanks to Cindy S. who typed my handwritten manuscript; to Barbara and Basie of the Boogie Brown Band for allowing the use of their name; to D.M., L. H., Kathryn B., and Cheri S. for reading the early drafts; to Sandi B. for her critique; and to Andrea Z. whose remarks made it all worthwhile.

* * *

Prologue

Headline and excerpt from The Palmaltas News:

MARISOL HOTEL TYCOON
STILL MISSING AFTER FOUR WEEKS

The family of Peter J. Harris has issued a statement to the media pleading for help and information in locating the missing heir to the Harris Hotel chain fortune. Mr. Harris, age thirty-five, represents his family in Palmaltas as the CEO of the Marisol Hotel, which was established here by his late father P. D. Harris, an American hotel entrepreneur. His mother, Alma Gutiérrez Harris, who died five years ago, was a notable figure in Palmaltas religious charities.

Mr. Harris, a native Palmaltan born and raised on the island, is a familiar figure at prominent social events. His sudden disappearance four weeks ago on April 21 left his family and colleagues stunned.

The police have stated that there is no indication that Mr. Harris left the island either by air or by sea. His sister states that none of his personal belongings is missing. His suite in the Harris mansion, which is across the street from the Marisol Hotel, appears just as it did on the day before his disappearance. The police have continuously combed the island, and, as yet, have found no trace of the missing billionaire.

Both family and officials deny that anyone has contacted them regarding a ransom. "He just seems to have disappeared into thin air," cried his sister, Lisa Harris Rivera.

However, his fiancée, the stunning Marla Hunter, director of a New York modeling agency, stated that she is positive that Peter will return soon. "He is much too responsible to abandon his business, his family, and especially me," she declared with confidence yesterday at a press conference.

Palmaltas resort area

A tanned, muscular man with short-cropped, silvery hair dressed in ragged shorts, a white short-sleeved shirt, and tennis shoes without socks walked along the beach that separated a line of hotels and restaurants from the Caribbean Sea. He took his time, inhaling and enjoying the salty sea air. In a casual, carefree manner he walked around the sunbathers, tourists who ignored him or turned up their noses at him. He didn't care. He barely noticed them himself. When he reached the Marisol Hotel beach, he sauntered over to his brother's boat concession where the hotel guests were already clamoring for Amos' attention. He waved at Amos who grinned back at him and said, "Fishing again, bro?"

He nodded yes and went inside the little portable building that proclaimed *Amos Soto, Glass-Bottom Boat Rides and Other Activities* on the outdoor sign. He grinned at how industrious his brother was and how he had become the seemingly lazy brother. Amos was industrious while he spent his days fishing with his new friend. At least that was the way their lives would appear to casual observers. He grabbed the fishing gear that he stowed in the concession and started to head out the door for the pier that marked the boundary between the Marisol beach and the condo beach on the other side.

At that moment Amos stepped inside the concession.

"You're up mighty early," he said.

"Yeah, but just in case one of them or both show up on the beach this morning, I want to be in position."

"You really think she would get up this early?"

He laughed. "I doubt it, Amos. However, if she is involved in this thing with him then I want to catch her at it."

"Trust me, she is involved. At least, you've got yourself a good cover, bro."

His brother laughed. "You were the one who dared me to do this."

"Yes, and I still think you can pull it off. They don't seem to care about what they say in front of tourists or Marisol employees like me."

"That in itself indicates reckless danger."

Amos laughed and said, "You're safe enough here but get yourself in place just in case."

His brother laughed, too, and waving good-bye headed for the pier to wait for his new fishing buddy.

Telephone conversation between Palmaltas and Omaha, Nebraska:

"So, Amy, how about it? Can you come to my wedding? Surely school will be out then."

Stunned by the invitation that her best friend had just given her, Amy managed to say, "Uh yes, school will be out May twenty-nine."

"Great! Then do you think you could fly here Wednesday, June fifth?"

"Oh, Donna, you know I would love to, but there's no way I can afford a trip to Palmaltas."

"My dear, I don't expect you to pay. We, David and I, are offering you an all-expense trip."

"Why-why?" Amy sputtered. She had never met David Díaz. Why would he be so generous, she wondered.

"Why are we doing this? You have to ask? Other than the fact that you are my closest friend, I-uh, well, I do have an ulterior motive."

"Aha," exclaimed Amy, although she was puzzled more than ever.

"You're fond of Jeremy, aren't you?"

"Of course I am. I love that little boy." Amy felt that Donna's question had veered the conversation off track. Donna knew how fond she was of her son. There could be no ulterior motive in that fact.

"Then I have a proposition for you," she said.

"Donna, just tell me what's going on. Get to the point."

"My honeymoon, you little idiot. That's what. I need someone, someone I trust, to care for Jeremy for two weeks while David and I island-hop around the Caribbean. Jeremy adores you and you haven't seen him in two years. Are you game?"

Amy laughed. "Am I game? Oh Donna, I would love to look after Jeremy. Two weeks in Palmaltas with Jeremy? What a dream!"

"Only you, Amy, would consider spending time with a six-year-old a dream."

"But I love children, especially Jeremy."

"And well you should, Miss Dedicated School Teacher."

"Uh, Donna, I have a silly question to ask."

"Ask anything."

"Is-is there bougainvillea in Palmaltas?"

"Well, of course. Every tropical bloom you can imagine abounds here. Why do you ask?"

"Because it's always been my dream to go someplace exotic that has brilliant bougainvillea. So many of the books that I read describe it and I want so much to see some."

"You do have strange dreams. Aren't there any men in any of those dreams?"

"I-I suppose so but you know how unlucky I am with the men I fall in love with."

"Well, my first husband wasn't the cream of the crop but David, however, is literally Prince Charming."

"And I am so happy for you."

"I know you are, honey. So come to the wedding, take care of Jeremy, and, who knows, maybe you'll meet someone. The men here are gorgeous."

"Just don't fix me up with anyone. Blind dates are my worst disaster. If I meet someone, it has to be completely natural."

Donna laughed. "As cute as you are, with that lush dark brown hair and brown eyes, all you have to do is prance around in a bikini when you take Jeremy to the beach, which will be everyday, by the way, and hordes of men will descend upon you."

"That sounds very intimidating. Just living in luxury in Palmaltas with Jeremy for two weeks is more than I could ask for. Uh, you do live in luxury, don't you?" Amy joked.

"Just wait until you see my condo. But I'll omit any descriptions. David gave me carte blanche to decorate however I wished. I doubt if your wildest imagination could conjure my décor."

"Wow, then I can't wait to see it."

"Oh say, have you read about our current mystery?"

"No, I don't think so. Palmaltas news doesn't make it to Omaha."

"Too bad. We have a missing billionaire. He's handsome, dashing, and a friend of David's. I really like the guy and I was hoping that you two would click."

"What? You mean you were planning to fix me up with someone? With a dashing billionaire? Donna, get real!"

"Well, if he doesn't show up soon, you won't have to worry about meeting him."

"What do you mean by missing? Has he been kidnapped? I mean, if he's so rich?"

"We don't know. Nobody does. He just simply vanished about four weeks ago. Personally, I think he wanted to get away from his fiancée, a highfalutin' society dame from New York."

"Highfalutin'? Dame? That's the kind of language you speak nowadays?"

"No, I guess it sounds silly but it fits her."

"Are you telling me that you want to fix me up with a man who is already engaged?" Amy asked, slightly indignant.

"Well, she is a bitch and Peter is rather a doll."

"I take it that Peter is your missing billionaire."

"Oh, yes."

"Personally, Jeremy and the bougainvillea are all I want."

"Goodness, what a nut you are. By the way, there are some books available about Palmaltas. Be sure and read them to familiarize yourself with the island's background, history, and culture."

"My reading slips during the school year but I'll try to find time to read some before I leave."

Donna gave her the necessary details for the trip. Amy couldn't believe that in two and a half weeks she would be flying to the Caribbean. She was grateful that she had had the foresight to acquire a passport when she graduated from college. At age twenty-eight this would be her first time to use it.

After hanging up, Amy sat back, stunned, enthralled, and invigorated. She thought back to the beginning of her friendship with Donna. They had been college roommates during their freshman and sophomore years. At the beginning of their junior year Donna married Paul Risot and became pregnant, whereupon Paul immediately abandoned her. She asked Amy to move into her apartment with her and help her with the baby. Amy did so and together they cared for Jeremy and both finished college. Donna became an executive assistant and Amy, a first grade teacher. Jeremy was the cutest, most lovable little boy that Amy had ever seen. He inherited his dark good looks from his father and his friendly, outgoing personality from his mother. Amy dearly loved that little boy.

Then two years ago, Donna and Jeremy went to Palmaltas, an island in the Caribbean, for a short vacation. While there she met and fell in love with David Díaz, a local restaurateur who offered her a secretarial position. She accepted and she and Jeremy stayed on the island. Now she and David were planning an island wedding.

Amy felt that to fall in love on a tropical island and live there happily ever after seemed an impossible dream. Yet, Donna had accomplished it. And now she was going to spend two weeks in Palmaltas. No, counting arrival, rehearsal and wedding days, it would be two and a half weeks! And with all expenses paid plus cute little Jeremy, Caribbean beaches, and bougainvillea. What more could she want?

Well, she thought to herself, not a missing dashing billionaire, no matter what Donna said. No, she definitely didn't want that.

One

Amos was getting ready to fry an egg for his breakfast when his brother walked through the small living room to the front door of the cabin.

"Where are you going at this hour, bro?" asked Amos.

"I'm going over to the condo to discuss doing a favor for Daniel."

Amos burst out laughing. "You don't fool me, bro, you're doing yourself a favor."

His brother smiled back. "Well, I want to check out Saint Amy to see if she really is all that she's cracked up to be and if my new bud is telling tall tales about her."

"But why this early? You've got plenty of time. I thought you said that she wasn't scheduled to arrive until later in the day."

"I know but I want to make sure that Ossie won't say anything."

"He won't. Ossie can be trusted. He knows our history and our family. Besides, he's the one who gave me the idea for this whole thing."

"Yeah, but he doesn't know that."

Amos grinned, shook his head, and waved him out the door.

~ * ~

As the plane circled Palmaltas, which was west of Jamaica and south of the Caymans, Amy's window seat gave her a breathtaking view of the island. Her eyes absorbed as much as possible. First, she gazed over green flora, pink beaches, pounding surf on southern cliffs, a brief rooftop view of what appeared to be a congested city on the western side. Then her gaze shifted to white clouds perched atop a cluster of small mountains, followed by what must be the U.S. military base. On the eastern end there was another rooftop view of, presumably, the elegant resort area where Donna and Jeremy lived. Donna had sent her a tourist brochure of the island along with her own vivid comments, so Amy would know what to look for as the plane encircled the island. But nothing that she had read had prepared her for the close-up beauty of the Caribbean Sea. While descending, the blue of the water changed intermittently to turquoise to indigo to even violet with glittering rays of sunshine dancing on the shimmering waves. All quite overwhelming for someone used to the plains of Nebraska, she thought. Her heart leaped into her throat as she anticipated the descent onto the small airfield next to the Palmaltas Airport.

She quickly went through customs, having nothing to declare, not that any of the officials seemed interested anyway. Entering the open lounge area where tropical plants with pleasing fragrances awaited the incoming visitors, Amy expected to see Donna rush toward her with an affectionate greeting. Donna was nowhere in sight.

Instead, a rather scruffy-looking, but well-built man dressed in cut-off, raggedy jeans and a dingy-white, short-sleeved shirt was holding a placard, which said, "Welcome, Amy Ann." Did he mean her? Her full name was Amethyst Elizabeth Andrews but Donna sometimes called her Amy Ann. Surely there were no other passengers on her flight with that name. She was not surprised that Donna had risen in social stature to be able to provide a personal chauffeur for a wedding guest but Amy thought she could have provided someone who looked more reputable than this one.

She approached him with caution and as she drew closer she noticed he had the most incredible pale blue eyes she had ever seen.

His features were rugged yet pleasant although he needed a shave. He was muscular, tanned, and obviously quite fit. His most notable features were close-cropped silver hair that she imagined had been bleached by spending a lot of time in the sun and those pale blue eyes. She had never seen anyone with such coloring before and she was embarrassed to find herself staring intently at him. He emanated a masculinity that suddenly made her feel uncomfortable, as if he were studying her with disdain. She shook herself slightly and proceeded toward him with her head held high, trying to project confidence.

She asked him if he represented Donna Risot or David Díaz.

"Yes, ma'am," he replied in a deep, forceful voice that inexplicably sent shivers down her spine. "If you are Amy Ann, then please follow me. We will first collect your luggage."

Figuring that Donna knew what she was doing and would never have sent anyone disreputable to pick her up, she followed him. She noticed that the other passengers on her flight were lining up for hotel limousines and that made her feel good and slightly superior. They were tourists; she was a guest. Perhaps her feelings were a little silly, but the idea of a personal chauffeur was making her giddy, no matter that the "chauffeur" looked like he belonged on the beach or out on a fishing boat.

He led her to a long, black limousine, which impressed Amy immensely. To think that this beachcomber-looking person was actually attached to such a mode of transportation was astonishing. When they reached the limousine he stopped and, muscles rippling, opened the backseat door for her. He gave her a sardonic grin as she slithered onto a padded leather seat of luxurious comfort. Her giddiness was giving way to simply being awestruck. He put her bags in the trunk, then entered the vehicle on the driver's side and pulled away from the curb. She glanced around at the passing scenery where to her left was the splendid Palmaltas Hilton, to the right, tall condominiums with, Donna had told her, the U.S. military base beyond. As they passed the Hilton, smaller hotels cropped up with condominiums between. Just as they reached the famous Marisol Hotel, the road turned right but the chauffeur made a sharp turn to the left onto a private driveway, which led beyond the Marisol to a very tall condominium.

He drove up to it, hopped out, smiled smugly, and opened her door.

She didn't know why, but she still felt there was something in his attitude that seemed rather condescending. Inexplicably he made her feel uncomfortable. At least, she thought, she wouldn't have to deal with him anymore.

"Here you are, Miss Amy Ann," he said pronouncing her name emphatically. "I hope you enjoy your stay in Palmaltas. If you would like a tour of the island, the condo management provides guides who would be happy to show you around."

"Oh, thank you. How would I get in touch with them?" She was certain that she didn't want this scruffy, superior-acting individual to take her anywhere. She didn't know why, but he was making her nervous with his pale blue eyes seeming to pierce right through her.

"There is an office just off the foyer. Ask for Daniel. He's the best."

"Why, thank you, I will do just that," she said, relieved that he had recommended someone other than himself. With more confidence than she felt, she gave him her brightest smile and shook his hand while giving him a five-dollar tip.

He gave her a sly smile and pocketed the money. Then he handed her bags over to a uniformed doorman who nodded to him but said nothing. Nonetheless, there seemed to be some kind of interplay between the two men and Amy wondered if she was the cause. Shaking this ridiculous assumption aside, she turned to the doorman who bowed and asked her to follow him. Obviously, he was expecting her.

From a chauffeur to a doorman, what next would she encounter, she wondered. She already felt pampered, in spite of the enigmatic chauffeur, and she had yet to see Donna.

The doorman was older than the chauffeur and had graying hair. However, he was very handsome and very courteous. Was this a ploy on Donna's part to introduce her immediately to two handsome Palmaltans? Surely Donna didn't think she would be interested in a scruffy, almost rude chauffeur or a doorman. But then, she thought, wasn't that the stuff from which romance novels were made? And if

Donna was anything, she was a romanticist. But Amy's imagination was running away with her. These were the employees of Donna's condo. She would have met them anyway.

The doorman accompanied her to the fourth floor, which in Nebraska would have been the fifth floor. Palmaltans, for some reason, didn't count the ground floor, she assumed. He rang the bell to Donna's apartment. The door opened to the exuberant greeting that Amy had expected at the airport.

Donna grabbed her and gave her a bear hug and swung her around although Amy, at five feet four inches, was only an inch shorter than her friend. Donna's brownish-blonde hair was coifed into a simple pageboy hairdo that somehow managed to appear quite elegant. She was dressed in a silk lounging pants outfit with a flowery print. Amy was soon to learn that Donna loved vivid tropical prints.

Finally releasing her, Donna turned to the doorman and said, "Thank you, Ossie, for your help."

He smiled, bowed, and left.

"Aren't you going to give him a tip?" Amy asked.

"Oh no," said Donna. "He would be insulted. He's a very dear friend. All of the condo employees are as you will find out."

"But I gave the chauffeur a tip and he took it," explained Amy.

"What? Daniel took a tip? I can't believe he would do that. He's such a doll, don't you think?"

"Oh, the chauffeur wasn't Daniel. He was some beach bum kind of guy who was, well, I wouldn't call him rude but he-he seemed out of place in that limousine."

"Now that's just weird. Daniel promised us he would take very good care of you. I'll have to talk to him about that."

"Oh, don't worry about it, Donna. I'm here, aren't I?" she said, laughing.

"All right, but I will ask him what happened." Then she exclaimed, "Oh, Amy Ann, let me look at you. You are still so adorable and still have those big brown eyes!"

"Let's not get maudlin here, Donna. Of course, my eyes weren't going to change."

Ignoring her comment, Donna said, "I'm so glad you're here. Now, come meet David."

She indicated the tall, dark, attractive man who was standing in the middle of the most extravagantly exotic room that Amy had ever seen outside of the movies.

As for David he was smiling and opened his arms to give her another bear hug.

"I'm thrilled to finally meet you, Amy Ann," he said as he released her. "Donna has told wonderful stories about you."

"Oh?" she said, assuming that he meant flattering stories. He seemed genuinely sincere to meet her and she felt equally so toward him. "Well, I'm thrilled to be here and I'm so happy for both of you."

With their enthusiastic greetings behind, Amy gazed around at the enchanting room.

"Oh, Donna, only you could pull off a décor of orange and green floral prints." The pattern seemed to be everywhere, covering two cushiony sofas, and a love seat. Even the draperies were made of the same material. The deep pile carpet matched the palm green of the material and Amy felt an unbelievable comfort as her feet sank into it.

She couldn't stop herself from gasping while taking in the tropical splendor of the room. "Coral walls to go with orange and green. Only you, Donna, only you," she repeated. "And a white circular staircase! How on earth do you keep it clean?"

She laughed. "I have a cleaning service."

"What's upstairs? The bedrooms, I presume." Not giving her time to respond, Amy glanced up and saw the domed ceiling, from which hung a modernistic crystal chandelier with hundreds of twinkling glass rectangular shapes harboring tiny light bulbs. "How on earth do you reach the chandelier to change the bulbs? From the upstairs balcony?"

"The bulbs have a ten-year warranty. It's the cleaning that's the most perilous. But no, reaching the chandelier from the balcony would be quite awkward. The cleaners bring in ladders once a month. I just leave when they come. I can't bear to watch."

"I can understand that," Amy said as she continued to gaze about her. And to think she was to have the privilege of living in this paradise for two whole weeks, a thought that immediately reminded her that someone was missing.

"But where is Jeremy? I'm dying to see him."

"Out on the beach. Come, I'll show you."

Donna led the way to the draperies and drew them back to reveal a spectacular view of the Caribbean, the colors of which Amy still couldn't conceive really existed. She gasped in amazement as they stepped out onto a large balcony furnished with a rattan table and four chairs with cushions made of the same floral pattern as the interior furnishings. Below the grilled railing was a swimming pool and beyond that was the pink sandy beach.

"What a view," she said admiringly. "But why do you let Jeremy go out there alone? Isn't it dangerous?"

"If he goes out to play by himself, I stay here on the balcony until I see that he checks in with the pool and beach lifeguards. Both they and Jeremy know that he's not allowed to go into the water unless I, or David, accompany him. They are employees of our condo and are paid to care for all of the residents here. They are wonderful young men and we couldn't ask for a better arrangement. Later on I'll introduce you to them."

"But aren't there a lot of strangers such as tourists on these beaches?"

"Not really. They generally stick to the beaches pertaining to their hotels. There is a pier that marks the boundary between us and the Marisol whose guests are discouraged from coming over here."

Amy could see the pier from the balcony and there did seem to be a lot more activity on the Marisol beach than on the condo's beach.

At that moment Donna waved and yelled at Jeremy who was playing in the sand. He waved back and came running toward the building. A few minutes later, as long as it took the elevator to reach their floor, Jeremy came bounding into the room and into Amy's arms, two years melting away with another bear hug. He had been four when she last saw him but he still remembered her and all the fun times that they had together. She was grateful to Donna for keeping her memory alive with him. He was full of "remember" questions: "Remember that story about the purple dog?" or "Remember the game with the marbles?" Of course she remembered. She dearly loved the child and had very fond memories.

After the reunion with Jeremy was complete, Donna led Amy upstairs where, from the balcony, she gazed down upon the living room, the open door to the outside balcony, and the beach and sea beyond. The chandelier, which up here was just above eye-level, seemed to tinkle a melodious welcome. What had she ever done to deserve such magnificence?

"I'm sure you need to rest and freshen up after your long trip," Donna was saying as Amy gazed about almost numb.

Although Donna's observation was on the mark, Amy's adrenaline was flowing and she wondered if she would ever calm down.

Donna opened a door into a lovely bedroom furnished in rattan, which included the bed headboard, night table, and an intricate wing-backed chair.

"My, you certainly do like that pattern," Amy commented as her eyes swept over the light quilt with its orange and green print.

"I designed it myself," Donna said proudly, "and David arranged to have the whole apartment decorated with it. Orange is not a popular color, but I've always liked it."

"Wow, do you mean that David can do stuff like that? Turn your designs into fabric and such?"

"David is a man of many talents." She smiled with satisfaction. "I'm sorry that you don't have a window view but only the master bedroom has that. It's over the kitchen and dining area. However, we usually eat out on the balcony, at least Jeremy and I do. David is slightly amused at my love for the sea view."

"I can understand how you feel. But don't apologize for this darling room. I love it, but somehow I doubt that I'll spend much time here. If I'm not on the beach with Jeremy, then I'll probably be out on your balcony. Believe me, Nebraska never had it so good."

Donna laughed. "I couldn't agree more. Oh, Jeremy's room is between this one and mine. We each have our own bathrooms. Well, I'll leave you to relax and unwind. Join us later for cocktails. David brought up your bags while you were reminiscing with Jeremy." She paused, and then hugged her again. "I'm so glad you're here, Amy."

"Me too, and those are two of the truest words I've ever spoken."

"By the way..." Donna paused hesitantly. "...here are some newspaper clippings that I've saved about our ongoing mystery of the missing heir. If your eyes aren't too tired from your trip you might want to browse through them."

Ordinarily Amy would have been annoyed at this little maneuver of Donna's to interest her in some man that she had never met. But the exhilaration of just being there overcame any annoyance, and she was slightly bemused at her obvious little ploy. Besides, the man was missing and even if he did reappear during her two-week stay, Donna and David wouldn't be around to introduce them. And since Amy loved mysteries anyway, she told her that she would be glad to glance through the clippings.

After a shower and a change of clothes, she sat on the bed, propped up by two enormous fluffy pillows, and began to read about the disappearance of one Peter J. Harris. She found the articles puzzling. She could understand if the police could find no record of him flying off the island. But how could they determine that he had not sailed away? Surely, there were plenty of charter boats on the island and a man as wealthy as Mr. Harris could hire someone to take him anywhere and buy his silence. From what she had read about the island, Palmaltas was as famous for anonymous, secret bank accounts as the Cayman Islands or Switzerland. He would have access to his money and no one would be the wiser. Somehow she didn't think this was much of a mystery. The man had simply taken off for parts unknown. He had a playboy reputation, it seemed, so it was possible, even probable that eventually he would be sighted in Monaco, the French Riviera, or Río de Janeiro, just like in all those Riviera-type movies she had seen.

Then a sobering thought overtook her. What if Mr. Harris had disappeared as a result of foul play? If his body were to be discovered, then she would feel guilty at dismissing his disappearance so frivolously. She didn't know the man. Donna apparently did and liked him. Suddenly another emotion hit her, one that she didn't want to admit, even to herself. She was curious about Peter Harris. Deep down she wanted to meet him. He was a wealthy man who could provide a lifestyle that she had never dared to dream existed. After all, Donna was marrying an affluent restaurateur who had the means to let her decorate her home any way she desired plus much, much more. Why couldn't she, Amy Andrews, meet someone like that? Then more guilt followed this little fantasy. The man was missing. He had a fiancée who certainly must love him, no matter what Donna had said about her. Who was Amy to think she could find a place in his life if indeed he reappeared alive and well? No, there was no way a simple Nebraska schoolteacher could compete in the rich league of a Peter Harris.

Two

When Donna came up later to see how she was resting, Amy put forth her theories about the mysterious disappearance of Peter Harris.

"Yes," she said, "I can see how you have jumped to these conclusions, but you don't know Peter. He's not like that. Despite his wealth, he maintains a responsible job and a lot of people depend on him."

"But you said his fiancée was a bitch and that's pretty strong language from you. Maybe he finally realized that and this is his way of getting away from her."

Donna laughed. "You know, I honestly thought that at first, too. But he's been gone too long, almost six weeks, and Peter's not a coward. He has ended several engagements and broken a few hearts. This lady is no different."

Amy interrupted. "You want to fix me up with a man who has the habit of breaking engagements?"

"They were all gold diggers," she replied stubbornly. "He has to be very careful."

"Oh, give me a break, Donna! So, you think this latest fiancée is a gold digger, too?"

"The very worst from my point of view, but she has put on one whale of an act for Peter. The main reason she has fooled him is that she's supposedly independently wealthy herself."

"So she doesn't need his money?"

"Who knows? She may not need it, but I think her gold digging is not only for his money, but for his prestige, his mansion here on the island, although he shares that with his sister, and anything else Marla can conjure that belongs to Peter."

"How on earth did you turn on this Marla with such vehemence?"

"You'll see what I mean when you meet her. She's a bridesmaid." Apparently noticing Amy's astonished expression, she hastened to explain. "Peter was to be best man and he wanted Marla to be in the wedding party."

"That was presumptuous of him."

"Wasn't it? But David was all in favor of Marla being in the wedding, also. He and Peter thought that if I and other socialites gave Marla a chance that we'd change our opinion of her."

"You're a socialite?"

"Crazy, isn't it?" she said laughing. "I guess I am because I'm marrying David. Anyway, Peter knew I already had chosen someone else to be maid-of-honor. Now Peter apparently won't appear and I'm stuck with Marla as a bridesmaid. And that's another thing that discredits your theory that Peter might have sailed off voluntarily to playboy heaven on the Riviera. He wouldn't deliberately miss David's wedding."

"Oh," was Amy's feeble reply. "By the way, who is the maid-of-honor? Some Palmaltas high society dame?" She exaggerated the last word.

"Not at all, although in my book she's a class act anywhere. Besides, high society in Palmaltas isn't exactly like high society in other places. This island was developed from corruption and deception. The wealthy people here became that way through generations of fighting and backstabbing, stealing, and what have you. But many are snobs, nonetheless, just as you would expect from the high echelon of any country. The difference is how they or their ancestors reached that position."

"Oh, I wouldn't be too sure of that. A lot of blue-blood families have skeletons in their closets, not that I know any, of course. I'm just thinking about some of the novels I've read about the rich high and mighty."

"There's not much blue-blood in the rich high and mighty of Palmaltas, believe me."

"But you're marrying a wealthy Palmaltan and you're not exactly painting a very charming picture of his way of life."

"Oh gosh, I'm sorry. Not everyone is that way. Not David. Not Peter. Their families may not have a perfect background but they represent all that's good about Palmaltas, especially David. Besides, being a so-called blue-blood isn't necessarily a good thing anywhere."

"Spoken like a woman in love."

Donna smiled. "Well, getting back to Marla. She's from New York and not a Palmaltan."

"But you're from Nebraska and I assume you're accepted here."

"Touché. But I made an effort to fit in with everyone. She is, or was, a very highly-paid fashion model with her own agency."

"Well, that sounds rather admirable," said Amy, who was willing to be open-minded regarding Marla.

"But she flaunts her beauty and power. She ignores the maxim, 'When in Rome do as the Romans do.'"

Amy smiled thinking how Donna really had it in for this Marla person.

"Let's forget her for now. Tell me about the wedding. Just who is the maid of honor?"

"Why you, of course. Who else would I choose?"

"Oh, Donna," Amy gushed and embraced her with affection. "I-I'm so honored."

That evening Donna, Jeremy, and Amy dined on the outside balcony, although Amy felt that she consumed more of the atmosphere than actual food. Surely, not even the Hilton or the next door Marisol could compete with the ambience that she was experiencing: a full moon over the Caribbean with its waves splashing on the beach below and the fragrance of tropical blooms mixing with the sea air as it drifted through the swishing palms upon a light, nocturnal breeze. She was relaxed and at peace in this lovely setting with two dear friends. Wisely, David had returned to his own condo, leaving them to themselves. Amy assumed that he realized old friends would want to reminisce about things unknown to him.

"So," said Donna, "how are your parents? Still on the farm?"

"Of course," Amy replied dreamily. "Dad is sort of semi-retired now. My brother Tag has bought up most of the surrounding acreage and does most of the work."

"Tag, what a funny nickname. I'm sure you must have told me what his real name is. I just can't remember it."

"Price. It's an old family name but that's not as bad as my sister Polly's name, Pearl."

"Oh, I get it. Price-Tag. Yeah, I'd want to be called Polly instead of Pearl, too. They're twins, aren't they and a lot older than you?"

"Yes, to both questions. However, they're only five years older than I."

"Do you think Pearl is a worse name than Amethyst?" joked Donna. She added, "Although, Amy is just as pretty a nickname as Polly."

Amy laughed and said, "We're both named after great-aunts. I always thought Pearl was a quaint, old-fashioned name and Amethyst just down right silly."

They fell silent for a few minutes as they indulged in a luscious tropical fruit and rice salad. Amy held up a small, round green fruit and stared at it for a few minutes.

"This isn't a grape, is it?" she asked.

"No, it's a quenepa, a Caribbean fruit that grows profusely all over the island. Didn't you read about quenepas in any of the books about Palmaltas that I suggested?"

"I don't remember. I may have just glossed over something like that."

"Oh gee, I wanted you to familiarize yourself with descriptions of the island, the people, and especially the food. Along with the fruit that we have here, there's nothing that I love more than Palmaltas pizza."

"Good heavens, Donna, I'm only going to be here for two weeks after you leave and as you yourself said, I'll spend most of my time at the beach with Jeremy. Local cuisine isn't at the top of my list of things to sample."

"Well, I hope you will take a tour into the capital, Bay City. It used to be rather a seedy place but the government has done a lot to improve the waterfront area. It's now a haven of touristy shops and nightspots but it didn't used to be like that. I'm sure Daniel would be happy to take you there or you could take the bus, which used to be rather ramshackle and circled the island only twice a day. Now, the bus service has been modernized with brand new buses with large sightseeing windows and a regular schedule that runs every half-hour. Lots of tourists go into Bay City on the bus. The sad thing is that most Palmaltans don't benefit from them. The rich just get richer and the poor just stay that way."

"But you're marrying into a rich family."

"I know, but David is hell-bent on changing things. He wants to go into politics but we don't really have free elections here. They're just a pretense. If David is to win public office then he has to curry favor with the powers that be."

"Then how is he going to change things?"

"I don't know. Right now I don't want to think about that. But whatever he chooses, I'll stand by him. I know he'll do the right thing."

"Of course he will," Amy said, trying to encourage her, although she didn't know David well enough to know just what he could do for his country.

"Anyway," Donna said, "let's talk about the wedding. The rehearsal is tomorrow night."

"Wait a minute. What am I going to wear? Won't fittings take some time?"

"Oh, don't worry. My bridesmaids are going to wear colorful, flowered-print sarongs that I designed."

"What?" cried Amy. "You're kidding, I hope."

"Not at all. You'll just wrap the material around you, pin it with an orchid, and bingo, a beautiful, form-fitting, exotic gown."

"Donna, you're just too much."

"Hey," interrupted Jeremy. "This isn't fun talk. Amy, I want to play games with you."

"And that's exactly what we're going to do as soon as we finish eating. I guess this conversation isn't exactly little boy talk."

"No, so stop talking and eat."

Donna and Amy laughed and did as he bid.

After several rounds of Chinese checkers, Jeremy was marched off to bed and Donna and Amy settled down comfortably on one of the living room sofas to sip decaf espressos laced with rum.

"Donna, this is pure, blissful decadence," Amy murmured.

"Glad you like it."

They lapsed into a comfortable silence, while the night noises of the surf rushing to shore, the breeze riffling the palms, and distant laughter mixed with the rhythm of bongo drums wafting through the open balcony door surrounded them with a sense of tranquility.

Suddenly Donna spoke, jarring Amy's nerves with her question.

"So, are you going to tell me about it?"

"What?" Amy asked innocently although she knew exactly to what Donna was referring. She had foolishly thought the subject could be averted.

"Why you broke off your engagement to Rick just before Christmas. You've never given any reasons, just cleverly avoided the issue."

Amy knew that she was going to have to confide in her sometime. It might as well be now. "This is very painful, Donna, but it's simple really. After Thanksgiving I went to a teacher conference in Iowa. I gave Rick the key to my apartment to water my plants and feed the goldfish. The conference was boring so I came back a day early."

"Uh-oh," Donna uttered, clearly anticipating, more or less, what Amy was going to say next.

"Yep, I walked in on Rick in my bed with another woman."

"Oh no! But why yours? What was wrong with his apartment?"

"I'll never know. I threw him out and never spoke to him again."

"Honey, that's just terrible, but good for you for standing up to him."

"What else could I have done? The worst part was that he never contacted me again, no apology, nothing. I still have his ring. He's never asked for it back."

"Then sell it. Spend the money on something frivolous."

"I've thought of that but I'm afraid to have it appraised. What if it's worthless? That everything was a sham? I don't want to face that."

"Amy, I'm so sorry. I can see the sadness etched on your face. But don't you worry," she said, suddenly very cheerful, "you're in Palmaltas now. A lot can happen here. Believe me, I know."

"And I'm so happy for you, Donna. Let's see, you said you met David at a cocktail party, right?"

"Actually, it was the opening of a little art gallery on the ground floor of this condo. Jeremy and I were staying at the Marisol and were just walking around when we saw an advertisement in the lobby for the gallery. You know how I love art shows so we wandered over there and bumped into David. The rest is history."

"Lucky, lucky you."

"Yes, I am. I got rid of one bum and found Prince Charming. Now, hopefully, the same will happen to you."

"Maybe," said Amy doubtfully, "but don't worry about me, Donna. Just being here is more than I could ever dream."

"I'm not worrying about you, Amy Ann. Believe me, I'm not. I have great faith in your seductive powers."

"Your faith is misplaced but thanks for the vote of confidence."

They laughed, clinked their cups, downed the rest of their espressos, hugged each other, and said good night.

As she lay in bed that night, Amy couldn't put her conversation with Donna out of her mind. She had not told her the whole story, of course. She was afraid she might sound like she was wallowing in self-pity and the last thing that Donna needed during this, the happiest time in her life, was a friend crying her heart out and bemoaning her fate.

Friendship was wonderful and invaluable and no one could have a better friend than Donna. They had been through a lot together, especially during the aftermath of Donna's first marriage. They had a friendship based on trust, security, and best of all, comfort. They were comfortable with each other. They had fun together, sometimes just doing nothing such as lounging around, reading or joking or gossiping. There had never been jealousy or competition between them. Disagreements sure, but they usually just joked them aside.

Her thoughts roamed back to their conversation about Rick. Just before Christmas break, she confided her heartbreak to some of her school colleagues. One told her that he thought that Rick had asked her to marry him because she would make a politically correct wife. How better as he climbed the corporate ladder, and later perhaps politics, than to have an attractive, intelligent, wholesome, schoolteacher spouse? His statement had jolted her. There had never been any real passion between them, but she had been enamored of the handsome young junior executive. Rick had laid out a future of comfort, wealth, and security. Naïvely, she had been very content. Then the shattering discovery. No apologies or attempts to rebuild their relationship had been forthcoming. Rick simply slinked away, supposedly to search for another politically correct little dupe. As she looked back, she felt that Rick really didn't like relationships; he just used women to further his career and his physical needs.

The real mystery of Rick was why he had chosen her apartment in which to pursue his extracurricular activities. Was it the thrill of doing something illicit behind her back, flaunting it yet not expecting her to ever find out? And to think she might have actually married him.

She forced her thoughts back to her much happier current circumstances: Donna's wedding; playing in the sand with Jeremy; wading in the surf. She fell asleep as exuberance from her trip and her arrival dissolved into a pleasant dreaminess, which unexpectedly included the image of a scruffy beachcomber.

~ * ~

Amos walked up from the beach to his small cabin where he found his brother sitting in an old chair on the porch.

"Enjoying the night view, eh, bro?"

His brother took his time in answering. "It's the best in the world. I've missed coming here."

"That was your fault, not mine."

"Yeah, I guess so. How did the fish fry go tonight?" he asked although he knew what Amos would say.

"Just like always, bro. Happy, hungry tourists and lots of music. Did you do that favor for Daniel?" he asked with a grin.

"Uh-huh."

"Well, how did it go?"

"Let's just say that I wasn't impressed. Oh, she was pretty and curvy but she acted like a Miss High and Mighty."

"Ah, that's a shame. You think you'll see her again?"

"Yeah, I'm sure I will but I can handle her type."

Amos gave him a serious look and said, "I hate to think what that means considering what you've been through recently."

His brother grimaced. "Not what I've been through, Amos, but what you have observed. It's more like what I'm going to have to do in the near future."

"The sooner the better, bro, the sooner the better."

Three

The next morning, Thursday to be exact, Amy awoke to an energetic exuberance that she had not experienced for a long time. She shook off any lingering image of the mysterious beachcomber-like chauffeur, reminding herself that there was nothing logical about one's subconscious. This was to be her first full day in Palmaltas. What adventures awaited her, she wondered. Surely just walking out on Donna's balcony was adventure enough.

Donna and Jeremy were already up when she descended the stairs.

"Hey, sleepyhead," yelled Jeremy.

"What do you mean, sleepyhead? It's not even eight o'clock yet," she retorted.

"He's right," chimed in Donna. "This is going to be a busy day, and tomorrow, too. Then you'll have two whole weeks to lounge around."

"You must be kidding. If Jeremy's an early-to-bed-early-to-rise kind of kid, then I doubt if I'll be lounging much. So what's on the agenda?"

"First, breakfast. Plant yourself on the balcony and Jeremy and I are going to serve you your first Palmaltas breakfast."

"Oh really, Donna, let me help you. With all you've got going on, you don't need to cater to me."

"Uh-uh, Missy. Jeremy and I are giving you first class service. You helped me back in the old days when Jeremy was a baby. Now it's my turn. So park yourself out there and relax. Besides, I love doing stuff like this. Here, take this mug of coffee with you. You still like it black, don't you?"

"Of course." In mock obedience she walked out onto the balcony, sank into one of the chairs, and gazed out upon the eastern sea. The sun had long since risen and she knew she was going to have to set her alarm in order to get up in time to sit on the balcony and observe the sunrise. She could just imagine how gorgeous it would be.

Donna served a tropical fruit platter of melons, bananas, mangos, and papaya. Amy was quite anxious to try the mango.

"Well, how do you like the mango?" asked Donna.

"Delicious and juicy," Amy said as mango juice ran down her face. "No quenepas this morning?"

"Oh, do you want some? I was just trying for a variety."

"No, this is fabulous, although I really liked the tart little things."

Hot cinnamon rolls followed the fruit.

"And," said Donna, "these are to make you feel like you're back on the farm. They're made from my grandmother's recipe."

"You got up this morning and made rolls from scratch? I'm impressed. Thank goodness you're leaving." She laughed. "I'd become a blimp if I ate like this everyday."

"Oh, this is just to welcome you. We usually just eat cereal."

"Cereal is fine with me."

After breakfast Donna gave her a tour of the condominium, first showing her the agency where Daniel worked. Donna introduced them.

"Daniel, this is my friend Amy Ann who you were supposed to pick up yesterday. What happened?"

Daniel, a handsome young Palmaltan with black hair and bronze skin, assumed an embarrassed expression.

"I'm so sorry, Miss Donna, but something came up and a friend offered to help. I apologize if he did anything wrong."

"Oh no," interposed Amy. "He did exactly as he was supposed to do." She immediately liked Daniel and didn't want him to get into trouble.

"Well, that's a relief," said Donna, who then led Amy onward with the tour showing her next a restaurant, a beauty salon, a grocery store and pharmacy, a clothing store, and finally a laundromat, all located on the first two floors. The condominium was a virtual world unto itself.

Then she led her out the back to the pool area and introduced her to the tall, tan, muscular, young lifeguard.

"Eddie, this is Amy Ann, who'll care for Jeremy while David and I are on our honeymoon."

"A pleasure, Miss Amy Ann. I look forward to seeing you."

Amy thanked him and followed Donna to the beach where she repeated the procedure with an almost identical young man.

"Amy, this is Bert, our beach lifeguard."

"Hey," he said, "nice to meet you. We've got one of the best beaches on the island."

"And I'm sure I'll spend a lot of time here," she said.

"Hey, that's great." He was suddenly called away by a mother with a toddler who had just found a crab in the sand.

"They seem nice," said Amy. "Are they brothers?"

"No, I don't think they're related but who knows on an island this small? They hang out together, work out in the condo gym together. Oh, I forgot to show that to you."

"Don't worry. The last thing I want to do is work out in a gym."

"Don't be so hasty, Missy. A lot of good-looking men go there."

"Give it up, Donna. I'm not here to hunt men."

Donna laughed and said, "Okay, now let's see, you've met Daniel and Ossie and Eddie and Bert."

"Ossie?"

"The doorman. Ossie's short for Osvaldo."

"Everyone seems to have English first names but many seem to have Spanish last names. Why is that?"

"Palmaltas, about two hundred years or so ago, became a haven for pirates, ruffians, escaped slaves who intermarried with what remained of the local Indians. Both the Spanish and the English occupied the island for a while. We have all kinds of names here."

"Oh yes, I remember reading about the history of the island. Your Peter Harris sounds English."

"His mother was Palmaltan. His father was an American who came here to establish the Marisol. English is the prevailing language on the island but Spanish names are mixed in with English ones."

"And your David is a bona fide descendant of the Palmaltas mish-mash?"

She smiled. "Exactly. And look at what a dream he is."

Amy thought that all of the men she had seen so far on this island had been rather dreamy even, she hated to admit, the bogus chauffeur. And Peter Harris? Was he just as handsome? He must be since Donna seemed to be so fond of him and so determined to pair her up with him if he ever surfaced. The last thing Amy wanted her to know was that, yes, she was just a tad curious about the missing tycoon.

They lunched at the condo beach cantina, sipping lemonade and eating ham and cheese sandwiches with big slices of fresh pineapple, all very wholesome thought Amy.

"Can I go see if Peppy is out today?" asked Jeremy.

"Not today or tomorrow, sugar. We've got too much to do to get ready for the wedding," replied his mother.

"Who's Peppy?" asked Amy.

"Some little beach pal of Jeremy's that he seems to have met recently. It's wonderful the friends he's made here and sometimes he meets the children of tourists from the Marisol. Bert and Eddie are very careful about who he plays with."

"Peppy's not little," Jeremy said with a pout. "He's big."

"Peppy sounds like a name for a pet," Amy joked. Luckily Jeremy seemed to think that remark was funny and he very quickly resumed his happy disposition, forgetting all about playing with Peppy on the beach.

The wedding was going to be held in a conference room on the third floor of the condominium. A magnificent winding staircase led down from a landing that opened onto various small rooms, which would be used as dressing rooms for the wedding participants. Amy felt very nervous at the idea of walking down those stairs in high-heeled sandals and a tight-fitting sarong.

Donna, David, Jeremy, the new best man, and Amy spent the afternoon arranging the conference room for the wedding. She had asked Donna why she hadn't hired someone to do this, but she had replied that she wanted to do it herself because she loved to decorate. They set up chairs, arranged flowers, and streamed white ribbons about, all under Donna's supervision.

Peter Harris' replacement was a man of middle height, rather dark and robust, and very friendly. Amy guessed his age to be middle-thirties. His name was Martin and he was one of David's restaurant associates. Amy was amused at these wealthy men doing Donna's bidding. She wondered if Peter Harris would have been so amiable.

The reception was to be held in the banquet room at David's restaurant, La Concha Blanca. Amy was relieved that David's own caterers would take care of everything for the reception. There was no reason for Donna to wear herself out before the wedding and honeymoon.

The rehearsal began at seven o'clock. There was another bridesmaid besides the infamous Marla: Martin's cute, perky wife, Lily. She was tanned, short and plump, with a head topped with dark brown curls. Donna told Amy privately that Martin and Lily originally weren't part of the wedding party but when Peter disappeared and David asked Martin to substitute they felt that Lily should be included also.

"All I wanted was you, Amy, as maid-of-honor and Peter, of course, as best man. Now I have you plus two bridesmaids."

"Who will accompany Lily and Marla?" Amy asked, since she knew she would be standing next to Martin.

"Two government officials who are friends of David. I don't like them much but David has the right to choose whomever he wants."

Donna had predicted earlier that Marla would probably arrive late in order to make a grand entrance. And that was exactly what she did.

"I hope she doesn't do this tomorrow night," whispered Donna.

Amy stared in awe at the gorgeous, statuesque blonde whose satiny hair had been swept back into a French chignon. She had the bluest eyes Amy had every seen; not even the aquamarine of the Caribbean could compete with those eyes. Later Donna cattily commented that she was wearing tinted contact lenses. For the rehearsal, all of them wore casual attire but denim on Marla seemed positively elegant.

Donna introduced Amy to Marla who barely acknowledged her, turning instead to the men of the wedding party.

"Don't mind her," said a female voice behind Amy. "Frankly, I think she's uncomfortable with women and just doesn't know how to act."

Startled, Amy turned to see a smiling Lily standing next to her. "Well," she said, "Donna had forewarned me about her, but I didn't want to prejudge her. But surely if she's a former model and now has her own agency, it would be her business to get along with women and like them, also."

"Oh, I wouldn't be too sure of that. A conglomerate runs the agency. Marla just lends her name to it. She loves prestige. That's one of the reasons that she latched onto Peter, the prestige of landing one of the world's richest, most eligible bachelors."

"You don't think she might actually be in love with him?"

"Oh, she's probably convinced herself of that. And together, they do make a striking couple."

This last remark irritated Amy more than she wanted to admit. "What do you think of his disappearance?" she asked. "Do you know him well?"

Lily paused, answering the second question first. "Yes, we know him fairly well, Mart more than me. I've always thought he was a nice guy in spite of his reputation with women and was quite surprised when he became engaged to Marla."

"Why?"

"I'm not sure. She just doesn't seem real to me, like she's always acting, playing a great role for the guys. I was just surprised that Peter fell for it. Look at her over there, laughing and joking, completely at ease with David, Mart, and the others. But if you or I joined the group she would clam up and disappear."

"Do you mean she's afraid of sharing the limelight?"

"Yes, I think she's very insecure."

So far there had been nothing about Marla that had turned Amy against her. She certainly didn't look insecure but if she were, she could empathize with her. Amy had a sinking feeling that Marla would be the perfect mate for Peter Harris.

"Back to my other question, what do you think happened to Peter?"

"I think he has been kidnapped and that an exorbitant ransom has been demanded but the family and the authorities are keeping it quiet in hope of getting him back safe and sound."

"Does Martin agree with you?"

"Oh yes. That's been his theory from the very beginning."

"Would his family pay?"

"Yes, his sister Lisa would. She adores him and has gone into seclusion until he reappears."

"The newspaper accounts that I read mentioned the family of Peter Harris and you just mentioned his family. Who is there besides his sister?"

"New York cousins, especially one who came here to learn from Peter's tutelage. That's another thing that bothers me. This cousin is trying to run the Marisol without much experience. I just can't imagine that Peter would purposefully go away and leave the business to him."

"Can't Lisa help him?"

"She's too devastated by Peter's disappearance and I get the impression that she doesn't much like him."

"How sad," was all that Amy could say about people she didn't know.

"Yes," continued Lily, "as a result she won't be attending the wedding so you won't get to meet her. I think Donna particularly wanted the two of you to get to know each other."

"How do the sister and Marla get along?"

"At first Marla snowed Lisa completely, just as she did Peter. But since his disappearance I think Lisa has been appalled at Marla's behavior because she continues to go out and socialize and be seen everywhere."

"In other words, Lisa thinks Marla should put on a serious, worried demeanor until Peter returns."

"Well, not exactly. Marla does put on quite a good show everywhere she goes, especially playing up to the press at how concerned she is by Peter's disappearance. She acts serious and worried, but is she really?"

"So, like you and Donna, Lisa now suspects other motives."

"I imagine that's how she feels."

Amy smiled, grateful for Lily's apparent need to gossip, and turned to the rehearsal, which was now getting under way.

The rehearsal was performed several times and Amy didn't stumble once as she descended those awkward stairs, although she felt very shaky the first time. Donna, Lily, and certainly Marla glided down with the greatest ease and poise.

They went to La Concha Blanca for the rehearsal dinner. The restaurant was positioned midway between the Palmaltas Hilton and the Marisol with small hotels and condominiums flanking its sides along the beach. It had a perfect location for luring tourists and wealthy residents. It was a blend of classy and tropical airiness with a palm-thatched roof and wide doors that opened out onto a view of the beach and sea. Palm-thatched umbrellas sheltered tables scattered here and there on the beach. A charming bar with deep, padded chairs also had a broad view of the sea. David settled everyone into a small private room and served champagne and lobster salad. Donna told Amy later that the restaurant menu catered native and seafood cuisine. Amy found herself between Martin, who politely entertained her with local stories, and Marla, who ignored her.

~ * ~

The wedding day dawned with a beautiful, clear sky. Amy had set her alarm, hoping that it couldn't be heard outside her room, and had very quietly sneaked downstairs, made coffee, and sat out on the balcony, sipping the hot liquid as the sun slowly made its appearance, briefly turning the sea into a bright crimson. Now this was paradise, she thought over and over.

"Aha! Thought you'd get the jump on me, huh?"

"My goodness, Donna, how could you sneak up on me like that?" Amy almost spilled her coffee. "How are you? Wedding day jitters?"

"No, come to think of it, I'm just happy, really, really happy."

"Oh, Donna, that's wonderful." They both sat back, relishing the quiet, cozy comfort that only two friends can enjoy.

"You know," Donna said after a while, "this is the way life and friendship are meant to be. I'm as comfortable with David as I am with you and Jeremy."

"Donna, what a sweet thing to say and how wonderful that you feel that way about David." A bittersweet melancholy swept through Amy as Donna's comments reminded her of her own thoughts that she had the night she arrived.

"Yes, you not only have to love someone but be friends with him as well. That's why I wonder about Peter and Marla. I can't see her being friends with anyone."

"Oh, let's not talk about Marla on your wedding day. By the way, what do you think of Lily and Martin's theory that Peter was kidnapped and his family is keeping it quiet?"

"I think they're probably right but David and I have agreed not to speculate anymore."

"You're absolutely right. Forget Peter and certainly Marla for today and tomorrow and the rest of your honeymoon. Later, you can cope with his disappearance. But today is going to be glorious.

And it was. The wedding was indeed beautiful. Draped in a white sarong, Donna presented a lovely vision. A wispy, white veil hung from a narrow, white band that circled the top of her head.

"Dorothy Lamour herself never looked so pretty," Amy said to Donna.

"And who is Dorothy Lamour?" asked Donna while they waited upstairs for the procession to begin.

"Do you meant you never watched those old Bing Crosby-Bob Hope *Road* pictures?"

"Was that her name?" asked Donna absentmindedly, obviously not caring one way or the other.

Lily and Marla preceded Amy who made it down the stairs gracefully, giving thanks silently as she did so. Donna followed hand-in-hand with little Jeremy who was proudly "giving" her away.

The only hitch came after the ceremony when Donna ascended the stairs, turned and tossed down her bouquet. She aimed for Amy, and just as Amy was about to grab it, Marla snatched it, beaming proudly as if Amy were invisible.

"See," she pronounced, "that proves that my Peter will be back soon."

There was momentary silence from the assembled guests, then Martin's booming voice proclaimed, "Here, here, to all young lovers everywhere!"

Someone laughed and others joined in the merriment. Peter's prolonged absence was not going to cast a shadow over this wedding party. Marla's statement raised hope that he would indeed return and soon.

But Donna wasn't placated. "That bitch!" she exclaimed to Amy in an angry whisper. "My bouquet was meant for you."

"It's the thought that counts," said Amy.

"But-but I want, oh, never mind," she mumbled, apparently resigned to the circumstances.

Limousines escorted them the short distance to the restaurant, which had been closed to the public for the owner's wedding party. David had gone all out with not only the traditional, elaborate cake but a smaller groom's cake, also, as well as table after table of rich elegant hors d'oeuvres and champagne punch. An orchestra played love songs and for Donna and David it was a perfect evening. Amy danced with the two government officials a few times but mostly she stayed with Jeremy, a very happy little boy. Wistfully, she wondered if she would ever be as lucky as Donna.

Donna and David left for the airport in the condo limousine decorated by Daniel and Ossie with the usual newlywed accouterments. They would have quite a job removing their own handiwork but presumably the two men didn't mind. Amy thought the decorating bit was a bit ridiculous considering how close the airport was to the restaurant.

After the departure of the newlyweds, Marla again provided a jarring note for the end of the day's festivities. Everyone watched as she made a point of addressing the society editor of *The Palmaltas News.*

"Take this down, my dear. Peter Harris will return soon and then you will have the wedding of the century to cover."

Amy moaned inwardly. Marla almost made her wish that Peter Harris, a man she had never met, would never return, almost. Deep down inside of her, of course, this unknown man had piqued her curiosity more than she wanted to admit. But Marla irritated her. Why were there women like her, women who acted as if they were the only ones who mattered and all other women were the enemy? Amy wanted to like Marla but she made it very difficult, especially when she answered the society editor's question.

"Do you know something that the authorities aren't telling?"

Marla took her time in responding, smiling ambiguously. "I can't give out any information at this time." She walked away, oblivious to the cries and questions from the editor and other wedding guests.

Amy wondered, was she putting on an elaborate act or did she really know something?

Four

Saturday morning, June eight. The wedding was over. The newlyweds had departed. Alone at last with Jeremy, Amy's Caribbean vacation had begun.

She hadn't set her alarm but she awoke early anyway in eager anticipation of this day and the days to come. It wasn't that she was expecting anything momentous to happen. In fact, just the opposite was true. She was looking forward to strolls along the beach, collecting seashells, a tour with Daniel around the island, perhaps a ride, also, on the bus.

Sitting on the balcony watching the sunrise and sipping her coffee, she felt more at ease and at peace with herself than she had in years. Maybe more than in her entire life, she thought. Perhaps she wasn't completely happy, but this tropical atmosphere was doing much to alleviate the pain of Rick's treachery. She thought about growing up on the farm in Nebraska, of the flat land and how different it was from the profusion of flora that abounded here. Palm trees, she had never seen a palm tree before coming here.

Her mind wandered back to childhood, playing with her older siblings, Tag and Polly, and the various animals that inhabit a farm.

She had been content with Nebraska, with teaching school, and looking forward to a life with Rick. But Rick himself had shattered all that and she had begun to feel imprisoned, despite the open land and space, as if she could never escape the boundaries of Nebraska. Then, miracle of miracles, Donna's invitation had changed all that. Here she was in a new world hopefully recreating or rejuvenating her own persona. After all, in two weeks she would have to return to her old world.

"Hi, Amy, I'm hungry."

"Oh, Jeremy honey, I didn't know you were up. What would you like?"

"Cereal and milk."

"Well, that's easy enough." She arose and went into Donna's neat little kitchen and quickly poured cereal and milk into a bowl and carried it out onto the balcony along with a glass of orange juice.

"Can you call me Jerry? That's what my friend Peppy calls me."

"Of course, honey, if that's what you really want. Sounds like a reasonable nickname to me. Peppy is the one with the strange name."

"He says it means Joe."

Amy laughed. "The things some kids come up with."

"Why? What do you mean?"

"Peppy doesn't mean Joe. It means active, energetic. Now take my brother Price. Do you know what his nickname is?"

"No."

"Tag. Do you get it? Price-Tag."

Jeremy laughed a little uncertainly.

"When he first started kindergarten, the older kids teased him by calling him Price-Tag. It sort of caught on. People who have known him all his life still call him that."

"Do you?"

"I call him Tag. That's the way I think of him."

"Does he get mad?"

"Oh no. He likes to be called that. He has plenty of names for me, too."

"Like what?"

"Oh, silly names such as Amy-Wamy or Sissy-Wissy. Does Peppy like his nickname?"

"Yeah. He's neat. Can we go to the beach today so you can meet him?"

"I think that would be a very good idea."

"Peppy has a brother, too, but he works a lot."

"Then he must be a lot older than Peppy."

He frowned as if in deep concentration. Children didn't perceive age the way adults did and she remembered that Jeremy had described Peppy as being big. Presumably Peppy was a year or so older than Jeremy and his brother was a teenager who worked a part-time job.

"I-I don't think he's older than Peppy," he said finally, after eating the last of his cereal.

"Oh well, it doesn't matter. I'm looking forward to meeting them both. I'm going to fix myself some toast and pour another cup of coffee. Why don't you get dressed for the beach and then we'll straighten up the apartment and make a day of it outside? Do you want me to fix sandwiches or shall we eat at the beach cantina?"

Jeremy laughed. "All I have to do is put on my swim trunks. Let's eat at the cantina. That's fun."

"Great, then that's what we'll do."

~ * ~

"This looks like a good spot to spread our beach towels," Amy said as soon as they passed the pool area onto the beach.

"Oh no. We have to go further down by the Marisol beach."

"Why?

"Because that's where Peppy always is."

"Really? Your mother lets you go that far when she's not with you?"

"It's not far. The lifeguards can always see me and they know Peppy."

"Do they watch out for him, too, like they do for you?"

"Amy, that's funny. I like to sit and talk and fish with Peppy on the pier. The lifeguards are Peppy's friends."

"Pier? Oh, I've never been on a pier. Yes, let's go."

Jeremy was right. The Marisol beach and fishing pier were very close to Donna's condominium. Amy remembered when she first arrived looking out at the pier from the balcony and how Donna had explained the pier as being some kind of boundary. She began to spread their things out on the sand while Jeremy went running toward the pier shouting for his friend.

"Peppy, Peppy! Here's my friend Amy."

There was no one in sight except a rather grubby looking fisherman standing next to the pylons that upheld the pier. He was holding a fishing rod and was bending over his tackle box. When he heard Jeremy, he raised his head and grinned.

"Jerry, old buddy! How goes it? Did your mom get married okay?" He held out his arms and Jeremy rushed into them.

Amy was horrified. How could this rough-looking personage be the "little beach pal" that Donna had described? Had she not ever met him?

As she approached the two of them, she noticed that the man had a stubble. Apparently shaving wasn't part of his daily grooming habits. He wore cut-off jeans, ragged with a few holes, a dingy-white, short-sleeved shirt, and sneakers with no socks. He was well-muscled, tanned, and obviously quite fit. His most notable features were this close-cropped silver hair and pale blue eyes.

"Oh no," she gasped to herself. Peppy was the chauffeur!

Releasing Jeremy, he grinned mischievously at her, causing unexplainable shivers to run up and down her spine. Amy noted again what a very masculine man he was and seemingly a very strong one. Next to him, Rick, who was lean and fit, would seem soft. There was something about Peppy that disturbed her and she wasn't sure if she was going to like him. After all, he had posed as a chauffeur, supposedly doing a favor for Daniel. But why had he accepted her tip if he wasn't supposed to? Perhaps he was unemployed. His attire certainly suggested that he was.

He walked toward her, hand outstretched, still grinning that strange smile. She assumed he was mocking her from their first encounter.

"Ah yes, the famous Miss Amy," he said in his deep, manly voice as he grasped her hand firmly, causing an electric shock to rapidly course through her body.

Oh damn, she thought, *I've been out of circulation too long*. Despite her burning body she tried to maintain a cool and aloof demeanor.

"Yes, but are you really Peppy? Jeremy's mother led me to believe that you were a child. And why were you posing as a chauffeur when I arrived?"

"I wasn't posing, just doing a favor for a friend. So Jerry's mother thinks I'm a kid?" He turned and winked at Jeremy. "Telling tales out of school, huh, old buddy?"

Jeremy stood there looking puzzled.

"No, Jerry and I are old fishing pals," he continued. "We meet once in a while, sit on the pier, fish, and exchange stories. His mother never came out on the days we got together."

"What kind of stories does Jeremy tell?"

"Well, let's see. He talks about his mom, his new stepdad, and he told me a lot about you."

"About me?"

He seemed amused at her question. "Most definitely. About the pretty lady who used to play games with him. And I must say I'm impressed with anyone who can teach a four-year-old to play gin rummy."

"I'm six now," interrupted Jeremy.

"Yes, but you were four when I last saw you," she said. "Well, he's a bright little boy. It was easy to teach him."

"Jerry and I have gotten to know each other quite well, sitting up there on that pier, fishing, playing cards, and swapping yarns."

"What kind of yarns have you told him?"

"Fish stories, mainly."

That seemed reasonable, she thought. Mr. Peppy appeared fishy to her.

"What do you do for a living, er-Peppy?"

"At the moment I'm-uh-unemployed. Living at my wit's end as a beachcomber," he said calmly, apparently without shame.

"And previously?" she asked rather haughtily, not sure if she was relieved that her previous assessment of his unemployment had been correct.

"I was in business," he said slowly, indicating, she thought, that she shouldn't pry further.

Somehow she felt that his business had been illicit and that he was now living off ill-gotten gains, if indeed he was living off anything. Even she knew that drug dealing was rumored to be rampant in Palmaltas and she wondered if that were the reason he came to the resort area, to sell drugs to rich tourists. She had only known him for a short while, not counting their first meeting at the airport, and she was already very suspicious of him. How she wished that Donna had met him. He probably avoided Jeremy when the child came to the beach with his mother, figuring she wouldn't approve of such a playmate. She then wondered just how trustworthy the two lifeguards were if they let Jeremy "play" with Peppy.

He repeated his question about the wedding. "So did your mom get hitched okay?"

"Hitched?" asked Jeremy. "No, she got married. It was real pretty, wasn't it, Amy?"

"Yes, it was," she replied.

"So now, it's just you two, is it? Holding down the fort until the honeymooners get back?"

Amy resented not only his knowing so much about Donna, Jeremy, and her, but his visible interest in them as well. His information apparently had come from Jeremy who was just a child and couldn't be blamed for any indiscretions. She thought that Donna had not warned her son enough about speaking to strangers, which she deemed a very lax parental thing for her to have neglected, considering all the tourists that came here. Perhaps most of the tourists stayed in the vicinity of their hotels, but she still should have lectured Jeremy on the necessity of avoiding strangers. It was true that Donna said she allowed Jeremy to play with the children of tourists under the supervision of the lifeguards but playing with an adult? And Peppy did not appear to be the average tourist, at any rate. But Amy answered his question as succinctly as she could, hoping to imply that she didn't welcome such inquisitive liberties.

"Yes, we're doing just fine, thank you."

"Hmm," was his reply. Turning to Jeremy, he said, "So, Jerry, what do you want to do? Fish or build castles?"

"Both!" yelped the exuberant child.

Peppy laughed and, putting his hand on Jeremy's shoulder, led him down to the wet sand near where the surf occasionally lapped.

He turned to her and said, "Would you like to join us, Miss Amy? You could be our sand princess."

"No, thank you," she responded coolly. "I'm going to relax in the sun and read." At least, she contemplated, they would be directly in front of her and she could watch them out of the corner of her eye as they built their castle. Why would such a man spend his time playing with a small child? No, she didn't trust Mr. Peppy, who most definitely had obtained Jeremy's trust.

"Peppy, you don't have to call her Miss Amy, just Amy," said Jeremy.

"Well, that's up to her," said Peppy, slyly glancing back at her.

She ignored them both and began to read the latest time-travel adventure by her favorite author.

She must have dozed off because when she opened her eyes she saw that the sun was not only higher in the sky but hotter as well. She jumped up from her towel and shook off sand that had been blown on her by the light breeze. The aquamarine waters beckoned to her flirtatiously. Suddenly she realized that Jeremy and Peppy were no longer in front of her. The castle seemed to be finished and abandoned. She turned toward the pier where she saw them positioned on the end, fishing.

She couldn't believe Peppy would do anything to Jeremy in broad daylight, especially with her about, so she decided to take a plunge into the water, finally her first swim in the Caribbean. After all, Jeremy had been playing with this man for quite a while and nothing had happened, so far. Nonetheless, she would keep an eye on them.

When she approached the castle, she stopped and reluctantly admired the handiwork. The sandy architecture was complete with towers, turrets, and a moat. No wonder Jeremy was so fond of Peppy, especially someone who could entertain a little boy with such an endeavor.

She waved to Jeremy as she stepped into the water and cupped her hands to her mouth and yelled, "Very impressive!" She pointed to the castle, and Jeremy and Peppy waved back but kept on fishing.

Tentatively she sank down to immerse herself into the cool, gentle surf. Not the best swimmer in the world, Amy was terrified of deep water and of putting her head under. So she just dog paddled around and floated lazily on her back, never drifting far from shore. This was a lifestyle she could get used to, she thought to herself.

As she floated and kicked, she suddenly noticed another male figure approach Jeremy and Peppy on the pier. Although she was sure that the child was in no danger, she nonetheless decided it was her responsibility to make her presence known to all strangers.

With reluctance, she left the water, shaking herself dry, and walked toward the pier. As she came closer, she saw that the man was exceedingly handsome with brown skin, curly black hair, and the same island features that Donna's David had. He was dressed in dark shorts, white shirt, and sandals, much neater than Peppy.

He sat down on the pier, turning his back to her, with Jeremy and Peppy. Jeremy was obviously as familiar with this stranger as he was with Peppy.

Jeremy stood up when he saw her approach and shouted, "Amy, I've caught some fish. Amos says he'll have a fish fry for us tonight!"

"Amos?" she asked.

"Yes," said Peppy as he and the newcomer both stood up. "Miss Amy, this is my brother Amos Soto."

"What?" she gasped. Never had she seen any two brothers more unlike each other than these two. The only feature they had in common was their deep bronze skin. Amy assumed Peppy was the older with his strange but attractive silver hair, although they both had a youthful air about them. Peppy's pale blue eyes were in stark contrast to the sparkling coal-black ones of Amos.

They both seemed amused at her reaction and she felt terribly ashamed and embarrassed.

"Same father, different mothers," said Amos, laughing, with that lovely lilting accent of the Caribbean that she had noticed from David, Martin, Lily, Ossie, Daniel, and the two lifeguards. He added, "Happy to meet you, Miss Amy."

"Oh, I apologize for my reaction. Yes, it's nice to meet you," she said dubiously, not knowing whether she wanted to meet him or not.

"No problem, Miss Amy," said Peppy. "We're used to that reaction from strangers."

Amy wondered why Peppy didn't speak with the same rhythmic accent of his brother. His speech sounded American without any regional accent.

"Jeremy has certainly misled his mother and me about his young friends."

"That's what you said earlier," said Peppy. "But don't you worry, Miss Amy, he's in good hands with us."

Had her distrust of him been that obvious?"

"Donna knows me very well, Miss Amy," said Amos.

"Yeah," piped Jeremy, "and so does David."

"Well, one or both of us misunderstood you regarding Peppy and I remember you saying this morning that Peppy's brother was big but you didn't say his name." She had an urge to tell both of them to drop the "Miss" bit but decided to wait until she got to know them better if, indeed, meeting them on the beach became a habit. But she still had misgivings about Peppy. Something about him didn't ring quite right. Maybe Donna and David did know Amos, but what did that signify? Why did they know him and not Peppy? She decided to tread lightly and remain cautious.

"Would you like to fish, too, Miss Amy?" asked Amos.

"Yes, please do, Amy," pleaded Jeremy.

"All right, but don't ask me to put a worm on the hook."

Her three male companions laughed and teased her since the bait they were using was shrimp. They fixed a rod for her and Jeremy handed it to her.

"Okay, so now what do I do?"

"You mean you've never gone fishing before?" Jeremy was incredulous.

"It's been a long time, not since I was a little girl on my folks' Nebraska farm. We had a pond for fishing, but my sister and I usually just skipped rocks while our brother tried to fish. That really irritated him."

"Yes, I can imagine," said Peppy. "Pesky sisters."

She wondered if he was talking from experience and if he and Amos had sisters.

"Here, I'll show you how," offered Jeremy who whisked the line into the water and began explaining what to look for and what to do if she should be so lucky as to catch something.

The four of them settled down to a companionable silence and much of her uneasiness regarding Peppy and his brother melted away. They seemed to be genuinely fond of Jeremy and she couldn't believe either would harm him. Besides, for Amy this was heady stuff sitting, next to two such ruggedly masculine men.

"So, Amos," she ventured, "are you in the same business that Peppy was in?"

He hesitated, giving what she thought was a questionable look at his brother, then replied, "No, I run a tourist-guide boat concession over here at the Marisol."

"Really!" she exclaimed, quite surprised. "What kind of boat?"

"Sailboats and glass bottom. The tourists eat up that kind of stuff. It's a good business."

"I can imagine. It sounds like fun. I would love to go on a glass bottom boat and observe the sea life below. It must be magnificent. The water here is so beautiful."

"Then please someday soon you and Jeremy must be my guests."

"Oh, thank you. How wonderful, but I'll pay for us, the regular tourist-going price."

"No, no, you are friends. It will be my pleasure."

"Come on, Jerry," said Peppy, "lets check out our castle and see how it's stood up."

Jeremy jumped up happily. "Okay, Peppy."

Amy remained alone with Amos as they raced down the pier to the sand. For some reason, she felt much more comfortable with

Amos than Peppy. Amos had such a friendly smile as compared to his brother's cynical one. One thing was certain, she was more assured of their respectability, at least that of Amos, now that she knew where he worked.

"Tell me, Amos, about Peppy's name."

"What do you mean?"

"Jeremy says it means Joe. Why does he say that?"

He laughed melodiously, showing white, even teeth. "Pepe is a Spanish name. You know, Pablo translates to Paul, Pedro to Peter."

"And," she said, "José is Joe. Where does Peppy come in?"

"You don't understand. José is Joseph, so Pepe means Joe. It's spelled P-E-P-E."

"That's crazy."

"No, not really. Paco is Frank, short for Francisco."

"But you're not Spanish."

"We're Palmaltan, a little bit of everything."

She laughed, "I guess so, but I kind of like Peppy better than Pepe. It's cute the way Jeremy pronounces it."

"Yes, he's a cute kid."

Jeremy and Peppy rejoined them at that moment. She looked up at Peppy. "Amos just explained your name to me. Like Jeremy, I'm staying with Peppy instead of Pepe."

"Jerry! You have to call me Jerry the way Peppy does."

She laughed. "Okay, pip-squeak, Peppy and Jerry."

"And Amy and Amos," added the appealing child.

"So, will you come to our fish fry tonight?" asked Amos.

"Yes, yes! Amy, you have to say yes!" demanded Jeremy.

After a moment's hesitation she agreed. Why not, she asked herself. Amos, at least, seemed respectable enough and Peppy seemed devoted to Jeremy, although she was puzzled why this should be so. Nevertheless, she was here for fun and a fish fry sounded like fun. "Where are you having it?"

"Over there by my concession at the Marisol. I hope you won't mind a group of middle-aged tourists. It's a nightly event for the hotel."

"Oh no, the more the merrier," she replied, greatly relieved that Marisol patrons would be attending. What could be safer than that? In fact, relief flooded through her as she realized that she apparently had nothing to fear from these two very different siblings. A fish fry on the beach? Like Jeremy, she was excited.

Amos went back to his concession and Amy and Jeremy asked Peppy to join them for lunch at the condo cantina.

"Thanks," he said with a slight smile. "I brought a sandwich. See you after while?"

"Yes," she said slowly, "we planned to spend the day out here."

"Good," was his reply as he turned back to his fishing.

His attitude irritated her a little but she tried to behave just as nonchalantly as he did.

After their lunch and a quick refreshing break in the condo, they rejoined Peppy at the pier, or rather Jeremy did. Amy returned to her beach towel and her book and occasionally took a dip in the water. Peppy affected her in a way that she didn't want to acknowledge. How could a beachcomber, of all people, set her emotions swaying?

Around four o'clock Peppy walked down to her and said he had to leave, giving no reason. He took her hand and squeezed it, causing her heart to palpitate and her body to tremble. "I'm so happy to finally meet you, Miss Amy, and not as your chauffeur," he said, winking at her.

With that he was gone, leaving her breathless. She watched his backside, a very sexy one she admitted to herself with a wry grin, as he ambled eastward down the beach.

"Come on, Jer, we should leave also and get some rest before the fish fry revelry."

"Huh? What is rev-what you said?"

She laughed and hugged him. "Fun. It just means fun."

Besides getting some rest, she also knew she needed time to get her feelings under control. Mister Peppy, fake chauffeur, beach bum fisherman, had her reeling out of control, reeling emotions, not fish.

~ * ~

That evening Jeremy and Amy made their way down the beach, past the pier, to the Marisol. The sky was clear with twinkling stars gradually blinking their appearance and the full moon rising on the horizon. Couples strolled barefoot, hand in hand, as the tide crept upward on the sand. The smell of salt air intermingled with the aroma of fish frying as they approached the group gathered by Amos' concession.

"I hope Johnny will be here," said Jeremy.

"Who's Johnny?" she asked.

"My friend. Johnny, Amos, and Peppy are my bestest friends."

"Best, not bestest. My, my, but you are a friendly little rascal. Hasn't your mother ever warned you about talking to strangers?"

"Oh yes, all the time. But Mom and David know Amos and Johnny. And since Peppy is Amos' brother, I know he's okay. Everybody knows Amos."

That was understandable, she thought. Amos did run a boating concession on a prominent beach next to the beach where Donna's condo was located. It was only natural that she should run into him from time to time, and he was most definitely a friendly, likable guy.

When they arrived at the gathering, Amos greeted them and introduced them around. They were assuredly the youngest people there as the group was composed mainly, as Amos had stated earlier, of middle-aged tourists. But, they were friendly and quite boisterous.

"Is Johnny coming tonight, Amos?" asked Jeremy.

"No, not tonight, Jerry. Here, I've been waiting to serve you the fish that you caught." He handed the child a plate with a portion of fish and fried cornmeal.

Amy doubted that Amos would remember which fish was Jeremy's but it was a good trick to get the boy to eat. She had noticed that eating wasn't Jeremy's greatest interest in life. He could barely sit still for a whole meal. She hoped that with all his energy he consumed the nutrients that he needed.

"Where's Peppy?" she asked.

"He thought he'd do some fishing out in front of our cabin. He's not one for touristy fish fries."

"Is that so?" A tinge of disappointment pricked her and she was irritated at her own reaction to Peppy's absence. She didn't want to admit to herself that the main reason she had looked forward to the fish fry was that she would see Peppy again. His touch had electrified her. Had hers not done the same to him? Mentally, she shook herself, trying to rid her mind of thoughts of a scruffy beachcomber who should not have affected her so sensually.

"Where is your cabin?" she asked, hoping that Amos hadn't sensed her disappointment.

"Farther down the beach, past the Palmaltas Hilton. Across from the airport is a group of small cabins."

"Oh yes, I might have noticed them when I arrived," she said, thinking back to her arrival and the sardonic chauffeur who had turned out to be Peppy. Had she really noticed anything else besides him, she pondered.

Amos turned back to his tourists, a group from New Jersey. Their main topic of interest was the local mystery of the missing hotelier. Several of the people in the group asked Amos for his opinion but he just smiled and shrugged and replied that the world of the wealthy elite was beyond him.

Amy inquired if the police had asked him if he had rented or sold a boat to Peter Harris.

Laughing, he replied, "Yes, they asked me and I told them that no, I didn't."

Inexplicably, a chill ran down her spine. He answered with the words that she expected, but his amused tone made her wonder if he knew more than he was indicating. If she had wanted to get away for a while, them Amos would be the person she would appeal to for help. And Amos worked for the Marisol, which was run by the missing man. But, she reminded herself, this was only conjecture. Amos appeared to be a straightforward guy with a legitimate business. Would he get mixed up in such a scandal, if indeed this was a scandal? Perhaps, if the price were right. However, if anyone she had met so far could be involved in clandestine activities, it would be Peppy. Of course, Peppy would have access to Amos' boats and he was unemployed. Was that why he wasn't working? Had Peter Harris paid him an exorbitant amount to whisk him away to a secret location? She shook herself again.

She was fishing for nonsense. How could a naïve nitwit like her, who had just arrived on the island, solve a mystery before the local authorities did?

Suddenly someone started playing bongos and after he served the fish, Amos bounced around to a calypso and sang Harry Belafonte's "Day-O". Amy wondered if he were doing that because the tourists expected it or if he really did things like that with or without tourists around.

Shoving aside her suspicions and some of her inhibitions, she and Jeremy bounced, jiggled, and writhed to the rhythm along with everyone else.

"Amy, this is fun," said the happy child.

"Yes, Jer-Jerry, it certainly is."

Later, after Jeremy had been tucked in for the night, she settled on the balcony and absorbed the pleasant night noises. At first all seemed quiet but the sounds of crickets, swishing palm fronds, and waves lapping on shore soon invaded her subconscious. She sat there quietly when suddenly she realized that in only a few days three different men had occupied her thoughts. Rick had been the topic of conversation the night of her arrival. Then the mystery of Peter Harris brought that enigmatic figure to the forefront. But today had been the shocker. An unemployed loafer had distracted her emotions more than she wanted to admit. Rick was no more, ancient history. Peter Harris intrigued her. Yes, she wanted to meet him. But Peppy? He had brought burning sensations to the surface of her soul. Why? How? Perhaps it wasn't Peppy doing anything, just her starved feelings crying out. But no, she feared it was far more than that.

~ * ~

Late that night, Amos walked in the cabin and said, "Well, bro, what do you think of Miss Amy now?"

He looked up and said, "I think that maybe the High and Mighty act was just a cover for nervousness although she's still a little uppity. However, I assume that's because she's so protective of Jerry."

"She's very pretty and seemed nice to me," Amos said.

"You are more respectable than I am," he said, laughing. "I'll be impressed if she really does want to be friends with a lonely fisherman."

Amos hooted. "You? Lonely? That will be the day!"

"I have to be careful, Amos, very careful."

"Yeah, there are a lot of things to be careful about. At least Donna has gone and you won't have to do those disappearing acts regarding her appearances on the beach with Jerry. I can't imagine how furious she would have been if she had seen her son's new best friend."

"Not to mention David's reaction."

"I know, bro. He would be angry, too, considering how you have treated him. At least Ossie can be trusted. He knows part of what you are doing but he couldn't know about Miss Amy."

"That's personal, Amos."

"It's all personal, bro."

He nodded in agreement with his brother. There was more than one reason for his friendship with little Jerry. While Amos got ready for bed, he smiled to himself and silently considered the attributes of Miss Amy. Her bikini had shown that physically she had all the right ones. Her caution regarding Jerry indicated a propensity for love and responsibility. Only time would tell but was there enough time? And how much time did he need to determine whether Amy could be trusted?

Five

A new day brought a new resolve. Amy decided that if she had any more encounters with Mr. Joseph "Peppy" Soto then she would treat him with civility and respect and nothing more. She had to be strong and stamp out any physical urges that might come unbidden. He was Jeremy's friend and should be treated as such. He was Amos' unemployed brother, not Peter Harris' accomplice or even abductor. And that, she insisted to herself, was that.

But she was excited, nonetheless. She was determined to get as much out of her two weeks in Palmaltas as she could. Last night's party had ignited her energy and burnt away the lethargy that had crept upon her since her fiasco with Rick.

Peppy was on the pier and Jeremy joined him happily. Amy put her new resolve to work by casually waving to him as she spread her towel on the sand. Gradually, as the days progressed, she began to realize that he was treating her with the same civility as she was treating him. His behavior should have reassured her and, in a way, it did. But deep down inside her, she wanted something to happen. Was she expecting this hard, rugged male to throw her on the beach and ravish her, she wondered? This thought exasperated her. She wasn't some forlorn, loveless female yearning for a sexual adventure. Or was she? No, no, she told herself, she wanted to be friends with Peppy, nothing else.

On Tuesday she joined Jeremy and Peppy in their fishing venture on the pier. Of course, they didn't spend all of their time there. Jeremy loved to play in the sand and shallow water and Peppy and Amy took turns playing with him. Until now she had avoided their quiet fishing time on the pier.

"Tired of the sand, are you?" asked Peppy, with his casual, rather sardonic tone.

"No, not exactly, but I did think you guys might want some feminine company. Tell me, Peppy, what do you do with all this fish that you catch?"

"Give it to Amos for his fish-fry parties."

"Oh." At least he was doing something constructive. "But surely you don't catch enough everyday."

"No, no. He or a helper goes to the fish market in Bay City every afternoon and brings back fish from the day's catch."

She wondered if he was the helper since so far he had left the beach everyday around four o'clock. There were many things she wondered about Peppy but he was not forthcoming about his personal daily life.

They saw very little of Amos during the day because he was quite busy with the tourist trade. Their days that first week began to follow a pattern of fishing on the pier, playing in the sand, flopping around in the water, strolling along the beach and collecting shells, and joining Amos' parties at night. Sometimes Peppy joined them in these activities and sometimes not. However, he never attended Amos' night parties.

Although she maintained a certain suspicion about him, Amy gradually became comfortable in his presence. While at times she still considered his attitude to be cynical, there were moments when she found him to be rather sweet and vulnerable, especially when playing with Jeremy. But he always, always had the aura of solid, impenetrable masculinity. Such men had frightened her off in the past and now to find herself becoming friends with one was intoxicating. Certainly Rick had been masculine but not in the sense that Peppy was. Rick lacked Peppy's ruggedness and Rick was a coward. She couldn't feature Peppy in that role but yet something had driven him to idle away his days on this beach. Peppy, however, never offered to enlighten her and she didn't pry. The irony was that it was Peppy who maintained a polite distance between them and not her. She soon told him to drop the Miss from Miss Amy, which he did.

Those first few days were spent in contentment and she knew she shouldn't desire more. She was doing exactly what she had told Donna she wanted to do. She never dreamed a man like Peppy would factor into her daily activities. She kept telling herself that she had all she needed. But being in close proximity to him everyday caused her heart to palpitate and certain parts of her body to burn, conditions which exasperated her while she fought to keep calm around Peppy. He projected an air of relaxed amusement when he was with her and Jeremy. She tried hard to do the same.

Amos had promised them a ride in one of his glass bottom boats but the Marisol kept him booked solid and there was never any room for them. Amy realized she was more disappointed than Jeremy who apparently had ridden it before with Donna.

Sensing that they, or at least she, needed a change of pace from the routine that they were establishing with Peppy, she suggested to Jeremy that they should hire Daniel to give them a tour of the island. He thought that would be fun and readily agreed to the plan. But she reluctantly admitted to herself that the main reason she wanted to get away from Peppy was to find out if he would miss her and if her feelings toward him would or would not be reciprocated.

Thursday afternoon, she told Peppy in as cool a manner as possible that they wouldn't be at the beach the next day.

Before she could tell him what their plans were, he tweaked Jeremy's nose, and said, "Hey, no problem. I'll see you whenever." Then inexplicably he tweaked her nose, too, winked, and walked away.

What on earth had those actions meant, she wondered? Or had they meant anything? She trembled with rambling thoughts as they trekked to the condo. Her emotions were reeling. She had wanted him to ask what they were going to do and had hoped that he might offer to take them on a tour of the island. No, no, she admonished herself, she mustn't let Peppy affect her this way. She and Jeremy needed some time away from Peppy. She needed to get a grip on herself before she made a fool of herself in front of him.

~ * ~

"Okay, Pepe," said Amos, "when are you going to make some moves on your sand princess?"

"All in good time, brother, all in good time. I talked to Daniel a while ago. He's taking her for a tour of the island tomorrow."

"Then maybe you'll pay attention to our other problem for a day or so."

He laughed. "Why? Have you heard anything new?"

Amos replied seriously, "No, but I'm getting nervous."

"Don't worry, brother, it will soon be resolved anyway."

"I hope you know what you're doing. I think this may be more serious than we thought."

"But you just said that you haven't heard anything new."

"It's just a feeling I have."

"In that case, we have to be sure before we make any moves."

"What kind of moves do you have in mind?"

"I'm sneaking back into the Marisol executive offices to continue my search."

"When?"

"Maybe tomorrow night"

"Well, you haven't found anything so far and I don't like it. It just doesn't make sense that he would endanger the family business."

"He might have gotten careless and left something that I haven't had time to find."

"I still don't like it. Promise me that this will be the last time. Stay away from the hotel. Whatever he's doing, he wouldn't endanger the Marisol."

"All right, all right. Tomorrow night is the last time."

"And Miss Amy?"

He laughed. "Ah, Miss Amy. As I said, all in good time."

After Amos had settled down for the night and he could hear him snoring, he pondered just what he was doing with Amy. He may have tried to sound lighthearted with his brother but he knew he didn't have "all in good time" with her nor, for that matter, did he and Amos have much time left for their other very real problem. He was boasting when he told Amos that it would soon be resolved. He needed tangible proof and so far neither of them had that kind of proof.

~ * ~

Daniel proved to be a delightful tour guide. Not only did Amy consider him handsome and charming, but quite informative as well concerning the island. As they pulled away from the condo, he began a discourse on the history of this end of the island before it was taken over by developers during the middle of the twentieth century.

"This is where escaped slaves and shipwrecked sailors landed although the northern shore has the calmest surf as you'll soon see as we pass the Hilton and the airport. The U.S. Navy now uses those waters."

They made a turn to the left at the Palmaltas Hilton, passing some beach cabins on the right where Amy assumed Amos and Peppy lived. The airport was across the road. Past the airport lay the massive military base encircled by high metal fencing and tall palm trees. The beach along this stretch of the road was long and flat and deserted. A few navy ships could be seen anchored offshore.

"Don't they need a dock or a wharf to bring supplies in?" she asked.

"They do that in Bay City where commercial freighters and tour ships anchor. They have their own vehicles to transport their supplies and equipment from the city, over the mountains, to here. I think that was part of the original arrangement with the Palmaltan government. May not make sense but that's the way our government works," he explained laughing.

"Anyway," he continued, "Caribe Indians, who were later decimated by the Spaniards except for a few who escaped into the mountains, originally inhabited this part of the island. The Spaniards set up a small settlement here where the military base is. When the English gained control of the island, they founded Bay City because they thought they could better defend the island there due to the shelter of the bay. Didn't make sense, really, but it didn't matter. Nobody ever attacked."

"I thought the Indians were called Carib," said Amy, wondering at his pronunciation, which sounded to her like *kah-ree-bay*.

He laughed again. "The Spaniards said Caribe because that's the way the Indian name sounded to them, I suppose. A few of us today still have Caribe blood but for the most part the Indians of the Caribbean died from the white man's diseases and harsh treatment. The Europeans neglected Palmaltas for long periods of time and it became a refuge for ruffians of all sorts including shipwrecked sailors and runaway slaves. They intermarried with the remaining Indians as did the Spaniards and English for the brief times that they governed the island."

"Yes, I have read some about the people who have migrated here." She paused then said, "Oh, this is beautiful."

They had just passed the military base and were climbing small hills that skirted the mountain range. The terrain had changed drastically to dense foliage on both sides of the road. As they continued to climb, she asked Daniel questions about himself.

"Is there a girl, someone special in your life?"

"Yes," he said rather disarmingly, "there are three that are very important to me."

"Three?" she retorted, surprised that he would admit it. "Are they all Palmaltans? Or tourists? They must keep you busy." She figured Daniel to be quite the island Romeo. He certainly had the best opportunity to meet attractive incoming young tourists and she supposed those tourists would be bowled over by his good looks and charm. His answer surprised her.

"Yes, they are Palmaltans," he said calmly. "My wife and two little daughters and yes, they keep me very busy."

"That's wonderful," she said, feeling silly at jumping to the wrong conclusion. "Tell me about your daughters. I love children. I teach first grade in Nebraska."

He proceeded to entertain her with tales of his toddlers while continuing to indicate points of interest. At the summit on one hill, he stopped so that they could see all of Bay City spread out below, occupying the entire western end of the island.

"Oh," she gasped, "this is so different from the other end." Then she remembered how congested it had looked from the air when she arrived. She had not thought much about it then because she had been so excited in her expectation of seeing Donna and Jeremy.

"Yes, it certainly is," he replied rather bitterly, his manner changing from lighthearted to serious.

"Do you live in Bay City?"

"No, we live in one of the beach cabins near the Palmaltas Hilton."

"Then you must know Amos and his brother Peppy-er-Pepe."

"Yes, Amos is everyone's friend."

"And Peppy?"

"I don't know him well enough. He's older than Amos."

Amy thought that he seemed reticent to speak about Peppy but she was curious and wanted to know as much as possible.

"But what is his story? Why is Amos so industrious while Peppy does nothing?"

"I don't know anything about him. I think something must have happened to him in the States. He was educated there, I think. But I'm just guessing. A lot of people come here with tainted pasts to begin a new life. He was born here and has Amos here. We don't ask questions, just accept people as they are."

She fell silent. She sensed that Daniel didn't want to discuss Peppy, perhaps in deference to his respect for Amos. But her curiosity was piqued. What had Peppy done in the States to warrant a return to Palmaltas, to do nothing except fish? Drugs? That seemed the most logical reason. Despite the presence of the military base, Palmaltas didn't have an extradition treaty with the United States. That much she knew from reading about the island. Perhaps Palmaltas was still a refuge for ruffians. But was Peppy a ruffian? Or a drug dealer? Or a thief? Or worse? She couldn't bear to think of him as any of these things. His American education explained his American accent. And why had he, of all people, substituted for Daniel when she arrived? Had that been a coincidence or something else? Somehow, she thought Daniel wouldn't give her a straight answer to any of these puzzles so she left her questions unasked.

The drive down the hill to Bay City was quick but, as soon as they arrived at the outskirts of the city, Daniel drove through narrow, crowded neighborhood streets until he came to what seemed the hub of the city. He parked alongside a central plaza and, as they alighted from the limousine, she asked him if there were any major tourist attractions in Bay City.

He laughed and said, "There's a hotel that was made famous by a very popular novel but if you haven't read it then it won't mean much to you. I'll show it to you anyway."

Amy had not read any novel about Palmaltas, just a few reference books, but she was interested in a hotel that would inspire someone to write a novel.

He led her and Jeremy, who had been very quiet during the journey from the condo, across the street and down a block where he turned right. A few doors down, a freshly painted sign stated very simply, *Bay View Hotel.* The brick façade was painted beige and the ground floor contained a neat little lobby next to a small coffee shop. Amy wanted to tour the other floors but Daniel said she couldn't unless she registered as a guest. The little hotel was charming and if she had been a regular tourist to the island she would have preferred it to the others on the eastern end including the Palmaltas Hilton and the Marisol. As they stepped outside from the lobby she glanced upwards at the wrought-iron balconies that faced the Bay of Palmaltas. The hotel was darling, she thought, and she wondered what had happened there to inspire a writer to use the hotel as the setting for a novel.

"It's a lovely little hotel," she said to Daniel.

"It didn't use to be that way. At one time it was a haven for hookers and low-lifes and it didn't have a view of the Bay at all. There used to be warehouses here across the street blocking the view but the government knocked them down after the book came out."

A cobblestoned promenade led down to the piers and wharves, but Daniel, it seemed, was taking them on a riding tour of the island and was not inclined to do much walking. The Bay View Hotel seemed to be his only concession to getting out of the car. However, as they left the city, he did drive past the busy bay with its touristy little shops, docks, piers, wharves, fishing boats, ships, and freighters. Daniel explained that the tourist shops had replaced rowdy bars. The area had been cleaned up for the tourists. Amy would have loved to spend more time around the bay but Daniel was obviously anxious to show them the south part of the island, which turned out to be much different from the other parts that she had now seen.

The road started to climb upwards and she saw that rugged cliffs dropped dramatically to surf pounding on jagged rocks. The view was electrifyingly beautiful and certainly dangerous. The road ran alongside the cliff edges giving them a perilous view of the rocks below. Daniel, accustomed to the terrain, took the road curves much too fast, it seemed to her, and she found herself clutching her seat and closing her eyes. Daniel and Jeremy chattered about fishing as they twisted and turned and climbed, ignoring her feeble protests to slow down.

However, Daniel did stop the car once and pointed downward.

"That's Black Water Cove down there. Pirates used to hide out there, centuries ago. Then it remained fairly deserted for a long time. Now, as you can see, tourists come in droves."

Amy looked over the cliff and down to the crowded little beach. A paved path with a handrail led the way down the cliffside. She tried to imagine what the beach would look like without the bikini-clad bodies, both male and female, littering its pink sand.

"Yes," she said, "it certainly looks like a popular spot."

"Yes," replied Daniel rather bitterly, "someone writes a book about us and suddenly the whole world wants to come. Mind you, for the most part I don't care. I make a good living because of it. But a lot of people haven't benefited at all. And you'll never see a Palmaltan native enjoying the cool waters or sandy beach of Black Water Cove."

"Why not?"

"The big hotels bring their guests here from dawn to dusk. It's not worth the hassle of getting here and finding a spot to spread your towel and fend off strangers. Very few Palmaltans enjoy their own homeland as much as rich strangers do."

"My friend Donna said that her husband David Díaz wants to change all that."

"Yes, but he's going to have to do something soon or the Palmaltan people are going to be pushed away with nowhere to go."

"So David should persevere no matter what?"

"I pray and hope he does. But, Miss Amy," he said turning even more serious, "be careful who you tell about David. Not many people know of his ambitions. If he makes a wrong step then he'll never have another chance."

"Oh no, it's that bad?" Quickly changing the subject, she asked, "What do you think of the missing man, Peter Harris?"

"Not much. He can stay missing for all I care. I never paid attention to him. I work for the condo not the Marisol."

Amy was shocked at that reply, considering all of the praise that she had heard from Donna about Peter. Then another thought occurred to her. "Do you suppose that he, like David, was plotting to undermine the current government and got caught?"

His laugh was bitter. "Not likely. He is or was what you might call a playboy who spent his money on parties and women. Some say he worked hard and that he deserved to spend his money however he pleased. I disagree. When all Palmaltans have enough money to support themselves and enjoy life, then he'll have the right to do what he wants. And Peter Harris is, or was, a friend of David Díaz but I'll bet David never discussed politics with him, just business. I've heard that Harris sent a lot of Marisol customers to La Concha Blanca and David couldn't afford to alienate him. No, David has to be very careful. We all do. What makes me mad is that there's enough money coming into this island from tourists alone to make all of us at least comfortable, but most people don't get a thing."

"Who does?"

"The government, the hotel conglomerates. Then there's money from the U.S. Military. No telling how much they pay for the right to be here. Then consider all those banks that do business here."

"What about drug money?"

"That's kept hush-hush. I suspect only government officials are involved in that."

"That's terrible."

"Of course, but the crazy thing is, they don't need drug money. Like I just said, everyone on this island could be well off just from tourist money alone. This could be one of the best island paradises in the whole world. But greed and government corruption are going to ruin us. I don't think we'll turn into another Haiti, not with the U.S. Military here, but it's a possibility."

"So you need men like David Díaz."

"Desperately, and we don't need men like Peter Harris."

A sudden thought fluttered through her mind. Instead of the government doing away with Peter, what if other secret, more militant revolutionaries had kidnapped him? That would make a lot more sense in view of the fact that Peter seemed to be allied with the government. Yet Donna had been genuinely fond of Peter but was that because he was an associate of David's, she wondered? This was nonsense, she told herself. Peter and David were not her concern or the overthrowing of the Palmaltan government.

But her thoughts wouldn't stop as Peppy's figure floated through her mind's vision. He was a Palmaltan who was nothing more than a scruffy beachcomber, wasting away his life on a sunny, sandy beach while someone like David was willing to make sacrifices and take chances to better his country. Even Peter Harris made more of a contribution than Peppy. The Marisol brought tourists and their money, some of which found its way to Amos and Daniel and Ossie, all native Palmaltans. Why was Peppy so different?

"But," she persisted, "you and Amos and others like Ossie and the lifeguards benefit from the tourist onslaught. Why can't more Palmaltans do so?"

His smile was more of a scowl. "We are tokens, lucky tokens mind you, hired to give a false front of how prosperous we Palmaltans are. The tourists see handsome, smiling, friendly faces and think all Palmaltans are the same. They leave the island thinking what nice people we are. About the only part of Bay City that they see is what I showed you today such as the cove down there, the shops around the bay, and the Bay View Hotel, which incidentally is also owned by the Harris hotel family. But I don't complain for my family or myself. We are lucky and yes, even happy. I complain for my people."

"What? Peter Harris also owns that little hotel?"

"His family does but I assume he is the principal stockholder or CEO or whatever that kind of person calls himself. The Bay View was always owned by outsiders anyway."

He started the car and pulled away from the view of Black Water Cove. Amy settled back and tried to enjoy the rest of the trip, which turned out to be quite short. Daniel pointed out some mansions perched on the cliff tops, stating that they belonged to government officials. Jeremy had fallen asleep. Local politics were not very entertaining for a six-year-old.

The road began to descend and they were soon on level ground and approaching the condo. Once there she roused Jeremy and thanked Daniel for an enlightening day. That night she decided not to go to Amos' fish fry, feeling that maybe Jeremy needed to get some rest if they did indeed take the trip she was planning. She had a longing to see Peppy but after listening to Daniel, she felt that maybe she needed to stay away from him for a while.

The next day, Saturday, Amy felt brave enough to take the bus tour around the island. Originally, as Donna had explained to her, there had been only two bus stops on the entire island, one at the airport and one at the central plaza in downtown Bay City. Now there were bus stops at all the hotels. After leaving the condo and greeting Ossie, she and Jeremy walked over to the Marisol where in due time the bus arrived. The bus route retraced Daniel's tour as they proceeded around the island's east end, turning left at the airport, passing the base on the left and the lovely flat beach on the right. They again climbed the mountains and enjoyed the view of the lovely vegetation even more through the bus's wide windows.

As they reached the summit of the last hill, she marveled once more at the view of Bay City below. The bus progressed smoothly down into the city straight into the hub of the crowded little city, bypassing the residential neighborhoods that Daniel had shown them yesterday. Amy was not surprised. The bus was run by the government and was filled mainly with tourists who were going to Bay City to check out the Bay View Hotel and the shops around the bay. Naturally the government would prefer that the tourists not observe these neighborhoods. She felt that Daniel, on the other hand, wanted her to know of the plight of his people. There were Palmaltans who occasionally got on or off the bus, but for the most part the people who had boarded in the resort area stayed on until they arrived at the plaza.

At the plaza Jeremy and Amy began to walk around it. There were trees and benches and ice cream and hot dog vendors, even eager shoeshine boys whose enterprise seemed outmoded. Lively tourists and subdued Palmaltans mingled creating a contrasting throng of humanity. Yet strangely she felt comfortable there, even welcome.

Amy purchased mango sherbets for both of them, much to Jeremy's delight. As they ate, they walked down the promenade to the bay, which was entrenched with tourist shops selling souvenirs and trinkets. She tried to imagine what this part of the city had looked like when there was nothing but bars here. Normally, she loved places like these but she immediately discovered that Bay City residents were not the proprietors. Only people from the prominent hotels and condos, which were advertised in each doorway, ran the little shops. Many were foreigners, mostly Americans, Europeans, and Asians.

"It's just not fair," she said absentmindedly.

"What isn't?" asked Jeremy.

"Life. Oh, never mind. Let's walk out on one of the docks and watch the ships unload and listen to the seagulls. Later we'll go back to the plaza for one of those Palmaltan hot dogs. They sure look good."

"Yeah, Amy, that's a great idea."

They spent a leisurely day walking around, feeding pigeons in a little park on a hill that overlooked the bay and eating hot dogs in the plaza that turned out to be even more delicious than they looked.

When they finished eating Amy wanted to inspect the Bay View Hotel again but Jeremy tugged her hand and said, "Look, Amy, there's the bus."

"Oh," she said, "I guess we had better start back now."

The bus didn't return the way it had come but followed the south side of the island just as Daniel had done yesterday. What a strange way to run a bus line, she thought, but since buses circled the island punctually all day, she supposed people got to where they wanted to go when they wanted. Servicemen, though, would have a longer time returning to the base than they had on their trip into Bay City.

Once back at the condo, she flopped on the sofa as the ever-energetic Jeremy brought out his Chinese checkers game. While they played, her mind focused on her vacation. Except for the two excursions to Bay City, she assumed her remaining days on the fascinating and diverse island of Palmaltas were to be spent on the beach with Jeremy and Peppy. There could be worse fates, she assured herself, but deep inside her soul, she yearned for something more, something to put the final stamp on her breakup with Rick. But would a daily rendezvous with a down-at-heels beach bum, albeit a sensual and enigmatic one, and a six-year-old chaperone suffice?

Six

"Where was Miss Amy today?" asked Amos when his brother came to the concession that afternoon to drop off his fishing gear.

"I wandered over to the condo and asked around. Bert and Eddie hadn't seen her but Ossie said she took Jerry on the bus. I guess Daniel's sightseeing tour wasn't enough."

"Maybe that shows she's interested in the island."

"I hope so."

"Or maybe she just takes you for granted. You haven't been much of a Don Juan with her."

"Yeah, but I kind of like taking it slow with her."

"Whew! I've never known you to do that! You take it too slow and you'll run out of time. She's only here for a couple of weeks and you've got only one week left."

"I have to be sure about her. I can't make any mistakes now."

"The biggest mistake might be not doing anything at all."

"Maybe, but I want to be certain, really certain." He waved good-bye to his brother and ambled down the beach, his thoughts on Amy. There was one thing of which he was positive: how much he wanted to hold her and run his hands over the curvy contours of her body and crush his lips over hers.

Yes, he had surprised not only Amos with his restraint but himself as well. But this was too important. He had made mistakes before with women he cared for only to be deceived by them, especially the last one. He tried to convince himself that his ego was bruised more than his emotions. Luckily, he had Amos on his side looking out for him and so far Amos approved of Amy. But it was how he felt about Amy that mattered the most in the long run and right now he didn't have a long run.

He gave a grim smile. He had always thought of himself as being the one who controlled his relationships with women. But the latest one had fooled him completely. He had thought he was in love at last and had found the perfect match. Then Amos had seen and heard her conspiring with someone he had dismissed as inconsequential but trustworthy and his world started to unravel. If Amos' plan worked and he was sure it would, the two scoundrels would be exposed and he could turn his attention to Amy who so unexpectedly was beginning to capture his heart. For the first time in a long time he looked forward to each day because he knew he would see her on the beach with Jerry. These few days with the two of them had opened up feelings that he never knew he possessed, feelings of contentment and even joy.

~ * ~

Around midnight Pepe crept out of his tiny room, listened to Amos and his snoring, and left the cabin. It was a clear night with stars twinkling but no moon was out. The beach was deserted except for the lapping waves. He walked along in a casual manner but he didn't feel casual. He had done this before without results and this was going to be the last time. He had to trust Amos who didn't want him inside the Marisol. He walked on, passing hotels and restaurants, until he reached the back entrance of the Marisol. All was quiet. The front of the Marisol stayed open twenty-fours a day but the back part was closed and locked at midnight. He waited in Amos' concession for the night watchman to walk by on his rounds. When he finally appeared and disappeared, Pepe reached up to where various keys for the hotel hung from a hook, grabbed two, and then began to look for a penlight that he knew Amos kept in a drawer. When he found it, he crept carefully across the sand to the back entrance.

He turned one of the keys in the lock and slipped inside. He walked quietly to the elevator, entered, and punched the code for the executive suites. When the door opened, he went directly to the office door marked Peter Harris CEO and with the other key, opened it.

Being careful so that the light never wavered toward the ceiling-to-floor window overlooking the beach, he began to search the desk. This time he would take his time and not rush through the papers as he had on previous times. He read everything carefully but nothing seemed out of place. In fact, the hotel seemed to be running smoothly and that was exactly what Amos thought he would find. But somewhere in this office there had to be something that indicated treason. After all, Amos had heard the two of them conspiring on the beach, not knowing or caring who Amos was.

He went through all of the file cabinets, a painstaking and time-consuming effort, but found nothing. At four o'clock he gave up and left as he had entered. While walking back along the beach, it suddenly occurred to him that the evidence might be kept in the Bay View Hotel. That would be a much harder place to break into because too many people milled around in front of the office at all hours of the day and night.

He took his time strolling along the beach, inhaling the salty aroma of the sea, and enjoying the calm lapping of the waves on the shore. He thought about Amos and his connection to the Marisol. He grinned to himself. Amos was a man of many talents that included more than charm and hospitality for visiting tourists.

But his thoughts drifted to Amy, as they always did. How he wished that he were strolling along the beach with her, both of them carefree and wanting only to be alone together. Could or would that ever happen?

When he reached the cabin he walked into his room and collapsed on the bed with visions of Amy circling in his mind. He soon fell into a deep sleep.

~ * ~

The next day Peppy joined them on the beach just before noon. Amy's heart fluttered at the sight of him but she managed to gain control of herself when he sat beside her on the beach towel.

"Wow, you're kind of late this morning."

"Uh-huh, keeping tabs on my hours?"

"No, of course not."

"Seems like you have been missing for two days."

Not responding to that statement, she cautiously brought up the subject of downtrodden Palmaltans to see if she could get any kind of rise from him.

"Do you ever go over to Bay City?" she asked.

He rolled over onto the sand, with one arm folded over his eyes, his muscular, tanned body glistening in the sun. The sight of him like this made her wonder at her own restraint with him. He took so much time in answering that at first she thought he wasn't going to answer at all.

Finally, he simply said, "Sometimes. Why?"

"We took a couple of trips there the past two days. I was disheartened at how shabby and crowded the city is, except for the parts that the government has cleaned up for tourism."

"So that's where you were, huh?" he asked laconically.

"Yes, Daniel, the real chauffeur," she said with a tinge of sarcasm, "took us Friday and then we went by bus yesterday. By the way, on the day of my arrival, did you take Daniel's place on purpose or were you really just helping him?"

He grinned slyly. "I managed to send Daniel on an errand. I was very curious about St. Amy and wanted an early peek at the woman Jerry was so fond of."

"Well, I never! That-that was so rude!"

He burst out laughing, rolled over, and made a move to grab her.

"Oh no, you don't. There are things I'd like to discuss with you, things Daniel told me."

"Yeah, such as?" he asked without much enthusiasm.

"I think it's a shame that not all Palmaltans get to share the wealth that's pouring into the island."

He sat up and stared at her for a few minutes.

"Do you really feel that way?"

"Of course," she said. "This is a beautiful island with beautiful, friendly people who don't seem to be very happy because they have to struggle for a living."

"Have you discussed this with anyone or is this just an observation?"

"With Donna some and quite a bit with Daniel."

"Hmm," was his only response.

She persevered. "How do you feel about David Díaz's desire to improve the island or do you know much about him?"

He raised an eyebrow and stared at her skeptically, and she thought, with surprise.

"David Díaz is Jerry's new stepdad."

"Yes, I know you know of him that way. But his political ambitions, what have you heard or think about them?"

He sat very still for a while then spoke somberly. "Amy, is this really important to you? You'll be gone soon. You live in another world."

"Yes," she exclaimed defiantly, "I do care. Not only because my best friends live here but also because I can't bear to see people suffer when there's no need for it."

He smiled then, more with concern than cynicism. "I certainly agree with that."

"But David Díaz needs help from all Palmaltans. Would you be willing to get out and really work for him?"

He evaded her question as his cynical smile returned. "Donna and Daniel have told you all this, huh?"

Suddenly she remembered Daniel's admonition not to discuss David's ambitions with anyone and her own private conjectures of Peppy being a fugitive from American justice. She quickly changed the subject.

"What do you think of the missing hotel tycoon Peter Harris?"

The question seemed to startle him and she supposed that was due to her avoiding his question and countering with an unrelated one. He took his time in answering.

"I don't think the opinion of an unemployed Palmaltan matters much. Why do you ask? Do you think of him a lot?"

"No, of course not. I've never met him. He was a friend of Donna and David's and he disappeared before I arrived. I've heard conflicting opinions about him and wondered what you thought."

"I'm flattered that you're interested in my opinion," he said sardonically. "But what kind of conflicting opinions have you heard?"

"Oh, Donna and a couple of her friends think he's a great guy and that he's been kidnapped for a huge ransom but the family and the authorities are keeping a lid on it. Others don't seem to like him at all. They seem to think that he was just a playboy who kept money that should have gone to Palmaltan citizens."

"He didn't take money from the citizens of Palmaltas. He took it, by way of the Marisol and the Bay View Hotel in Bay City, from rich tourists. My brother works for him, remember."

Surprised that he was defending the man although she supposed that was due to Amos' influence, she persevered in her argument. "But he didn't share it."

"You think people should share what they earn?"

"Yes, as long as there are people suffering!" she cried.

"Isn't that called socialism?"

"I-I don't know," she said stubbornly. "So what if it is? I just think there are better ways to distribute wealth than the way it's done here."

"Well, Amy, maybe you're right. And if you think David Díaz will change things then I support him."

He stared at her long and hard with his piercing, pale blue eyes. The sun danced on his silver hair and his tanned muscles rippled through his arms as he pushed himself up, brushing away sand from his sturdy legs. He gave her a quick smile as he called to Jeremy who was playing patiently by the water's edge.

"Hey, Jerry, how's the water?" He ran down and scooped up the laughing child and plunged them both into the water.

Amy watched them with mixed feelings. He had not shown particular interest in either David or Peter, although he had defended Peter while agreeing to support David. Or had he just said that to placate her? Had she done any harm in informing him of David's ambitions? Was she too trusting?

Her most confused feelings came from the sensual yearning that was coursing through her body when she was in Peppy's presence. How could she let him affect her that way? Was she really attracted to a whiskered, muscular, sardonic vagrant? Would her feelings change if Peter Harris were to return and somehow Donna contrived to get them together?

She watched Peppy playing with Jeremy in the water and yearned for him to scoop her up just as he had done with the child. A little demon seemed to lurk somewhere deep inside her, urging her toward Peppy and a chance for a romantic interlude. After all, this was her vacation and time was running out. But did she dare? Peppy seemed so aloof and unobtainable.

~ * ~

"So, what did you find last night?" asked Amos, sipping a beer and relaxing alongside his brother on the back porch of the cabin.

"Not a damn thing. I'm beginning to think that if there is anything incriminating to be found, it's at the Bay View."

"That makes sense, but you couldn't break into that place."

"I don't intend to but I might spy on the place. That shouldn't be too difficult."

"Maybe. Take Ossie with you and hang out with a bunch of guys on the corner."

"That might work." He hesitated a moment and said, "You're not going to believe what Amy told me today."

"What?"

"David Díaz seems to be working against the government."

Amos sat up and said, "How does she know that? Did Donna tell her that before she left?"

"I'm not sure but Daniel did while he was acting as tour guide. Why haven't I heard anything like that?"

"Daniel? Damn, bro, I think you and I have been left out in the cold. I think it's about time you speeded up some things."

"Yeah, and although I'm trying to be cautious regarding Amy, I'm going to have to speed things up with her, too."

"No argument from me there."

"The thing is that she has to want to stay here. I have an idea of how she can do that. I'll throw out a suggestion but it's up to her. If she's the one then she will do it."

"I can't believe how lazy you've been around her. The old bro would have ravished her by now."

He grinned. "Maybe I'm growing up. I'll know within the next few days if I've been right about her. In the meantime we need to get organized. We've got two problems to work on now."

"Two?"

"Our original problem and the David Díaz problem."

"And you, my bro, can add a third. The Amy problem."

He grinned. "At least that one is enjoyable."

~ * ~

While her days on Palmaltas grew fewer in number, Amy dreaded leaving more and more for various reasons. One, she hated the thought of leaving Jeremy, a little boy whom she dearly loved, but he had a loving mother and stepfather and didn't need her. He thought of her as he would a beloved aunt and would miss her once she was gone, but she felt she would miss him so much more. Two, she loved Palmaltas. If she could find a way to stay in Palmaltas, she would do it in a flash. The third reason was one she hated to admit to herself. She didn't want to leave Peppy.

Monday afternoon she and Peppy sat on her beach towel watching Jeremy collect shells. As casually as she could, she said, "I love Palmaltas, Peppy. I wish that I could live here."

She thought she noticed a tinge of surprise cross his face and wondered if she had said something wrong.

"You might," he said after a few moments, "ask David Díaz when he comes back if he has any ideas about you teaching here."

"Teach here?" Oh, she thought with relief, how wonderful that would be. "But would it be legal?"

"What do you mean?"

"Wouldn't I need a work permit or something?"

He seemed amused by her question. "In Palmaltas? Are you kidding? This is a place people escape. People come here, change their identities, nobody cares."

"Are you serious?" Was this what he had done with Amos as a collaborator? The idea was just too farfetched. Or was it?

"Definitely. There are some plus sides to corruption, you know."

"Oh you!" She threw sand at him pretending that he was joking but she didn't know what to think. Had Peppy indeed come here and changed identity? Did Amos really have a half-brother that Peppy could impersonate? Daniel accepted him as Amos' brother but wasn't that because he trusted Amos? There was no resemblance between Peppy and Amos whatsoever and only Amos spoke with a Palmaltan accent. Of course, Peppy had lived in the States according to Daniel. Why didn't Peppy show up at Amos' nightly tourist beach parties? Surely a beach bum would enjoy partying into the night. And Peppy's daily appearances were sporadic, never following any particular schedule. Where did he go? What did he do? Had he done something illicit in the States and had come here to do the same?

Pushing those thoughts aside, she playfully dodged the sand he threw back at her. Then he yelled at Jeremy and told him it was time to fish. Amy went with them, not wanting to dwell on her doubts regarding Peppy. She loved spending time with the two of them but desired for so much more.

That evening while Jeremy was playing in his bath, Amy considered the predictable routine that she and Jeremy followed. They arose early, immediately going to the beach after breakfast, usually having lunch at the cantina or returning briefly to the condo, back to the beach, returning to the condo for dinner, back to the beach and Amos' parties, always leaving early because Jeremy had to bathe and be in bed by nine o'clock. Yes, they were creatures of habit. But her routine didn't end with Jeremy's bedtime. After a story and a kiss, he fell asleep readily, happy and content, and she would go downstairs for a glass of wine and sit out on the balcony to listen to the night sounds.

And it was that peaceful time filled with the sounds of the splashing tide, the swishing palms, and the distant calypso and laughter from Amos' ongoing party that caused her to yearn for her vacation to be prolonged. Was she actually going to leave without any semblance of romance? She bitterly told herself that she had not come here for any such thing. What had she told Donna? Bougainvillea. And Donna had laughed and asked if her dreams had included any men. Well, she had the bougainvillea. The condominium grounds were covered with it, and she hated to admit that now she wanted something more than exotic blooms. She wasn't lonely exactly. Jeremy was nearby.

Her thoughts always returned to Peppy, to her doubts, to their conversations, and unbelievably to how comfortable she had become with him. She looked forward to each day because she knew she would probably see Peppy. But something was wrong in their relationship. He never came on to her or made advances. Something was amiss. Was he really Amos' brother, a true Palmaltan? If not, then why did Amos permit such a charade? And who was Johnny, the friend that Jeremy had mentioned and had never appeared? Since she was going home soon, would she ever learn the answers to her questions? Would Donna or David know? Would they have time after their return and before her departure to sit down and listen to her feeble conjectures? Would they help her to find a way to teach in Bay City? They, naturally, would be wrapped up in their reunion with Jeremy.

Should she just shove aside her doubts about Peppy and invite him up to the apartment for a glass of wine after Jeremy had gone to bed? Would Donna approve? What would Donna say about her trusted babysitter thrashing around in the sheets with a beach bum while her son slept nearby? No, she couldn't chance her censure. But she knew Peppy would never harm either of them and deep down she knew that if Donna knew what was going through her mind, she would laugh herself silly at her. Still, she shouldn't take any chances. She couldn't invite someone unknown to Donna up to her apartment. But Amy could hear that little demon deep inside her crying out, *Chicken, chicken, you're just afraid Peppy will say no, that you will be hurt again.* Her mind responded, *How silly, a lazy beachcomber could never steal my heart.*

No matter how hard she tried, she couldn't push Peppy out of her thoughts. He had become their one dependable friend despite maintaining an aloofness regarding his private life. His appearance had remained the same, the close-cropped hair and the inevitable stubble on his face. How did he keep both his hair and his beard cut so short? And why? Wouldn't a beach bum let them grow out? Those were his two physical features that irritated her the most. Amy liked clean-shaven men whose hair she could run her fingers through. How he chose to appear was his business, though, and whether she approved or disapproved, his appearance always caused her heart to beat faster, much to her own consternation.

Jeremy interrupted her thoughts. "I'm ready for bed, Amy."

She jumped up and went upstairs with him to his room. Tucking him into bed, she asked, "Are you sure that Peppy and Amos are brothers?"

"Of course. Johnny says they are and Johnny would never lie."

"Tell me about Johnny."

He smiled sweetly. "Johnny is nice, very nice, almost as nice as you, Amy."

"Thank you, darling. But is Johnny nicer than Peppy? He's a very good friend to you."

"I know. He's my best friend and Amos and Johnny are my friends, too, but Johnny's really great."

"My, my," she murmured as she kissed him good night.

Why hadn't she met Johnny? Just as she was about to turn off the lights, she asked one more question. "Is Johnny a brother of Amos and Peppy?"

"No, Amy." He giggled sleepily. "That's silly."

What a strange reply, she thought, but Jeremy was only six-years-old. He saw adults from a completely different perspective. He believed that Peppy and Amos were brothers. Why would they have lied to a little boy? Since Amos knew both Donna and David, she couldn't see any reason for such a deception. If only she could meet the elusive Johnny.

~ * ~

Walking to the beach the next morning, Amy said wistfully to Jeremy, "This is my last week here, Jerry. Let's give it all we can."

"What do you mean, Amy?"

She laughed, not admitting to herself and certainly not to Jeremy what she really meant. "Let's have a fishing contest with Peppy." She didn't want to have a contest with Peppy at all. In fact, that's what it seemed like they had been doing, competing to see who could maintain the most restraint. Or was she simply not Peppy's type at all? Or was this idea a remnant of Rick's deception, that she couldn't be attractive to any sensual male?

Luckily Jeremy jolted her out of her self-pity.

"Oh yes! That would be great fun, Amy."

He ran on ahead of her, shouting the minute he saw Peppy on the pier. "Peppy, Peppy, we're going to have a fishing contest with you!"

"Oh yeah? Well, we'll see about that," he said scooping up the boy in his arms and whirling him.

By the time Amy arrived at the pier, they had all three fishing rods ready.

"Hurry up, Amy, and get in position," said Peppy.

She smiled and sat down while Peppy handed her the rod. She thought to herself how she had become quite the fisherwoman during the short time she had been here. She could bait her hook, reel in her catch, and clean it as well as Jeremy could. She was quite proud of her new accomplishment. She knew this wasn't going to be much of a contest because Peppy could outdo either of them.

Jeremy was eager to start and as soon as Peppy counted to three, all of them cast their lines.

Amy was sure that Peppy would be the first to land a fish but he surprised her in the most pleasant of ways. He started by letting Jeremy and Amy take center stage in their fishing game.

Jeremy laughed with delight when he was the first to pull in a fish. He was equally happy when Amy was the second one to do so. He hooted uproariously when Peppy brought up an empty hook. She didn't know how Peppy did it, because many times she could see him struggling with a large fish only to lose it. Then Jeremy or she would reel in something smaller and Jeremy would tease Peppy relentlessly

This action endeared him to her, not only because he was considerate of them, but also because he seemed to thoroughly enjoy their company.

~ * ~

Wednesday afternoon when he stowed his fishing gear in Amos' concession, he said, "Ossie is coming over to the cabin tonight when he gets off work at the condo. We're going into Bay City and stake out the Bay View Hotel."

"Well, you may have to have more than one stake-out. Let's just hope that they get careless."

"Ossie thought he saw them going in the hotel together the other night."

"Man, I'm glad we've got Ossie. What was he doing there?"

"Just visiting some friends. It was purely by accident that he saw them."

"Well, good luck, bro. Be careful."

~ * ~

Ossie met him at the bus stop in front of the airport.

After boarding the bus, Ossie said, "I hope this isn't a wild goose chase, Pepe. Just because I saw them there once doesn't mean they'll do it again."

"Amos and I have suspected that something might be going on at the Bay View."

"But Amos has been spying on them at the Marisol, hasn't he?"

"Not for some time. He has to be careful. Mostly, what he heard from them came about by accident."

"Well, if nothing happens tonight, let's just go to a cantina and enjoy the music."

He laughed. "Good thinking, Ossie, good thinking."

At this time of night, the bus didn't make many stops and they soon arrived at the plaza near the Bay View Hotel. They joined a group of men who were friends of Ossie and stood on the corner joking and gossiping. Suddenly, he saw a limousine pull up in front of the hotel. He nudged Ossie.

"Damn, that's her."

"Uh huh," whispered Ossie, "and look who is greeting her in the entrance."

"So they have behaved themselves at the Marisol but it's here that they have carried on with their illicit business."

"It would seem so," agreed Ossie.

"Seeming so isn't enough. We need more proof but at least now I know that those two are into something together."

"And I bet you know just what that something is," said Ossie.

"Yeah, I'm afraid I do."

~ * ~

Amy and Jeremy spent Tuesday, Wednesday, and Thursday competing in the fishing contest with Peppy. Thursday afternoon Peppy announced Jeremy as the winner of the contest.

The little boy jumped up and down and ran over to tell Amos how he had caught more fish than Peppy. Amy couldn't understand why this rugged individual was so content to spend his days playing games with a little boy and his guardian while she wanted so much more.

Alone with Peppy at the edge of the pier with the sounds of waves lapping against the pylons and the mewing of seagulls above, Amy wished the moment could go on forever. To her great relief, he put his arms around her so tightly that she could feel the hardness of his body.

"Two more days, Amy," he whispered into her ear, his warm breath sending ripples of passion up and down her body. "Do you think you'll find a way to stay?"

Bravely she looked up into his hooded blue eyes and asked, "Do you want me to?"

Giving her a steely look, he said, "It's what you want that matters, Amy, not what I want."

"No, Peppy, what you want matters very much to me."

He smiled and hugged her more. "I hope you mean that."

"I do," she whispered.

At that moment he crushed his lips to hers sending her emotions reeling out of control.

"Oh yuk!" cried Jeremy, causing the two of them to jump apart.

"What do you mean 'yuk'?" joked Peppy, tweaking his nose.

"That kissing stuff. That's what Mom and David do. That's not fun."

"Just wait, young man, someday you'll see how wrong you are." Turning to Amy, he said, "I've got to go now but think about what we were discussing."

She nodded numbly. There was nothing else she could think about except that.

75

Seven

The next day, Friday, her last day before Donna and David returned, the three of them again sat on the edge of the pier, their usual perch, with lines in the water and seagulls mewing around them. Amy inhaled deeply, knowing that soon she would no longer be able to enjoy the unique salty aroma of sea air or the intoxicating presence that Peppy emanated.

"Well, guys, this is it, our last day together," she said in a melancholy tone and hoping that she was wrong.

"Oh no, Amy," said Jeremy. "Why can't you stay longer?"

"Your mom and new dad will be back tomorrow. The condo will be crowded."

"But David has his own condo."

"That's right, twerp, and I imagine you'll either move to his or he'll move to yours."

"Then," said Jeremy seriously, "you can stay in the empty one."

Peppy laughed. "Sounds logical to me. That might solve your problem of staying here longer."

"Yes," she smiled, wishing that his tone didn't sound so jocular. "Wouldn't it? But I'm sure Donna and David already have made plans for the extra condo. They couldn't possibly have known that I would want to stay. So, let's be practical and assume that I'm going home Sunday. Peppy, you've never come to Amos' nightly beach parties. Couldn't you come just this once?"

"I don't care for the company of silly tourists," he replied tersely.

"Yes, but tonight is special. Couldn't you come at least tonight? Sort of a going-away party for me?"

"Oh, please, Peppy," pleaded Jeremy, "please come. It'll be fun."

"Wouldn't lunch at the cantina be enough?" he joked.

"No, no!" cried Jeremy. "Lunch isn't any fun."

Peppy turned and stared at Amy intently. She felt a sudden sadness emanating from him, this strange, solitary man who had become such a pleasing companion to them. Of course, he would still have Jeremy to pal around with but she suddenly felt as if he would really miss her, more than ever after their brief interlude yesterday afternoon. If this were the case, then why wouldn't he spend this next to last evening with her? Why had he made only one serious pass at her? Did he really just consider her a platonic friend, but one he would really miss? Surely, his behavior yesterday indicated much more than that.

"You know," he said after a while, ignoring Jeremy's pleas, "you should talk to David about staying and teaching here. We need people like you."

"Oh, Peppy, that's so sweet of you. Yes, if I can find the time to bring it up, I will talk to him about it. Remember, though, there are children in Nebraska who need me also."

"Maybe so. But there are more qualified teachers in Nebraska than Bay City."

"Perhaps. Jeremy, where do you go to school?"

"On the base."

"What?" she sputtered. "But your mom isn't in the military."

Peppy laughed and answered for him. "No, but I'll bet that David has clout with the powers that be. All the kids on this end of the island attend the base school. Of course, that's another option for you, although I don't think you'd want to teach there."

"Why not?"

"The kids are a bunch of rich, spoiled brats."

"Not me!" cried Jeremy.

Amy and Peppy both laughed and hugged him.

Amos joined them and invited them to lunch at the cantina, his treat. "Since this is almost your last day, Miss Amy," he added.

"Why thank you, Amos. We'll be delighted. And since this is my last day with you and Peppy..." She gulped and paused at the sadness of that thought, then continued, "Can't you convince your brother to join us at your party tonight?"

Peppy put up his hands and said, before Amos could respond, "Okay, okay, I'll come."

"You make it sound like a death sentence," Amy said.

Amos laughed, always pleasant and easygoing. "Just wait, Miss Amy, he'll enjoy himself."

"It's Amy, Amos, not Miss Amy," corrected Jeremy earnestly.

"That's right," she said. "We're all friends here, no formalities."

"In that case," he said, "Amy, Jerry, and Pepe, let's amble over to the cantina and get some ham and cheese sandwiches."

Returning to the pier with their sandwiches and drinks, they sat and chatted amiably making Amy feel happy and peaceful with such nice companions.

"One thing I've regretted," she said as she chewed her sandwich, "is not meeting Johnny who seems to have made quite an impression on Jerem-Jerry."

Amos smiled. "Yes, I'm sure Johnny would like to meet you but there's work to do out on the island."

"Do you mean the interior of Palmaltas?" asked Amy, confused.

"No, not Palmaltas. Johnny and I maintain a little beach on a tiny island several miles offshore from here. We have a beach hut there and I take tourists over for a change of scenery. Besides, the snorkeling is great. Johnny runs the concession end out there and always has drinks and snacks ready."

"Oh, what fun," exclaimed Amy, who started to ask if Johnny was their brother, also, then remembered that Jeremy had said the idea was silly. "I wish we could have gone there."

"And Johnny's a great snorkeling instructor," added Peppy.

"Does Johnny just stay on this island?" she asked, a germ of an idea was creeping into her mind.

"Sometimes," said Amos, "during the height of the tourist season, but I often go over and spend nights there, too, or we rotate our jobs. That gives us a nice change of pace. The island is quiet and peaceful after the tourists have left for the day. You should see the sunsets," he added reflectively.

"Oh, I wish I could have. And you, Peppy, do you ever go there?"

"Very seldom. I leave Amos and Johnny alone to run their business."

Inexplicably, or so it seemed to Amy, the two men laughed and playfully slapped each other, causing her idea, now a suspicion, to grow.

"So, Amy," said Amos, "you are definitely going home?"

"Yes, I am. The day after tomorrow. Sunday," she said sadly.

"Unless David Díaz can convince her to stay and teach in Bay City," commented Peppy. "Of course, she has to give him the idea first."

"Oh, please, Amy, do it," pleaded Jeremy.

"Say, that would be great," agreed Amos, winking at Peppy.

What did that wink mean, she wondered? Did she dare hope that something might be happening between Peppy and her or was that just one brother teasing another?

"I don't know what David will say," she replied nonchalantly. "We shall see, but I'm not getting my hopes up. I do have a wonderful job in Nebraska."

"So the newlyweds are coming back tomorrow?" asked Amos, slightly changing the subject. "I'll be glad to see them."

"Yes, so will Jerry and I, although their return signals my departure," she said wistfully, not really daring to hope that there was a possibility that she might stay.

"Not necessarily, Amy," said Peppy, "but if we don't see you after tonight then may you have a speedy and safe trip home."

That was the last thing Amy wanted to hear Peppy say. Why couldn't he insist that she stay? She was crestfallen but tried her best not to show it.

"I second that," said Amos who gave her a big hug. "I've got to get back to work. If you do stay, then when the tourist business slows down, I'll take you and Jerry out to the island to meet Johnny."

"Oh, I would love that. Thanks for the sentiment anyway, Amos."

"See you tonight. We'll put on quite a show for you." He left them, waving back as he walked away.

"What a nice person he is," she said sincerely.

Peppy studied her for a few moments then answered. "Yes, he is. We've always been close, but the past few weeks have brought us even closer together."

"Oh?" She held her breath, hoping for not only a revealing insight into Peppy's mystique but also a selfish desire that she had contributed to their closeness, although she couldn't imagine how she could have done that.

"Yes, we were both raised by our mothers. Our father appeared intermittently in our lives. He was more concerned with business than with us. And I hate to admit it, but I almost fell into the same trap, putting business before family."

Desperately, she wanted to ask what kind of business and what family he might have neglected. That thought worried her. Afraid of the response she might receive, she asked instead, "Did you and Amos know each other when you were little?"

"Yes. I'm the older, of course, but Dad would take me to play with my little brother on some of his sporadic visits."

"Then you knew he was your brother when you were growing up?"

"Sure, we both called him Papa when we were little." He smiled ruefully. "Unfortunately, my mother never acknowledged Amos or his mother so Amos could never visit me. My mother was a very jealous woman."

Amy assumed therefore that Peppy's father had divorced his mother in order to marry Amos' mother. She could imagine her hurt feelings and jealousy. Hoping for more revelations about Peppy's past, she was disappointed when he fell silent and she realized no more were forthcoming. Although this was more than likely the last time she would have a chance to learn more from Peppy, she didn't want to pry. Maybe after the party she would have an opportunity. At least Peppy had convinced her that he and Amos were brothers. Why would he make up such a sad story for someone who would soon leave?

Her focus suddenly shifted to the elusive Johnny. Surely, Peppy wouldn't be reticent about answering questions about that mysterious personage. But Jeremy interrupted them and the time for questions passed.

"Come on, you guys, let's go play," said Jeremy, who, as full of energy as ever, pulled them both back toward the beach.

"Since this might be the last time the three of us will spend a day together, I'm going to construct the biggest and best sand castle ever," announced Peppy.

Amy and Jeremy were both thrilled and they spent the rest of that afternoon following Peppy's instructions by hauling wet sand, forming it, and applying it. Peppy formed the towers and turrets and gates. All three of them dug the moat and carried up buckets of water to pour into it.

At last it was finished.

Peppy turned to Jeremy. "Go tell Amos to bring his tourist party over here this evening before the tide washes our handiwork away."

"Okay, Peppy," he said, running happily over to the Marisol Beach.

Turning to her, Peppy said with a sly smile, "Now, mademoiselle, your castle awaits you." Suddenly he knelt before her and said, "Please may I be your own personal knight of the realm?"

Laughing, she tapped him on the shoulders and said, "I dub thee Sir Peppy."

Without warning he jumped up and kissed her hard startling her not only with his ardor and passion but also with his strength and muscular hardness. His arms enveloped her and she wanted to sink into them forever. His tongue penetrated her mouth with an energetic forcefulness that she never dreamed possible. He pulled her even closer and she felt that her entire being was being devoured. This was a masculine heaven that she never wanted to leave.

Much too quickly he released her, and disappointment flooded through her.

"That's not a goodbye kiss, Amy. I'll see you tonight."

Shivers of anticipation ran down her spine.

"But," he continued, "I want you to know how much I want you to stay. These past two weeks with you have made a big difference in my life. I just hope I haven't waited too late to beg you to stay."

"Oh, Peppy," was all she could say as tears started to stream down her face. What had she done to make a difference in his life? Now, at the end of her vacation she found herself longing for a scruffy beachcomber, a man without a job, possibly without a future. Perhaps, she thought, it was best that she was returning home.

Suddenly, in a different mood, he cupped her chin, tweaked her nose, smiled sardonically, then turned and ran toward the returning Jeremy whom he scooped up and whirled around. Gently dropping the boy he turned and waved to her then continued onward along the beach.

Tears continued to stream down her face. Never had Rick kissed her like that.

"Why are you crying, Amy?" asked Jeremy as he reached her.

"I-I'm going to miss Peppy," she replied.

They returned to the condo with Jeremy excited about one more beach party and showing off the sandcastle while Amy burned with a desire, a longing, that she had never experienced. Both of them were in a state of elation for far different reasons, but both of them were living for the moment. Jeremy, in his child's world didn't consider that Donna and David could very easily take him to more of Amos' parties after she had gone. For herself, Amy didn't dare dream what might happen but she knew that after tonight she had tomorrow night also. Would she, could she, possibly spend both nights with Peppy?

Inside the condo as they prepared for the night's festivities, she suddenly came down from the high she was on and considered her plight. Why had Peppy waited so long to kiss her? Why hadn't he pressed his advantage sooner, knowing that she had only two weeks here? Or should she be flattered by his caution? Did he really want her to stay? With an even more sinking feeling, she realized that it was she who had pressured him into attending Amos' party. Had he originally intended for the kiss on the beach to be a goodbye kiss? She knew he had sent Jeremy off to look for Amos just to get the child away so they could have a few moments together.

"Oh, stop it," she told herself as she showered. "Go to the party. Have fun. At least I'll have some semblance of a romantic tale to tell my friends back home."

Determined to stop analyzing Peppy and to try for nothing but a good time, she set forth with Jeremy for one more fish fry and one more night of calypso music.

~ * ~

"Amos, Amos," shouted Jeremy when they approached his bonfire, "have you shown my castle?"

"Not yet, Jer," he answered. "I was waiting for you." Amos gathered his group about him and he and the happy child led the chattering tourists to the endangered castle.

Amy stood still watching the happy, noisy crowd, and especially Jeremy, when something grabbed her and whirled her around. To her greatest joy she found herself imprisoned in the unyielding arms of Peppy.

"Oh!" She gasped as he began to kiss her hard, causing her lips to ache. Her body felt like gelatin and she was powerless to resist. *Oh please*, she pleaded to the powers that be, *please let this go on forever*.

Unfortunately, only too soon the others returned and he released her, saying to Jeremy, "Okay, kid, let's show Amy a good time."

"You bet, Peppy," replied the ebullient child.

The three of them filled their plates with fish as Amos began to play his bongos. It was going to be a rowdy night but Amy's thoughts were anticipating the end of the evening when Jeremy had been tucked into bed and Peppy and she had retired to the balcony with a glass of wine. She was certain now that she was going to ask him to accompany them back to the condo.

Abruptly, the bongos stopped. Someone, a local kid from what Amy could tell in the dark, was whispering to Amos, whose cheerful face immediately turned dour. He glanced at Peppy who quietly but quickly put his plate down.

He turned to her and said, "I'm sorry, Amy, but I have to go now." Then he grabbed her to him and kissed her again with an urgency of extreme sadness. "Please," he whispered, "don't go home. Not now."

Hastily, he released her and ran quietly down the darkened beach. No one had noticed them, not even Jeremy who had gone up to the food counter for lemonade. When Amos saw Peppy disappear into the night he resumed his bongo playing with just a little less enthusiasm, noticeable, she was sure, only by her.

But what had happened? What had caused Peppy to run off like that?

Suddenly, out of the darkness appeared two men dressed casually in print shirts and white trousers. They were of medium height with olive complexions, dark hair, and taciturn expressions. They wandered about trying to look uninterested at the group but Amy had the feeling that they had eyed everyone attending the party. Just as abruptly as they had appeared, they left by way of the Marisol back entrance.

When she found a chance she rushed to Amos and asked who the men were.

"Oh," he said a little too casually, she thought, "you saw them, did you? They come by once in a while to see that whoever is here should be here."

"What business is that of theirs? Who are they?"

"Oh, just Palmaltan policemen, going undercover, trying to act important for my benefit."

"But who were they looking for?" However, she was afraid she knew the answer to that question.

"No one in particular. Just trying to show me that they were around. Don't worry about it, Amy. They've been here before when you were here and you didn't notice them."

Maybe so, she thought, but tonight she noticed them because the music stopped and Peppy left just before their arrival. Was the reason that Peppy didn't attend Amos' nightly parties because he didn't want to be seen by the police? What could he be afraid of? What could he have done? Why would he be safe on the beach during the day and not at night?

As if reading her thoughts, Amos said, "Don't jump to conclusions, Amy. Peppy's okay. And please, please, think about staying."

Before she could respond, several of his tourists demanded his attention.

Stunned at what Amos had just said, she stood there in the sand, her mind almost numb.

"Amy, Amy," yelled Jeremy. "Let's go watch the water tear down the castle."

She turned to her little friend and, as if in a trance, she followed him past their pier over to the condo's end of the beach where the lonely, dark castle was being quietly eroded away by the creeping tide.

While Jeremy laughed and ran around, splashing the water, she sank to her knees and let her thoughts erupt through her shock. Oh, what had Peppy done? What did Amos mean, that Peppy was okay? Had the corrupt government of Palmaltas accused him of something he hadn't done? Or could it be something else altogether different? Was Peppy really a criminal of some sort? Or perhaps he was an undercover policeman from the States hoping to uncover a drug cartel, perhaps one involved with the Palmaltan government. And the mysterious Johnny out on the island? Did Johnny have anything to do with any of this? But she knew one thing. She had to stay at least a little longer. She had to have answers.

~ * ~

"Well, bro, is it all over with you and Miss Amy?" asked Amos, arriving late at the cabin. "Do you think she will stay? What was that 'if we don't see you after tonight then may you have a speedy and safe trip home' bit all about anyway? That's not exactly the way to win a lady's heart. You should have gotten down on your knees and begged her to stay. "

"I don't know, Amos. It's certainly up to her now and that's the way I wanted it: her decision."

"Yeah, but you didn't give her much encouragement."

"Damn those two policemen. I just couldn't afford for them to see me. It would have been disastrous for our plans if they had recognized me at this juncture. They know they'll never find drugs around your parties."

"Not if they're on to you-know-who. He could get both of us into a lot of trouble just by association. Wouldn't you know that the one night you show up at my party so do those goons. Well, Amy or no Amy, it's time you take care of the drug business."

"Yeah, there's a lot of business that I want to take care of. We need to plan a meeting. Get your friends together and let's make sure we're all on the same ticket on this other thing."

"Yeah," said Amos, "but what about the drugs?"

"When I get the definite proof I need, we'll take action."

"And you will get rid of him?"

"With the utmost pleasure."

"And Amy?"

"And I'll take care of Amy if she stays. If she does, then I'll know for sure."

Eight

Donna and David returned as happy as newlyweds could possibly be. Jeremy was thrilled and Amy, of course, was happy to see them. Most of their Saturday was spent unpacking and spending time with Jeremy. Amy was due to leave the next day and felt shut out, which she knew was quite selfish. Donna and David had no way of knowing how turbulent her emotions were and how desperately she wanted to talk to them, not only about the possibility of her staying and teaching on the island, but also about the appearance of the mysterious men at Amos' party. She wasn't ready to confide in Donna about her feelings for Peppy until she learned more about those men who were supposedly policemen. However, she left the Díaz family alone, not wanting to interrupt their return activities.

Finally that evening, after Jeremy had gone to bed and the three of them had collapsed on the living room sofas, Amy decided to bring up her problems. First though, she wanted to ask which condo they would live in, Donna's or David's. One luxurious condo would surely be vacated. What joy and relief, she thought, if she could secure a teaching position here and move into one of the condos. Then she could take her time solving the mystery of the two strangers and sorting out her feelings for Peppy.

To her profound surprise, they solved her quandary for her, at least temporarily.

"Amy," began Donna slowly, "we're sorry to have neglected you today, but must you go home tomorrow?"

"What?" she gasped, daring to hope. "What do you mean? I-I love this place and would love to stay."

"Then how would you feel about a proposition that David and I have for you so you could stay the rest of the summer?"

Amy shot up, almost spilling her drink. "Wha-what is it?"

"David wants to open another restaurant in the Caymans and use it as an undercover political base there for the ultimate purpose of overtaking the government here. It's too dangerous for him to use his restaurant here for that purpose but his followers can take trips to the Caymans for business purposes or pleasure without rousing suspicion. At least we hope so. But this is all very hush-hush and, whatever you do, don't mention it to anyone. Our social friends and acquaintances must think that David is expanding his business, nothing else. I just want you to see the whole picture."

"Yes, yes, go on," she said eagerly, wondering what Donna was trying to tell her.

"He wants Jeremy and me to go with him. How would you like to condo-sit here?"

Could this really be happening? Could her immediate problems be solved this readily?

"Are you serious? I would love nothing better. What are you going to do with David's condo?"

"Oh, Amy," she exclaimed, excited, "then you can stay? David wants to rent his for the summer. You can't believe the prices tourists will pay for the privilege of living here a few months. When we come back around the first of September we'll decide which one we'll sell."

"But-but, Donna, I can't afford to rent your condo."

"Not you, silly. You can stay here rent-free, water the plants, and take care of David's cat."

"Cat? What cat? Who took care of it while you were on your honeymoon?"

"He has a beautiful Persian cat that he would never trust to the care of strangers. A neighbor of his took care of it the past two weeks but she's moving now. We felt that it would have been too much of an imposition to ask you to care for both Jeremy and a cat at the same time. You do like cats, don't you?"

"I love animals of all kinds. I grew up on a farm, remember?"

"Then that's perfect," said David, speaking for the first time. "So how about it, Amy, will you do it?"

"Oh my, yes. I can't think of anything more wonderful. When-when will you be leaving again?"

"Not for a couple of weeks. We've got a lot of planning to do and we'd appreciate it if you'd continue to watch Jeremy for us until we leave."

"I would love nothing more."

"So, I take it that everything went fine with you two while we were gone," said Donna.

"We had a fabulous time together. I met Jeremy's friends who weren't so little, one of them being Amos who said you knew him. Did you know he had a brother?"

She laughed. "Oh, you met Amos, did you? Isn't he great? I wouldn't be surprised if he had lots of brothers. Did you meet Johnny?"

"No, Johnny was on some little island."

"That island is darling. Get Amos to take you there sometime."

"I hope to do so." Not wanting to discuss Peppy just yet, Amy decided not to postpone her inquiry about her other puzzle. "Last night at Amos' fish-fry party for the Marisol guests, a strange thing happened."

"What's that?" asked David as he finished his drink.

"Two strangers walked around looking at everyone. Amos said they were undercover policemen just trying to act important for his benefit. He tried to shrug it off as normal, but, well, I thought something was wrong. Do the police here spy on the tourists?"

David answered very seriously. "They weren't spying on the tourists, Amy. They were spying on Amos."

"But why?" she cried.

"They don't like the idea of native Palmaltans running their own businesses on this end of the island. They're afraid that men like Amos might be infringing on their drug trade."

"But that's ridiculous!"

"Of course. They were just scouting his party to see that nothing illegal was going on. They don't mind if tourists indulge in drugs, as long as they're purchased from them. That, of course, is one of the reasons that I want to change our government."

"And another reason that we were-are so fond of Peter Harris," added Donna, "is that he let Amos run his own concession and keep the profits. But since he's disappeared and his cousin runs the hotel, we're afraid Amos might lose his job."

"Oh, his cousin. Yes, I remember your friend Lily talking about him. She seemed to think he was doing a good job. You must be wrong, though, about Amos losing the concession. He seems to be firmly entrenched and quite happy."

"Well, let's hope so," she said. "And now, Amy dear, we're tired after our trip and getting resettled. Since you're not leaving tomorrow, and you can't imagine how relieved we are that you'll stay, you can sleep in tomorrow. I know we're going to sleep late." She winked at David and added, "Somehow I wonder if the reason you agreed so quickly to stay was that you wanted more than bougainvillea."

Amy smiled to herself and thought how little Donna knew.

As she lay in bed that night, her thoughts whirled and whirled. Amos and Johnny seemed to be legitimate. At least they had David and Donna's stamp of approval and that was enough for her. But Peppy? Why was he afraid of the police? Surely that had to be the reason for his sudden departure. And Amos was obviously aware that Peppy needed to avoid the corrupt ones. Oh, if only that were so, she pleaded to herself.

Then her thoughts leaped to Johnny. Was Johnny secretly harboring Peter Harris on that little island? If so, why? From what Donna said, Amos owed Peter his job. Were Amos and Johnny his allies or his abductors? No, they couldn't possibly be his abductors. From what she knew of Amos, he was a good man and apparently so was Johnny. Maybe Peter was forming his own plan to overthrow the government and was using the island as his base, not knowing that David was going to do the same in the Caymans. But could he do that with a daily invasion of tourists to the island? Or was that the perfect cover?

As always, her thoughts reverted back to Peppy. Was he involved with Amos and Johnny's enterprise, Peter Harris or not? She remembered his comment on how he left them alone to run their own business and how he and Amos had laughed. Then there was the problem of Peppy and the police. Who was checking out whom? Could he possibly be involved with drugs? Then there was Amos' plea for her to believe that Peppy was okay. Or was that just the love of a brother coming through? Did Amos want her to stay because he thought she could reform Peppy? And Peppy himself had begged her to stay. Surely Peppy wasn't involved in any wrongdoing.

No, she told herself, these were silly conjectures. How could a naïve newcomer like her solve the mystery of Peter Harris' disappearance and Peppy's fleeing the police from a few odd occurrences?

Then the memory of Peppy's kisses took hold and she finally fell asleep to a melancholy yearning that she be kissed and kissed again.

~ * ~

Sunday for everyone was indeed a day of rest. Jeremy was thrilled that she would be staying and that he could go with his mother and stepfather on their next trip. He was a happy little boy.

Donna and David slept in most of the day. Late in the morning Jeremy and Amy wandered down to the beach. They waved to Amos and walked over to tell him her good news. He was busy but managed to say how happy he was for her. Peppy didn't put in an appearance all day. She desperately hoped that Amos would tell him that she was staying.

When they returned to the condo, Donna said that David had gone after the cat whose name was Salty.

"Why is he named that?" asked Amy.

"His coloring is sort of salt and pepperish looking. He's beautiful and I'm sure you'll adore him."

"Of course I will. Donna, are you sure that you don't know Amos brother, who, it turns out is Jeremy's friend Peppy?"

"What?" She seemed genuinely astounded. "So Jeremy's little friend is Amos' brother? But that's wonderful."

"Yes, but he's not little. In fact, he's older than Amos."

"You're kidding! And all the time we thought Peppy was just a little kid that Jeremy had met on the beach, some tourist's child."

"How long had Jeremy been talking about him? I mean, if you never met him, then he must have known him only a short time."

"Yes, that's why I thought he was a tourist kid from the Marisol. Well, Amos is a great guy. I'm sure his brother is, too."

"Yes, I think so, but well, he's just a beachcomber type and doesn't do much of anything."

"That is strange since Amos is so industrious." Suddenly a mischievous gleam appeared in her eyes. "Wait a minute, Amos is one of the handsomest men on this island. If his brother looks anything like him?"

"No, no," Amy protested, not wanting Donna to know her feelings towards Peppy, feelings she wasn't sure of herself yet. "They're nothing alike. They had different mothers but the same father. Uh, you know..." She let her sentence slip away.

"Ah well, that probably explains a lot of things."

Unfortunately, Amy could see that Donna's eyes were still gleaming.

"But," she continued, "you like the guy, don't you? I mean, there's no problem is there? With him and Jeremy? Or you?"

"There's not a problem," Amy tried to state as matter-of-factly as she could. "Like Jeremy, I've enjoyed his company. I just thought it was strange that you had never met him. However, Daniel gave me the impression that Peppy has spent a lot of time in the States."

"Daniel? Did he give you a tour of the island?"

"Oh yes." Grateful that Donna had changed the subject, Amy launched into her tale of their two trips around Palmaltas. For the time being she didn't want to reveal her speculations on why Peppy had left the States.

"Amy, that's great," Donna said as she finished. "It sounds like you've been a busy little tourist."

Now that Amy hoped the subject of Peppy was closed, Donna wouldn't let go of it.

"By the way, is Peppy his real name or nickname?"

"A nickname. It's Spanish for Joe. His real name is Joseph."

"Amos and Joseph. How biblical. But you're mispronouncing it, silly. P-e-p-e is Spanish for Joe."

"I know. I'm just imitating Jeremy. I like the sound of Peppy, although he has less pep than anyone I know."

"Oh really?" she said with raised eyebrows.

Luckily for Amy, David returned at that moment with Salty who was not particularly happy to be in a new environment, and discussions of Peppy halted. Amy ignored Salty for a while, letting him adjust to his surroundings. Then cautiously she approached him as he burrowed into one of the sofa cushions. She sat down and carefully began to pet him. At first he hissed then gradually began to purr.

She looked up at David and smiled. "We'll get along fine, just fine."

~ * ~

"Good news, Pepe," said Amos when he entered the cabin that night. "She's staying the rest of the summer."

"Oh? She told you that?"

"Uh-huh. And she will be alone. No more babysitting."

"Is she staying in Donna's condo or David's?"

"Donna's. The Díaz family, all three of them, are going to the Caymans for the rest of the summer."

"Why are they doing that?"

"Amy says they are going to open more restaurants but I doubt that's the real reason."

"Yeah, I agree with you." He paused for a moment and said, "Well, well, well, I'll have Miss Amy all to myself."

Amos laughed. "And about time but what about David?"

"Let me think on that for a while."

He stepped outside of the cabin, kicked off his sneakers, and walked barefoot across the sand down to the water's edge. It wasn't David that occupied his thoughts but Amy. She was staying, really staying. He couldn't believe the joy that he felt at knowing that he would have her at his side. This feeling had been a revelation to him, a feeling about a woman that he had never had before. And the knowledge that she was going to be here for the rest of the summer freed him to pursue and solve his other problems.

~ * ~

Jeremy and Amy resumed their daily beach excursions. Donna joined them occasionally for lunch at the cantina but was much too busy preparing for their departure to flitter her remaining days at the beach. Peppy didn't appear at the beach at all the first week that Donna and David were back, leaving Amy dismayed and disappointed. She vacillated back and forth in her mind whether she wanted Donna to meet Peppy or not. She knew that she should introduce them since Peppy and Jeremy were so close. But Jeremy was going with her and David to the Caymans. He wouldn't see Peppy for the rest of the summer and therefore there wasn't an urgency on Jeremy's behalf. The main reason that she hesitated for Donna and Peppy to meet was that she didn't know what Donna's reaction to him would be. It was a silly and perhaps cowardly reason, perhaps, but nonetheless Amy was not ready for Donna to find out about her feelings for Peppy, especially since she wasn't sure about them herself.

She asked Amos about Peppy's absence and he just shrugged, laughed, and said, "Who knows what he's up to?"

She wanted to ask more because she had never seen Peppy "up to" much of anything but Amos was always busy and she didn't want to pester him. Since he didn't seem very worried, she decided that surely nothing was wrong.

Jeremy was so excited about leaving with Donna and David that for the moment he forgot about Peppy. However, when they found Peppy on the pier the following Monday, July first, the boy was ecstatic at seeing him. And, Amy hated to admit to herself, she was just as happy and relieved to see him also. The memory of his embraces and kisses never left her, lingering just below her subconscious.

"Peppy, Peppy," cried Jeremy, "where have you been?"

She was dying to hear the answer to that question also but his reply was far from satisfactory.

"Oh, scooting about the island," he joked as he playfully tousled the boy's hair.

Which island did he mean, she wondered, Palmaltas or Amos and Johnny's little island? And did scooting about mean he was running from the law, such as it was on Palmaltas? But here he was in plain daylight once again. He certainly wasn't in hiding. For the time being she decided to leave well enough alone. She still wasn't sure that she wanted to know the answers to all her questions.

"So, Amy, Amos says you're staying on," he said as they sat down beside him.

"Yes, for the summer at least."

"Well, I'm glad." He put his arm around her and gently hugged her, causing her heartbeat to race.

What were their days going to be like when their little chaperone Jeremy was no longer with them, she wondered? Acute anticipation was mixed with fear that she might not be able to handle this oh so manly male.

A partial answer to her question came sooner than expected. On Wednesday, Donna said she was taking Jeremy shopping and that he wouldn't be able to go to the beach with her. Donna invited Amy to tag alone but shopping for boy's clothes wasn't her idea of a fun day so she wandered out to the beach alone. Her heart leapt into her throat as she spied Peppy sitting on the edge of the pier. He waved her over.

"Where's Jerry?" he asked as she sat down.

"His mother took him shopping. They're leaving Sunday for the Caymans."

"So soon? And you'll be here all alone?"

It was a rhetorical question, as he knew perfectly well that she would be.

"Have you talked to David Díaz about teaching here?"

"No, I haven't had much of a chance. He and Donna have been so busy. Right now I'm just happy to be able to stay the rest of the summer, catsitting and all."

He laughed a pleasant, friendly laugh with none of his usual cynicism. "Catsitting? How did that come about?"

"David has a cat named Salty. That's the reason they asked me to stay."

"You mean all it took was a cat?"

"Well, you certainly didn't give me a reason to stay."

He lifted an eyebrow and glanced at her skeptically. "Are you sure?"

Not knowing if he was joking, she said solemnly, "Not in words anyway."

"So it's words you want." He put his arms around her and turned her face to his.

All at once she realized how much she enjoyed his company. Surely, she had nothing to worry about.

"Amy?" he addressed her cautiously. "I was wondering."

"About what?" she said, hoping that he was finally going to say the words she longed to hear.

"Would you go out with me Friday night?" The usually confident Peppy sounded unexpectedly shy.

"You-you mean, like on a date?" she asked, taken by surprise.

"Yes, I guess you could call it that." He hesitated then added, "I'll get all dressed up, even shave."

His eyes were twinkling now and she realized his old self-confidence had returned. Was he making fun of her?

If he was issuing a challenge of some kind, she decided to accept.

"Of course, Peppy, I would love to go out with you."

"Fine, then Friday night at eight o'clock we'll meet here at the pier, but wear your finest dress."

"Oh, Peppy." She laughed. "Of course I'll dress properly." She wanted to add "better than you'll ever dream" but she didn't want to hurt his feelings, if hurting his feelings were even possible. Perhaps he was nothing more than a beach bum fisherman but he was a friend for whom she felt a deep sexual attraction and, she told herself over and over, that's all it was. At last she was going to be alone with Peppy and she had to maintain a modicum of self-control and not allow herself any further feelings, but could she do that?

"But," she continued, "we don't have to meet here. Come to Donna's condo and meet her and David."

"No, Amy, this is our date and I hope that we'll have many more but for now just you and me. Please? Humor me and meet me here."

She smiled. "Okay, Peppy, then the pier it is. Eight o'clock here Friday night."

They lapsed into companionable silence and fished the rest of the morning, at times touching accidentally, smiling at each other, and on Amy's part, just feeling very, very good. Amos joined them for lunch at the cantina, happy as ever. In fact all three of them seemed very happy, she thought.

After lunch Amos went back to work and Peppy and Amy lay in the sand a while.

"Come on, Amy, let's see how far you can swim now that you don't have to watch for Jerry."

"Oh no, I'm terrified of deep water. I never put my head under."

"Silly girl, do you think I would let anything happen to you? Come on, I'll hold you and we can swim together."

Her body tingled with expectancy. Swimming alone with Peppy. Of course, there were others about, tourists on the Marisol side of the pier and condo residents on this side. But for all she cared, they didn't exist.

He pulled her up, grasping her hand, and ran with her into the water, turning to splash her. She yelped playfully and tried to splash back. Suddenly he grabbed her to him and kissed her so hard that she couldn't breathe. Not releasing her, he pulled them both under the water, still kissing. Amy was torn between rapture and terror. She wanted to breathe, to surface, but she also wanted to be in his arms. Then suddenly up they came with Amy sputtering and Peppy laughing.

"Come on," he said, "hold onto me and we'll go out into the deeper water."

"Oh, no thanks, if this is the kind of treatment I'm going to get."

His face became concerned. "No, Amy, I was just playing. Come on, I'll take you out past the breakers. You'll love it. Trust me."

Of course she trusted him but into deep water? So far out? Reluctantly she agreed. She held onto his back and with muscular agility, he propelled them through the breakers to calmer waters. He turned her around to face the shore.

"See how beautiful it is out here and how peaceful."

"Yes, it is beautiful," she said as she slowly turned away from the faraway beach scene and studied the light blue sky and the darkening blue of the Caribbean horizon. "It's wonderful, in fact."

He kissed her, softly at first and tenderly, then gradually with more urgency as she felt the hardness of his muscular arms encircling her. They were both treading water with a passionate rhythm. Never had she felt this way with any man. How long they stayed there she would never know. In some ways it felt an eternity and in others only a fleeting moment. She wasn't even sure when Peppy began swimming back to shore, still kissing her. The feel of sand beneath her startled her into complete consciousness.

"We-we're back" she gasped.

"Hmm, unfortunately. But, Amy, this is just the beginning. Remember, Friday night." Then he tweaked her nose and winked and began gathering his fishing equipment.

She waved goodbye to him still not quite understanding why he had to leave so soon. But she didn't care. As she returned to the condo that afternoon she was lighthearted and cheerful. Peppy was the antidote that she needed for getting over Rick. Peppy. Sexy, sardonic, exciting. Someone with whom she could have a summer's romantic interlude. And she dared not think of him in any other way.

~ * ~

He walked over to the concession and put away his fishing gear. "It's a go for Friday night, Amos."

His brother gave him a high five. "But you've still got a lot of work to do in the meantime."

"Yeah, but most of it's in place. Friday night will be the beginning of the rest of my life."

Amos burst out laughing. "I never thought I'd hear words like that coming out of your mouth."

"If all goes to plan, one person will be out of here."

"And the other will follow?"

"Yeah, that would solve a lot of problems."
"I hope it will be that easy."
"Keep the faith, bro, keep the faith."
Amos laughed again.

~ * ~

She entered the condo, humming to herself, never expecting the bombshell that Donna was about to drop on her.
"Amy, Amy!" she exclaimed, bursting with excitement.
"What's going on?" Amy asked lazily, not terribly concerned.
"Peter Harris has returned!"

Nine

"Wha-what do you mean, returned? The kidnappers have released him?"

"He wasn't kidnapped. He's just been hiding."

"Where?"

"I don't know. But this morning David had a meeting with some of his advisers. Not business but the covert anti-government stuff and they said that Peter appeared yesterday and talked to them."

"Do you mean Peter Harris is on the same side as David? I thought he was just some rich playboy out to have a good time."

"Amy," she said indignantly, "how many times do I have to tell you that he's a great guy? But his political leanings? They're just as much a surprise to David and me as they would be to anyone. His self-imposed exile apparently brought about a change of heart."

"Is that why he went into exile?" Could her silly conjectures have been right, she wondered, that Peter had actually hidden on that island with Amos and Johnny's help?

"We don't know but it certainly makes sense. But, and this is important, he wants to continue with the playboy façade, so don't tell anyone."

"Like who would I tell?" Amy asked, slightly piqued.

"Believe it or not, you do have friends here. You just don't think of them that way, I guess. Amos, Johnny, Daniel, your Peppy guy."

"I haven't met Johnny and I don't know how Amos feels, but Daniel and Peppy have indicated they support David's political ambitions."

"You mean you've actually discussed David with them? Amy, you've got to be careful. And whatever you do, don't discuss Peter's disappearance and reappearance. He wants to resume his old lifestyle as a cover for his clandestine activities."

"That's admirable, I guess," Amy added dubiously.

"So this is the plan. Friday night there's going to be a big party at the Marisol in celebration of his return. He's going to make a short speech stating that he's been on a voyage incognito getting much needed rest and relaxation. He'll claim that he had no idea that his disappearance had caused such a hullabaloo."

"And the authorities will buy that?"

"Of course. That's probably more or less what really happened. I think he went off on a junket with some rich shipping magnate perhaps to think about his future and had a change of heart regarding his politics. Besides, he wouldn't worry about what the authorities think. Peter can offer them enough money to do anything he says."

"Then why on earth would he want to join David and help overthrow a government he can bribe at will?"

"Amy, Peter really is a decent human being. He's a rich Palmaltan with a conscience and he cares for his people."

"Maybe so. You know him. I don't. And you say that David didn't know that Peter hadn't been kidnapped?"

"No, no. This has been a tremendous relief for David. He's overjoyed that his friend wants to help him. Now, you and I have some serious planning to do."

"We do? What for?"

"The party Friday night. Marla will be the official hostess."

"Do you mean she's known all along where he was? She acted that way at your wedding. What about his sister?"

"No, David says that Peter hasn't told Marla or his sister anything except what he wants the rest of the public to know. Marla likes to play-act a lot and this is one time that her performance has come in handy. Just how she really reacted when she saw Peter after his return we'll probably never know, but apparently she's going all out for his welcome back party. She thrives on publicity and will continue to hint, I'm sure, that she knew all along where he was. As for Lisa, poor thing, she's so relieved that Peter is back that she's willing to share the limelight with Marla."

"I don't know, Donna. It sounds like Peter is just using Marla."

"So what if he is? She's after him as her permanent ticket to the good life. Besides, they're still engaged. Anyway, Friday night is going to be the social event of the year for Palmaltas and do I ever have a plan for you. My dear, you are going to steal the thunder away from Miss Marla."

"Me? Are you crazy? Why-how would I do that?"

"When Peter Harris takes a look at you and remembers all the great things I've told him about you, then he'll forget all about his precious Marla."

"That's the most idiotic statement you've ever made, Donna. I could never compete with her and I would never want to do so. She's gorgeous."

"And so are you. Believe me, we're going to get you all dolled up."

"No, you're not. Besides, I have a date Friday night with Peppy."

"Amy, don't be absurd. You have beach dates with this Peppy everyday. This is important. Tell him you can't make it. If he's Amos' brother then he'll understand."

"No, really, Donna, I can't break a date with him."

"Yes, you can. I've always known that you and Peter Harris would be perfect for each other. Sometimes there are just things that one knows and this is one of them. So, put this Peppy business out of your mind."

She must have seen the pain on Amy's face and exclaimed, "My goodness, don't tell me! You've fallen in love with this beach guy, haven't you?"

Amy couldn't respond as tears ran down her face.

"Oh, Amy, Amy. It's all Rick's fault, isn't it? You were so vulnerable that the first man to cross your path was able to seduce you."

"He hasn't seduced me, not at all. But you don't understand. We're friends. Really, that's it." But it wasn't, of course, and she could tell that Donna wasn't fooled.

"Now listen to me, Amy Ann. Maybe you're sexually attracted to this guy and if Peter weren't in the picture, I'd say go for it. But we're talking about your future. And Peter's. Marla would be disastrous for him and for Palmaltas. Peppy would be disastrous for you. Do you honestly think anything more than a casual affair could happen between you and him? Break the date, Amy. This is a chance of a lifetime. If David and I were going to stay here this summer then we could ease you into Peter's life, but we have so little time left. We're leaving Sunday and Friday night something has to happen between you and Peter. Amy, as my best friend, do this for me, for Peter, for Palmaltas, but most of all for yourself. Cancel that date."

Amy thought that Donna's reasoning was beyond idiotic but Donna was adamant and reluctantly Amy let her wear her down into agreement. The only reason she was here on Palmaltas was at Donna's invitation and Donna was her best friend. Besides, she tried to convince herself, she and Peppy had been heading for a sexual collision and then what would have happened, she wondered? More than likely after he had gotten what he wanted, he would have abandoned her. But as she remembered the urgency of his kisses and embraces, she found that hard to believe. On the other hand, she wasn't experienced with hardened men like Peppy. And Peter Harris? Amy hated to admit that a little part of her wanted to meet the eccentric playboy. Leave Peppy for Peter? What a preposterous idea. If Peppy proved to be too much of a man for her then how on earth could she win the heart of an even more experienced man and compete with the likes of Marla? But she had promised Donna and Friday night loomed, not with anticipation but with fear.

~ * ~

Amy spent the next day, Thursday, on the beach with Jeremy waiting for Peppy.

"Did you know, Jeremy, that today is a holiday back home? The Fourth of July is Independence Day in the United States."

"Sure, Mom told me about it this morning. She asked me if I remembered fireworks."

"Do you remember them? You were four when you came here."

"I kind of remember them."

For a while they talked about the holiday and how it would be back home in Nebraska but Amy's mind couldn't stay focused and neither could Jeremy's. She was desperate to find Peppy and he was excited about the upcoming trip to the Caymans.

Peppy didn't appear at all that day. She could see that Amos was too busy to talk because he only shrugged when she asked where he was. Just before she and Jeremy left the beach, Amy debated whether or not to interrupt Amos and ask him if he would tell Peppy that she had to cancel their date. However, she really wanted to tell Peppy in person so she decided to wait until the next morning. She felt it was the least she could do, although there was nothing she dreaded more. If Peppy still didn't appear, then she would reluctantly ask Amos to pass along the message.

Friday morning, Donna announced that Jeremy would stay with her and she wanted her to do the same.

"I can't, Donna, I have to find Peppy to tell him that our date is off. I couldn't bear to stand him up."

"Just tell Amos to tell him and then please get back here soon. I want to make sure that the gown I've picked out for you fits."

"And if it doesn't?"

"Then we'll spend the afternoon making alterations ourselves."

"Oh, good grief!" Amy exclaimed, becoming more and more exasperated with Donna's attitude yet reminding herself once again that the only reason she was in Palmaltas was at Donna's request.

She rushed to the pier where there was no sign of Peppy. She could see quite a bit of activity at Amos' concession. She knew she was going to have to interrupt him and make sure that he would notify his brother of their date cancellation. This idea sickened her as she remembered Peppy's passion and Amos' friendliness. But she had promised Donna and she knew her reasoning was faultless. If she were to try for a future on Palmaltas, then it would have to be with someone like Peter Harris and not with her sensual friend Peppy. Her heart wasn't in it, though. She really wanted to go on a formal date with Peppy, wondering where he would take her all dressed up.

When she arrived at the concession, she was astonished to find that Amos was nowhere to be seen. The most gorgeous island girl that Amy had ever seen was running his concession. She was tall, with long, luxuriant black hair and beautiful bronze skin. Her eyes were almond shaped, the color of black coal. She was dressed in a white halter-top, tan shorts, and sneakers. Fleetingly, Amy wondered if the newly returned Peter Harris had replaced Amos with her, as she surely would fit into his playboy image. Then she considered that Peter probably had more pressing business to attend to than changing his personnel.

Hesitantly, Amy approached her.

"Miss, can you can tell me where Amos is?"

Barely glancing at Amy, she replied in a melodious voice, "Out on the island. I'm replacing him today and tomorrow."

Before Amy could ask if she knew Peppy, the girl was inundated with tourists.

"Miss Janice, are you taking us out today?" they clamored. In a professional manner she gathered them around her and began to give instructions.

Amy wandered away, relieved that Amos' job was still intact and amused at Peter's choice for a replacement. Did Marla know about Miss Janice? She thought probably not. And to think that Donna thought that she could compete with such women or that she even should.

But as she returned to the condo, her amusement gave way to depression with the realization that she had not been able to find Peppy in order to cancel their date. Standing up a friend was a lousy thing to do, to say the least, and she indeed felt lousy. Could meeting Peter Harris really be worth hurting, even losing, Peppy, she asked herself?

"Who's going to baby-sit Jeremy tonight?" Amy asked Donna as she twirled around in the satiny, pale blue gown she had chosen for her. It was a perfect fit.

"Daniel's wife runs a night-care center on weekends for condo residents with children. We all pay her salary. It's a great deal for those of us with kids."

"Sounds like it. You seem to have everything you could possibly need in this condo."

Donna laughed, "For the most part, I guess. They don't have a pet-care service yet."

"I'm glad of that. Then you might not have needed me."

"I don't think David would let Salty be cared for by strangers, not for a long period of time, anyway."

"So this soiree tonight is going to be held in the Marisol?"

"Yes, the Marisol banquet hall. It's quite elegant."

"I can imagine. Do you know, I haven't checked out the Marisol yet. Just the beach."

"Well, you're going to love it."

~ * ~

He shaved and dressed as he had not dressed in a long time. He couldn't wait to see Amy's expression when she saw him like this. He walked down to the pier and waited. The beach party was in full swing and so was the fancier party inside. He was thrilled that she had accepted his date. He was sure that her hosts David and Donna would want her to go to the Marisol party. He finally admitted to himself that he was falling in love with her and tonight would let him know for sure how she felt. The minutes passed and still no Amy. His disappointment became acute. He had never been so hurt. She wasn't coming. She must have chosen the other party instead of her date with him. He couldn't believe that she had deceived him. He decided to wait a little longer.

"To hell with Amy," he said out loud with bitterness. Enough was enough. He walked away, not down the beach past the revelry at Amos' concession but along the darkened, paved path between the Marisol and the condo next door. He didn't want to be seen.

~ * ~

Without doubt, elegant described not only the banquet hall but also the entire affair. An orchestra played waltzes no less. Rhythms,

Amy thought, incongruous to the tropics, but as she listened and took in the ambience, they seemed quite fitting. The men were attired in tuxedos and the women in evening gowns. At first she felt she had been transported back in time to the thirties and forties. The look and feel of the party were reminiscent of the old black and white movies from that era. But the outside tropical atmosphere clashed with the interior sophistication. Huge glass doors slid open to allow the guests to roam freely from one setting to the other, from the dance floor to the exotic tropical gardens.

Stepping outside, she listened as the lilting waltzes mixed with the beating rhythms of the beach calypso music. The night fragrances of tropical blooms and salty sea air combined to make a heavy perfume. The moon and stars cast dancing reflections on the sea beyond. Under normal circumstances Amy would have been thrilled beyond belief to be in such a place at such a time, anticipating the much awaited appearance of Peter Harris, the eccentric mysterious tycoon. But she was downcast and moody. She had not kept her date with Peppy and guilty feelings surged through her.

Immediately a commotion began inside as the waltz came to a halt. The calypso continued to beat in the background.

"What on earth?" Amy muttered more to herself than anyone else.

"Come, my dear, let's see if that's Peter finally arriving," said a slightly familiar voice.

She turned to see Lily whom she had not seen since Donna's wedding. Martin was right behind her.

"My dear," she repeated, "Amy, isn't it? Mart and I had meant to ask you over for dinner while David and Donna were honeymooning but the time just slipped away. Mart puts in such long hours that I never know when we'll be able to entertain."

"Oh, that's all right. I certainly didn't expect an invitation."

Lily continued speaking as they stepped inside. "But don't worry, while the Díaz family is in the Caymans we'll find time for you. Mart will become acting manager of La Concha Blanca while David is away."

Amy was amazed that Lily knew about her continued stay in Palmaltas. She wondered if Donna had told her or if David had.

Before she could ask, Lily said, "Oh darn, it's only Marla making an entrance. I do hope that Peter hasn't pulled another vanishing trick."

They looked toward the ravishing Marla who was reveling in the spellbound attention of the gathering.

"Peter darling will be here soon," she announced, "please continue as you were." She glided around the room, picking out men who were momentarily unattended by wives or dates.

"What an act," mumbled Lily sarcastically. "Don't you think it's strange that Marla arrived without Peter? You'd think the lovebirds would want to make a grand entrance together. But this way, they both make grand entrances. What kind of marriage could survive two super egos?"

Suddenly, Amy didn't care and couldn't stand being there anymore. She slipped away from Lily and Martin to find Donna and tell her she was leaving.

Naturally, Donna was upset. "No, you can't leave. Peter will be here soon."

"Donna, I don't care about Peter. He has Marla. I care about Peppy. I really do. I can't stand up a friend. Why don't you understand?"

"Oh, Amy Ann, I think I know how you feel. But this is just a passing thing with this Peppy. If he's Amos' brother, he'll understand, you know the class difference and all."

Amy was horrified at her friend's statement. "Oh, Donna, really!" She wasn't going to say it, but Donna was gradually, perhaps subconsciously, becoming a snob. "Peppy is different from Amos but not in that way and I wouldn't want to hurt either one of them. I'm not sure that Peppy will understand at all. I have to leave. I just hope I'm not too late."

Despite Donna's protests she dashed out through the front of the Marisol just as a black limousine with tinted windows pulled up. As an elegantly shod male foot descended from the back seat, she whirled back toward the hotel.

She had suddenly realized that if Peppy was still on the pier then the quickest way there would be through the Marisol, out the back way, and across the beach. As she reentered the hotel, the party guests lunged toward her presumably to greet the occupant of the limousine. Pushing her way through, she thought how crazy the elite of Palmaltas high society were. Peter or Marla or whoever! Let them put on an act! She didn't care. She left the now deserted ballroom through the sliding glass doors and ran through the opulent grounds, past Amos' beach party, only Amos wasn't there. The flamboyant Miss Janice was still subbing, and presumably she would tomorrow also. Amy ran onto the deserted, darkened pier with no Peppy in sight.

She walked disconsolately to the edge of the pier, leaned on a post, and finally sat down, overcome with guilt. The orchestra in the ballroom began playing again amidst laughter and cheers, the sounds drifting and mingling once again with the resonance of Miss Janice's boisterous, calypsoing tourists. She sat on the pier and moped selfishly, suddenly resenting the gaiety that both groups represented. She had no idea how long the parties lasted but finally the noise died down and at last ceased.

Looking back toward the Marisol beach, she saw the beautiful Janice closing up the concession for the night. Momentarily Amy wondered where she would go, where she lived. Out of the darkness of the hotel grounds appeared a male figure who embraced her and kissed her on the cheek. Amy turned away and stared out at the sea. Of course, anyone as lovely as Janice would have someone waiting for her, a hotel employee, no doubt.

Suddenly, a waft of male cologne encircled her. Startled, she turned and looked upwards. Peppy was standing there, leaning on a post, staring at her, his silvery hair glistening in the moonlight. He was wearing a white dress shirt, unbuttoned at the top and dark dress pants. Was this what he considered "all dressed up," she wondered? But he was clean-shaven and she realized with a pang how good-looking he really was. His expression was stern and she was again overcome with guilt.

"Oh, Peppy," she cried, "I'm so sorry. I tried to find you yesterday and today to tell you that I couldn't make our date. Donna practically forced me to attend that party for Peter Harris. I didn't want to go. I really didn't." She thought she must have sounded terribly childish. Would Peppy believe her?

His expression changed from stern to disappointment to hurt. Not bearing to look him straight in the eyes, she stared down into the water.

"And what were your impressions? Of this missing personage?" he asked, sarcastically.

"I-I didn't stay to meet him. I felt so guilty at skipping our date that I left before he arrived, if he ever did." She really wasn't sure if that was Peter arriving when she turned back into the hotel.

"And where did you go?"

"I came here. I've been here all evening, hoping you would show up."

Finally, he smiled, not a forgiving smile, exactly, but more of a questioning one. Slowly he walked closer to her and then pulled her up.

"Is that so?" he said as he grasped her in his arms, pulling her toward him with such force that she couldn't breathe. He tipped her chin upwards and stared deep into her eyes, penetrating her soul. Then he kissed her, long, hard, and passionately. Just as abruptly, he released her. "And will you accept another-uh-date with me?" he whispered huskily.

"Yes, Peppy, of course," she whispered back, greatly relieved that she had been given a reprieve.

"I'll meet you Monday morning here on the beach. And you'll be here?"

"Yes, I will," she said, disappointed that he had not made a formal date. He looked so handsome in the moonlight, dressed up and cleanly shaven. She so much wanted him to meet Donna and David before they left, but she wasn't going to pressure him. After her behavior tonight she knew she didn't have the right to make demands or requests. "You-you won't be here on the beach tomorrow?"

"No, Amos-uh-needs help on the island." He kissed her again, tenderly, then slowly released her. "I had plans for us tonight, Amy," he said sadly, "but, oh never mind. Come, it's late and your friends will be worried about you. I'll walk you back to the condo."

"Oh," she protested, "I don't think they'll worry about me. Donna knows I have a date with Amos' brother and that reason alone makes you trustworthy."

He smiled. "Amos will find that most encouraging. And as much as I would like to dally with you on the beach tonight, it's late and both of us should go home. We have the whole summer, Amy."

Dally? Was that what he thought their date was? But as he put his arm around her and led her down the pier and over the beach she could feel his strength and masculinity overpowering her and thought how wonderful a summer dalliance might turn out to be.

They walked back in silence, arm-in-arm, and she thought how silly her ideas had been of Amos and Johnny hiding Peter on their island. Wherever Peter had been, it had not been there. Probably Donna's guess was correct and Peter had been on some yacht somewhere in the Caribbean or Atlantic, having nothing whatsoever to do with his employee Amos or the less industrious brother, Peppy.

Her thoughts must have brought a smile to her face because Peppy asked, "What are you thinking? It must be funny."

"In a way it is. Someday perhaps I'll tell you."

"That sounds mysterious. Well, here we are, Amy. I think you can mange the elevator." He kissed her again and, as he released her, tweaked her nose, smiled and walked down the condo grounds past the pool to the beach.

Not wanting to go up just yet, she slipped into the shadows of a palm tree and watched Peppy as he walked back toward the Marisol, expecting him to pass Amos' darkened concession and plod onward to the northern side of the island where he stayed with Amos. But he stopped at the concession and, to Amy's astonishment, the beautiful Janice stepped out of the shadows. Arm-in-arm Peppy and Janice continued along the beach.

Then an image drifted before her mind's eye. An image of a male figure embracing Janice earlier. A familiar figure. Of course! That had been Peppy embracing Janice just before he joined her on the pier. Had he asked her for a date only because he knew Janice would be subbing for his brother? Was that where Peppy went every evening?

To Janice? Pangs of jealousy and envy darted through her. Was he treating her the same way as Rick? Did Peppy really care whether or not she had stood him up? He didn't walk her back to the condo because it was late. He had to get rid of her because he had another date with Janice. And what about Janice? She must have seen the two of them on the pier. How did she feel about Peppy two-timing her? Or was he? Was Peppy using her to make Janice jealous? Oh, how could she ever know if a man was truly sincere, she cried to herself.

And she had accepted another date with him, feeling guilty at having stood him up, while at the same time he had another woman waiting for him. Would she keep her Monday beach date with him? Her first inclination was to stand him up again. But no, if anything, she had to prove that she was trustworthy even if he wasn't. Besides, it was only a beach date, just like all the ones before except Jeremy wouldn't be with them. What was she going to do? How could she handle a man like Peppy without little Jeremy around? Oh, this wasn't what she wanted, not at all. The jealousy and the hurt wouldn't leave her. Peppy and Janice. Peter and Marla. How could she ever compete with beauties like them? She, Amy, a little Nebraska schoolteacher?

~ * ~

Donna was furious when she finally returned to the condo.

"You little nitwit! The minute you left, Peter arrived."

Briefly the memory of the elegantly shod male foot stepping out of the limousine flitted through her mind.

"Oh, was that him in the limo?" she asked laconically, not really caring.

"Yes! And get this, not only did he see you running away but after all the commotion, greeting and media inquisition were over, he began discreetly looking for you."

"How could you possibly know that?" Amy asked indignantly.

"Because I was the person that he first approached. Amy, he thought you were beautiful. When I told him that you were my guest, he asked if anything was wrong with you."

"Why would he ask that?"

"Because he thought you looked rather distraught."

"Well, I was. What did you tell him?"

"The truth. That you had missed a prior engagement to come here and left because you felt guilty."

"Well, thank goodness you didn't make up something. I hate being deceitful or having anyone be deceitful for me." Then the memory of Peppy's deception with Janice seemed quite ironic to her.

Donna laughed, her anger subsiding. "Oh, you little smurf, what a goody-two-shoes you are at times. No, I told him the truth because I thought maybe the fact that a beautiful young woman would abandon his party for another engagement might make him intrigued enough or at least interested to know more about her."

"Oh, Donna," Amy wailed, then added, "did it work?"

Laughing again, she said, "I have no idea. He was inundated by guests and the inevitable Marla who dragged him away from me. Everyone was clamoring for his attention."

"Did people accept his reason for being away?"

"Oh my yes. This was his social crowd. They'd accept anything he told them except perhaps the real truth."

"And how did Marla take his supposed R and R?"

"Beaming, saying his absence had brought them closer together."

"Maybe it has."

"I doubt it. Why would he be interested in you if that were the case? Besides, I will never be able to see Marla posing as a revolutionary's wife."

"But Peter can?"

"I don't know. Men are so stupid where that woman is concerned."

"How does David feel about Marla?"

"He doesn't say much but he says that Peter will make the right choice for a wife, that he has confidence in him."

"That could mean anything, especially if Marla has snowed David, too."

"No, I don't think she has," said Donna, defensively.

"So, have Peter and Marla set a wedding date?"

"Not that I know of. We left early, however. Tomorrow, actually today," she said looking at her watch, "is our last full day here and we've got lots to do."

Amy also glanced at her watch. "Three in the morning. I can't believe I came in so late."

"So, did Peppy show up?"

"Eventually."

"What did you do?"

"Nothing. It was really too late to do anything. We have another date Monday." She had no intention of mentioning his kisses or Janice, the other woman in his life.

"Do you mean to say that Peppy was late for your date? Amy, for crying out loud! You could have waited a while and met Peter. There you were, worrying for nothing."

"Yeah, I guess you're right, but how could I have known he was going to be late?" But, she suddenly asked herself, had he arrived earlier and not found her there and left? He must have because he said that he had had plans for them. What did that mean? She had felt so guilty at standing him up that she had forgotten to ask him why he had been so late.

"Now, don't get mad at me, Amy, or fight me on this."

"Why, Donna, what do you mean?"

"Look at it like this. You can keep seeing Peppy, if you like, but promise me that once in a while you'll hop over to the Marisol for brunch or lunch. The Marisol is Peter's domain and if he spots you, remember his brief glimpse of you impressed him to no end, then maybe, surely, he'll approach you. Just keep Peppy in the background to make him jealous."

Amy burst out laughing. How hard it was to refrain from telling Donna that that was what Peppy was doing to her, keeping her in the background to perhaps make Janice jealous. Except that, unfortunately, she was the jealous one.

"What's so funny? Come on, Amy. Play the field a little. I'm sure Peppy's nice since he's related to Amos and all, but you yourself said he was a beachcomber without much ambition. Here's your chance to find out if Peter Harris really is interested in you."

"All right. I guess a brunch once in a while won't hurt," she agreed, secretly musing that she did wish to meet the intriguing Peter Harris, now that Peppy's true colors were starting to appear.

"Atta girl. Oh, but be on the lookout for Peter's American cousin. He can be a nuisance although I imagine that Peter will send him packing soon."

"Do you mean the cousin that was in charge while he was away? Don't worry. I'm not here to spend time with anyone like that."

Laughing, they embraced and said good night.

As Amy lay in bed that night, she realized that she wouldn't recognize Peter Harris if she saw him. She got up, turned on her lights, and looked through the clippings that Donna had given her on her first day here. No photos. She guessed everyone in Palmaltas knew what he looked like. Oh well, she thought to herself, drifting off to sleep, at least he knew what she looked like.

~ * ~

Lying in his bed that night, he thought about the evening and how it had turned out. Amy had disappointed him tremendously. In fact, he had never been so hurt. But, he had given her a second chance. Would she come through the next time? He wanted so much to throw caution to the wind, grab her, hold her, and make love to her. If she had kept their date as promised, how different the evening would have been. Why did she really choose to go to the party instead of meeting him on the pier? Did Donna have that much influence over her decisions? There were things he had to know about Amy. He mustn't make another mistake. Obviously, he had made the right decision in taking his time with her.

Ten

Saturday was full of commotion as Donna, David, and Jeremy prepared to leave. David was in and out, much too busy to listen to Amy's desire to remain on Palmaltas as a schoolteacher. Besides, she told herself, she had the rest of the summer to decide if that was what she really wanted to do.

She and Jeremy went down to the pool in the afternoon, her first time there in the four weeks that she had been in Palmaltas. Eddie, the pool lifeguard, jokingly asked if they had been avoiding him.

"Oh no," she reassured him, "this trip has been my first time to see a beach and the sea. I just couldn't bear to miss any of it. Also, at first, I thought I was going to be here for only two weeks." She didn't add that the main reason they came to the pool today was to be in shouting range of Donna in case she called them from her balcony.

"So, how long are you going to stay?"

"The rest of summer. I'm going to condo and cat-sit for Donna and David. They and Jeremy are going to the Caymans for a while."

"Hey, that's great. Then maybe you'll spend some time at the pool."

"Maybe. It's certainly easier to swim in a pool than in the sea, and I need the exercise." Of course, she didn't add that she wasn't much of a swimmer and pools weren't all that attractive to her.

"You look pretty good to me." He grinned.

"Thank you," she replied demurely. Amy realized that Eddie must be almost ten years younger than she was. Was it possible that he was flirting with her? Or was this an act that he performed for all the tenants and their guests? No, she decided he was probably just a friendly teenager doing his job. But she enjoyed the attention that she was getting, not only from Eddie, but also allegedly, if she could believe Donna, from Peter Harris.

Then there was all the attention that Peppy had so suddenly showered her with: the embraces, the kisses. But what had they really meant? A way to impress the incredibly beautiful Janice? He had seemed so sincere. Yet, if she followed Donna's reasoning a few steps farther, she knew that Janice would be more suitable for Peppy than she was. Janice was an island girl and he, a scruffy beachcomber, although he wasn't scruffy last night. The memory of his cologne and overall appearance rushed through her. No, no, at best Peppy could only be a friend, no matter how he kissed her and the feelings that pulsed through her body at his touch. Peppy and Amos were not of her world and the lovely Janice was of their world. Amy hoped she wasn't being a snob. She hated to admit how much she envied Janice. Then her thoughts leaped to Peter Harris. How exciting to think he had noticed her and inquired about her. But wasn't his world also out of reach from hers?

Was there anyone here in Palmaltas with whom she belonged? She looked down at the pool from her lounge chair and gazed upon Eddie splashing Jeremy while at the same time flirting with a couple of teenage cuties in bikinis. Eddie and Bert, his cohort on the beach, were too young. Ossie, the doorman, handsome but too old. Daniel, the chauffeur, handsome and happily married. And always, always, Peppy and now Peter looming in the foreground of her mind. Peter Harris, the mysterious unknown, rich and powerful, but out of her league no matter how curious she was to meet him. And Peppy? Lazy? Shiftless? Yet sexy, attractive, virile. If she hadn't seen him walking away into the moonlight with Janice, she would have become involved with him and not wasted a moment thinking of Peter.

Donna's voice from the balcony broke into her reverie.

"Amy! Jeremy! Come on up!"

Amy waved back and called for Jeremy.

"What's up?" she asked as soon as they reached the condo apartment.

"David's taking us to the Palmaltas Hilton for dinner since this is our last night together for a while. There's a restaurant on top of the hotel. The food's almost as good as La Concha's but most of all it has a marvelous view of the sea and this end of the island."

Indeed, the view and even the dinner were marvelous, Amy thought. They dined on grilled swordfish, tropical fruit salad, a corn cake with raisins, and champagne, except Jeremy who had a child's chicken platter.

Their conversation was light and breezy. No mention was made of Peter Harris or his party. Amy sensed that David didn't want to discuss Peter, whether it was from fear of being overheard in case they mentioned his new anti-government stance or exactly what, she didn't know. She didn't mention that she might want to stay permanently and teach. More and more she was beginning to have her own doubts. Their conversation dwelt on subjects that interested Jeremy including Amy's cat sitting of Salty. It was a family evening and she knew how lucky both Donna and Jeremy were to have someone like David.

The new Díaz family left early Sunday morning and never in her life had Amy felt so alone. For the first time since she had been on Palmaltas, she decided not to leave the condo apartment. She had no desire to walk along the beach and get a glimpse of Janice. Of course, it was possible that Amos had returned but she didn't want to take the chance. Naturally, she could have stayed at the pool or the confines of the condo's beach but she wasn't in the mood for light talk with either Eddie or Bert.

When she plunged down into a cushion on one of the living room sofas, Salty hopped up, arched his back, and cried a plaintive, "Meow."

"Yeah, guy, I know how you feel. I guess I could watch TV but that somehow seems so out of place here in the tropics and a waste of time. And, you know, I never once saw Jeremy turn it on or even show interest in it. The beach was all that little boy cared about and who can blame him?"

Salty walked over her lap a few times, then rubbed his head under her chin and purred. She petted him a while, then both of them, perhaps bored with the routine, jumped up. Salty scampered away to the kitchen and she wandered out onto the balcony. She leaned over the rail, inhaling the early morning scents of sea air and tropical blooms. The pool wasn't open yet and the condo grounds were deserted. She retreated to the kitchen, poured herself a glass of orange juice and returned to the balcony where she sat and sipped. Gradually the peace and beauty of the scene below calmed her and a warm serenity spread throughout her being.

"Hey, Salty," she called out. "What's the matter with me? How could I have begun to feel so sorry for myself? You and I have it made here. A gorgeous condo complete with balcony and view. Forget men. Forget romance. This is just too beautiful to waste. I'm going to sit here and read today. Tomorrow I'll soak up that sunshine, go beachcombing and bring you back some shells. And eventually I'll make Amos keep his word and take me to that island of his. And I'll also keep my date with Peppy tomorrow. We're friends, he and I, damn it, Janice or no Janice."

"Meow," replied Salty.

~ * ~

Monday morning she threw off her covers, which were really floral-printed sheets. Each night she set aside the green and coral quilt that adorned the bed. Neither air-conditioning nor heavy bed covers were needed on an island that boasted a yearly temperature average of seventy-eight degrees. Sometimes it seemed much hotter on the beach with the sun beating down and Amy would soon learn that it could be much cooler inland. Ready to meet the day head-on, she jumped out of bed, her lethargy of the previous day completely dissipated. She quickly showered and dressed, fed and watered Salty, and tended to the litter tray, her one unpleasant task.

Since Peppy had not set any particular hour for their "date," she decided that he meant they should meet casually as they had done before when Jeremy was here. She wore her bikini under a wrap-around print dress and flopped a straw hat on her head. Just as she was leaving, she slipped into her beige sandals and bid adieu to Salty.

"Well, Salty, I'm leaving. No more lounging around, feeling sorry for myself. I'm going to plunge right in and see if I can compete with the likes of Marla and Janice. I'm going to change my habits by going down the front elevator and exiting out the front door. Maybe I'll even strike up a conversation with Ossie. Then I'll walk over to the Marisol for breakfast. So, what do you think? Will Peter Harris show up? Wouldn't that be great? Then I'll slither, like Marla or Janice, out to the beach for my day with Peppy. Maybe I can turn the tables and make both men jealous."

Salty arched his back, rubbed against her legs, and purred.

"Yep, I feel like purring, too. This is going to be a good day." Or was she just kidding herself? Compete for the likes of Peter and Peppy against the two most beautiful women on the island? A little tingling of fear ran down her spine but she had to try.

Because the morning was still early, the shops on the ground floor weren't open yet. But Ossie was in his position to greet residents to begin a new day. As she very seldom used the front entrance, always going out the back way to the beach, she wondered if he would remember her from her arrival. He did.

"Ah, Miss Amy, isn't it? You looked lovely Friday night."

"What? Oh, thank you. I guess you saw us when we were leaving to go to Mr. Harris' party?"

"Yes, and did you enjoy yourself?"

"Not really. I had to leave early before Mr. Harris arrived because of a previous engagement."

"Then we Palmaltans are keeping you busy."

"Yes-yes, I guess you are." She smiled and he countered with a very disarming smile. If there was one thing about Palmaltas that had impressed her, it was the handsome men it produced. Ossie's uniform wasn't ostentatious yet it lent him dignity as well as did his graying hair, moustache, and bronze skin.

"So, where are you off to now so early?" he asked.

"Breakfast at the Marisol. Maybe I'll get a glimpse of Peter Harris this time," she said lightly.

"And charm him, I'm sure," he said, bowing as she skipped down the steps.

Well, she thought, that was the plan.

The Marisol had a formal dining room but she found a little coffee shop toward the back of the hotel that faced the beach and the sea. As she sat down at a little table next to a window, she could see Amos opening his boat concession. Thank goodness Janice was nowhere in sight, she mused. She didn't want to be reminded of the view she had of her Friday night when she disappeared down the beach, arm in arm with Peppy. Today was Amy's day, a new beginning.

Beyond the boat concession was the pier with a few early fishermen. Whether Peppy was among them she couldn't tell, but for the moment she didn't care. She was going to have an elegant breakfast in a lovely tropical setting watching the morning sun send shimmering rays upon the water, which brightly reflected them. Sipping her coffee while awaiting her Palmaltan omelet, the rippling water almost hypnotized her. Spellbound by the beauty before her, she momentarily ignored the other patrons. When the waiter brought her omelet, a concoction of eggs, ham, pineapple, and cheese, she returned to her senses.

Glancing around she didn't see anyone that she could imagine would be a wealthy playboy and undercover revolutionary. She was the only solitary diner in the room among elderly couples and a few young honeymooners. Would Peter Harris, who lived in a mansion across the street, have breakfast here? That seemed unlikely yet Donna thought she might spot him here. Perhaps he came to work early and sometimes dropped down for coffee. But that seemed even more unlikely. Wouldn't he have a secretary or assistant who made coffee for him or would order from room service? And how would Donna know what Peter's morning habits were? But, she was here and determined to enjoy her meal.

The omelet was huge and was accompanied by a loaf of crusty soda bread and real butter. She thought that if she ever came again for breakfast that she would order the cinnamon roll that was listed on the menu. Surely it would be lighter than this combination.

Putting aside all thoughts of Peter Harris, she delved into the omelet. While engrossed in chewing a large mouthful, she happened to glance up and saw an extremely good-looking, well-tailored man sit down across the room and stare at her. She swallowed hurriedly, nearly choking.

He nodded and smiled. Suddenly panic overcame her. It was one thing to fantasize about capturing the heart of an intriguing man. It was another to face the reality of meeting one. Could that man possibly be Peter? Who did she think she was that she could possibly flirt with him?

He continued to stare at her and then unbelievably, he winked. Could this really be happening? What would she do if he approached? Could she handle this man? She had not been able to handle a rat like Rick and even a beach vagabond like Peppy left her breathless. Now she was faced with the possibility of meeting Peter Harris.

The waiter appeared at his table with a telephone. Gruffly, he answered. Although she couldn't hear the words that he said, she could hear the tone of his voice. He gave the phone back to the waiter, said something to him, and left in a hurry.

Amy breathed deeply, relieved that she wouldn't have to face him at that moment. Yes, he had flirted with her and, according to Donna, Peter knew who she was. But would he have gone any further than a mild flirtation? How could she compete with Marla?

The waiter crossed the room and stopped at her table.

"Mademoiselle, Mr. Harris hopes that you are enjoying your breakfast."

"Oh, my goodness, then that really is Mr. Harris."

"Yes, mademoiselle, Mr. P—"

"Then," she hastily interrupted, "then please tell him that I-I enjoyed my meal very much."

"I will do so."

Heart beating, she escaped to the ladies' room to compose herself before she went to the beach. So that was what Peter Harris looked like, handsome, yes, but unlike the other Palmaltan men that she had met. He had medium brown hair trimmed neatly, brown eyes, and a light tan. His attire was thoroughly professional and business-like, brown suit, white shirt, and navy tie. He looked as if he might have stepped from the pages of *Gentleman's Quarterly*, the quintessential American businessman. Of course, he had an American father and obviously took after him. Then she thought of Peppy's silver hair and blue eyes, so different from his darker brother Amos. Yes, Palmaltas produced gorgeous, gorgeous men, from Donna's David to Ossie the doorman to Daniel the chauffeur to Peppy and Amos. And now the most attractive, richest, eligible man on the island, Marla notwithstanding, seemed to be interested in her! Standing before the mirror, she told herself to calm down. Somehow she had to regain her composure and improve her self-confidence.

And how was she going to do that? By practicing on Peppy? Well, why not? After all, he had Janice and he may have been using her to make Janice jealous. Wasn't turn about fair play or something like that?

Peppy was sitting on the end of the pier, line dangling into the water, as she bounced up. Despite her resolve to take charge of her life, her heart beat faster as she sat down beside him. His rugged masculinity and provocative demeanor evoked sensual feelings that she didn't want to admit existed. Well, she told herself, she was just going to have to overcome these feelings and she couldn't do it by running away. She was going to spend the day with Peppy and, at the same time, resist any advances he might make. Perhaps Peter Harris might glance out his office window and see them side-by-side and realize that he had competition.

"You seem to be in a good mood," he said lightly.

"Yes, I think I am."

"Any particular reason?"

"Uh-no, it's a beautiful day and I'm still here and not on my way back to Nebraska."

He smiled "I'm thankful for that."

If she had not seen him with Janice Friday night, she wouldn't have questioned his sincerity. But why was he acting this way with her? As far as she could tell, Janice was nowhere in the vicinity. She wanted so much to believe that Peppy cared for her, that he wasn't using her. Then memories of Rick crept upon her. Was Peppy just a Palmaltan version of Rick? If that were the case then she had to keep her mind focused on Peter Harris and how she could use Peppy to her advantage.

Amos soon joined them. Another fisherman, a tourist type, yelled out, "Hey, Amos, you're not as pretty as Miss Janice. Bring her back."

Amos laughed good-naturedly and replied, "She's prettier than everyone."

His remark, though harmless, annoyed Amy. Amos was her friend and she felt that he shouldn't have made such a blanket statement in front of her. Then another thought intruded. Were the brothers competing for Miss Janice? Did Amos know of Peppy's involvement with his replacement?

Peppy, also laughing, got up, stretched, and said, "I'm going over to the cantina for a coffee. Want one, Amy?"

"No thanks, I just had plenty."

As he walked away, Amos commented, "You seem perky this morning."

Perky? She was perky and Janice was pretty? But Amos couldn't possibly know how she felt about Janice or that she even knew who she was. Amy knew she was being petty and childish.

"Amos, I finally saw Peter Harris."

His eyebrows shot up. "Wha-what do you mean? The party Friday night?"

"Oh, you knew about the party? You were gone that night. My, but gossip gets around this island fast."

"Everyone knew about his return party, Amy."

"You're right, of course. But no, I didn't see him at the party. I left because of my date with Peppy."

"What?" He seemed to be genuinely confused.

"I saw him a while ago in the Marisol Coffee Shop."

Noticing his stunned expression, she added, "Really, Amos, even the rich have to eat breakfast and it is his hotel."

Still looking at her in disbelief, he said, "Did he introduce himself to you? Did you actually meet?"

"Not exactly, he was called away but the waiter brought me a message from him."

"I see."

"Do you see him often?"

"Of course, I work for the Marisol."

"Yes, I know that your concession goes with the hotel but I just wondered if you ran into him very often."

At that moment Peppy returned and Amos got up and whispered something to him before he strolled back to his work. Peppy gave Amy a quizzical look but didn't enlighten her on what Amos had told him. She noticed that his Friday night grooming had not lasted. Apparently, he hadn't shaved in two days. His stubble had returned but his short-cropped hair had grown a little longer, displaying the silvery tones even more as the sunlight played on his head. He had been so handsome Friday night but now only the beautiful hair, bronzed muscles, and piercing blue eyes remained from his sensual allure of that night. Prince Charming was a scruffy beachcomber once again, a reversal of the Cinderella story and she didn't have a masculine version of a slipper to change him back. She supposed Janice preferred him that way. Amy wouldn't allow herself to think how she preferred him. At least, they were now beginning a new day together.

Eleven

"So, are you up for a little adventure?" asked Peppy, sitting beside her. He began to put away his fishing tackle.

"What do you mean?"

"I asked you for a date today."

"I know, but I assumed you meant the usual beach meeting with fishing, sunbathing, castle building. That sort of thing."

"What? You expect me to build you castles, too?" he asked with eyes twinkling. "No, I had something else in mind," he said slowly as his eyes drifted over her apparel. "I guess I should have been more specific Friday night. You're not dressed appropriately for mountain climbing."

"Mountain climbing on Palmaltas? Where? How?"

"There's a little mountain range between the military base and Bay City. Surely you passed over it on your trips to the city. Do you think you're up for a little hiking and picnicking in a tropical setting?"

"Oh, Peppy, that sounds like fun. I'll be glad to run back in and change."

"You're sure?"

"Of course I am."

"All right then. Put on some long pants, sneakers and socks, and bring a light jacket. I've got the backpacks we'll need."

"Where?" All she could see was his tackle box and rod and reel.

"At the cabin. You know, near the Palmaltas Hilton, across from the airport."

"How will we get there? Walk?"

"We could but let's save our energy for our mountain trek. No, we'll hop on the bus here in front of the Marisol and ride to the bus stop at the airport. Then we'll just walk across the road to the cabin."

"Will we take the bus to the mountains? I know it goes that way."

"No, we'll take Amos' jeep. We'll go up back roads after we pass the military base."

"Amos has a jeep?"

"Sure, why not? He-uh-has a good business. He can afford it."

"But-but, the island is so small and public transportation is punctual and inexpensive."

"We all like our independence, Amy, to come and go as we please."

"I suppose so," she said, thinking that no one would appreciate independence more than a loafer like Peppy. "But how does Amos come to work everyday if he leaves the jeep at his home?"

"He walks. It's not that far, really, probably not even a couple of miles."

"And he walks home at night after a day of sailing and dealing with tourists?"

"He doesn't always go out in his boats. Whether you've noticed or not, he has plenty of helpers. Besides, Amos is full of energy."

The beautiful Janice immediately came to mind but she didn't want Peppy to know that she knew anything about her. If she did mention that she had seen her subbing for Amos, she was afraid that her voice might give away the fact that she was jealous of Janice, a fact that she didn't want to admit even to herself. Surely, however, both Peppy and Amos would assume that she had seen Janice the two days that she had been working the concession.

"Yes," she said, keeping the conversation on Amos and away from his lovely helper, "but Amos stays late each night with his calypsos and fish fries."

"If he's tired, he might catch the last bus but knowing him, he probably walks back along the beach toward the Hilton, dropping in on other beach parties along the way."

"What a life." She sighed. "Do you ever partake in any of those parties? I know you said you avoid the parties at the Marisol because of the tourists." But after the one and only party that he had attended, Amy knew there were possibly other reasons as well.

"I sometimes crash.a private party near the cabin but I avoid all of the hotels and their parties."

"Who has the private parties?"

"People like Amos who work on this end of the island and either live in the cabins or in Bay City. Sometimes a group congregates on the beach that runs past-uh-our neighborhood and parties deep into the night. Then if there's anybody who lives in Bay City, Amos will take them home in his jeep."

"Like I said, what a life." She wanted to ask if women went to these parties but realized what a foolish question that would be. Men like Peppy and Amos would always have women around. Again, she pictured Janice. Had Amos hired her or had Peter Harris? Somehow she considered Janice more of a threat than Marla.

Although he couldn't possibly have known what she was thinking, Peppy's next question startled her.

"Would you like to go to one of Amos' private parties?"

"Are you serious?"

"Bear in mind it would be after he closed up here and long after your bedtime."

Was he just teasing her?

"How do you know when my bedtime is? We always left early when Jeremy was here because he had to go to bed early. Besides, you're the one who always left before the evening started."

"That's true. I just figured you were one of those early-to-bed, early-to-rise types."

"That's ridiculous," she stated indignantly. Of course, he was right but she didn't want him to know it. Not that her sleeping and waking habits were any of his business or anything to be ashamed of, she added to herself.

"Well, in that case, the next time Amos has an impromptu party or even a special occasion one, I'll tell him to pick you up if you're sure you'll be up and awake." He smiled with just a tinge of cynicism.

"For goodness sake, Peppy, stop treating me like a child. Of course, I'll be awake and I'd love to go. But why couldn't you come by for me?"

"I'd be at the cabin, more than likely. It would just be easier all around for Amos to drop by or yell up at your balcony. We're casual around here."

"Well, you certainly are." She fell silent while she pondered what she had gotten herself into. How wild were Amos' parties? Would the other women, if there were other women, be just as exotic and enticing as Janice? Could a little Nebraska schoolteacher fit into a group like that? But she couldn't back out. Besides, she trusted Amos, and yes, to a certain degree, she even trusted Peppy. No matter how wild the party might become, she was sure that neither one would let any harm come to her.

"Okay, that's settled. Now, run up and change. I'll meet you at the bus stop."

As Amy walked back to the condo, she wasn't sure how much of anything was settled. Nonetheless she found herself happily anticipating a mountain hike as well as a future midnight beach party. But how were activities like these going to entice Mr. Peter Harris? If she wanted to make him jealous then she needed to inhabit his world, not the world of the brother of one of his employees. Then she admonished herself to stop thinking of Peter. What would happen would happen. She needed to be open to all possibilities. After all, before she came here she dreamed only of bougainvillea, waves slapping upon sandy shores, crystal blue water, swaying palm trees, and a hot tropical sun. Well, she had sampled all of those. Now she had the opportunity to savor island life with real natives. What stories she would have to tell when she returned home, if she returned home, she thought dreamily. She would continue to haunt the Marisol, hoping for casual encounters with Peter and she would continue to see Peppy,

Janice or no Janice. But was she really strong enough and confident enough to follow through with these meager plans?

~ * ~

He watched Amy walking toward the condo, admiring the view of her behind swaying sensually from side to side. When she disappeared from view, he turned towards Amos' concession and walked over to it.

"Is she going with you?" Amos asked.

"Yes, so far she seems to be a good sport. Mind if I borrow that hat?" he asked, pointing to one of the hats that Amos had available for his tourists.

"No problem, bro. You really think you'll need it?"

"Just until we get to the cabin. By the way, is everything set for tonight?"

"Yeah, they will all be there. Do you think you'll make it?"

"I don't know. It all depends on how things go with Amy today."

Amos grinned. "I hope she works out but that was strange about her excitement on seeing Mr. Harris this morning."

"I wonder about that. Did she see *him* or jump to a conclusion about a tourist?"

"Time will tell, bro, time will tell."

He put on the hat pulling the brim down to shade his face, waved to his brother, and walked through the lobby of the hotel. Outside he walked to the main avenue, crossed it, settled on the seat of the bus stop, and waited for Amy. Coming towards him on the sidewalk was a jogger, an acquaintance that he didn't want to recognize him. He curled up on the seat and pulled the wide brim of the hat further down over his face. The jogger raced on by, not slowing down. He stayed in that position, wondering if he could fool Amy, too.

~ * ~

After changing into jeans, tee shirt, socks and sneakers, and grabbing one of Donna's light jackets, she rushed out the front, barely giving herself time to wave to Daniel and Ossie. At the bus stop she encountered a man nestled into a corner bench with a wide-brimmed straw hat pulled down over his face. On hearing her approach, he gingerly peeked out from under the brim.

"Peppy! I almost didn't recognize you. What's with the hat?" she exclaimed.

"Nothing. It just shades my eyes, that's all."

"Peppy, that's ridiculous. You're sitting in a bus shelter. Besides, you never wear a hat at the beach where the sun beats down on you all day. Where did you get it?"

"From Amos. He keeps all kinds of hats for his customers. I borrow one from time to time. I just put it on for a joke to see if I could fool you."

"Well, you would have if I hadn't recognized your figure and your clothes."

"How could you have recognized my figure? I was all doubled up in this corner."

"Good grief! What is this? Some kind of cloak and dagger routine?"

"No, just a feeble attempt at being silly."

She murmured, "Oh," not knowing what to think. Peppy had always been loose and laid-back yet serious at the same time. Silly wasn't part of his demeanor except when he was playing with Jeremy. Maybe, she considered, this was his way of loosening up both of them for their adventure.

"Where are your tackle box and rod and reel?"

"I always leave them with Amos at the concession."

They got off the bus at the airport, as planned, and ran across the road to the row of cabins that faced the beach and the sea. Peppy led her into the cabin, which, although small, was light and airy with simple furnishings and neat as a pin. A bowl of tropical fruit sat on the dining table. Absentmindedly, she picked a few quenepas and began to munch on them.

"Do you like those?" he asked.

"I love them. Donna had some when I first arrived."

He opened the refrigerator and took out the already packed lunches and put them in his backpack. Obviously, he had assumed beforehand that she would want to go on his hiking adventure. He entered the bathroom and soon emerged wearing jeans instead of the ragged cutoffs that he had worn to the beach.

The jeep was parked on a small driveway that led from the street to the cabin. They got in the vehicle and soon were off on their venture. As they drove past the military base, she asked Peppy how he felt about the Americans taking up so much of his island.

He shrugged and said, "Mixed feelings. We need the land. Bay City is too crowded. But we also need the revenue the military brings. Unfortunately, it goes to the wrong people. However, it's the U.S. presence that keeps our government from going off the deep end and conducting a reign of terror."

"A reign of terror?" she asked, horrified. "Why would they do that?" Apparently Peppy was more on top of island politics than she had realized.

"Our current president for life has psychopathic tendencies. At least that's my take on him. There's no telling what he would do if the U.S. weren't here."

"But the people are oppressed as it is," she said, dismayed.

"It could be worse."

They quickly passed the base and arrived at the foothills of the mountains where Peppy turned off from the paved road onto a dirt one. He wound around a few of the hills then pulled into a little clearing by the side of the road and parked the jeep.

They disembarked and put on their backpacks. Hers was a little heavy but not as heavy as his, which contained their lunches and drinking water.

"What's in here, anyway?" she asked.

"A light raincoat, flashlight, extra batteries, blanket, miscellaneous stuff like matches."

"My goodness, I thought we were going on a little hike. What do I need a raincoat for? It hasn't rained since I got here."

"It's almost time for our rainy season and clouds form on these mountains almost daily at this time of year. It pays to be prepared."

"Okay, Mr. Boy Scout, lead on."

He grinned and pointed to a faint path among the trees. "This is where we'll start."

They began slowly much to her relief. Walking was her favorite form of exercise, but being from Nebraska, she was used to mostly flat surfaces. She was accustomed to beginning at a slow pace, then to increasing her stride gradually to a more rapid one, and to decreasing it as she approached her destination. Amy remembered a friend back home who would start out almost running, outpacing her at first. But she would burn out quickly and Amy would end up passing her with ease and still full of energy.

As if he were reading her mind, Peppy said, "The reason we start slowly is to acclimatize ourselves. Walking uphill can be difficult at first if you're not used to it. But there's a reward for going uphill."

"Oh? What is that?"

"The return trip is downhill." They both laughed.

Peppy was in much better shape than Amy was, or at least more used to this terrain, and, as they gradually increased their pace, he maintained a faster stride. The scrubby growth in the foothills gave way to a dark canopy of taller trees and bushes. As a result grass didn't grow in the cool darkness and the ground was mainly dirt and small pebbles, and remarkably easy for walking.

She had hoped they would walk side by side, but she found herself lagging several yards behind him. However, it wasn't an unpleasant trek as she admired his figure from behind. Although more fully clothed than normal, she admired his stride and the confidence in which he carried himself. Shivers of anticipation ran up and down her body as she relished the idea of spending a day alone with Peppy in this wilderness.

When they had alighted from the jeep, nothing but the sounds of insects had greeted them but, as they became accustomed to Amy and Peppy's presence, many species of birds resumed their daily chorus. The air was sweet and pungent and occasionally Amy could see the sunshine filtering through the canopy of trees above them. All was still but not quiet. The surroundings enthralled her as they trekked onward and upward. They didn't speak, just listened and absorbed the mountain atmosphere making Amy more acute than ever of the primeval aspect of Peppy's attraction.

Soon they reached a sunny clearing and Peppy unstrapped his backpack and laid it on big, flat rock.

"Lunchtime," he said, "and we need a water break anyway."

"Lunch? So soon?"

"We got a late start. Remember?" He glanced at his watch. "Twelve-ten. Don't tell me you're not hungry."

After relieving herself of her backpack, she sank to the rock and realized how famished she was despite the heavy breakfast that she had eaten.

"Now that I'm not moving I realize that I am starving."

He laughed. "Yep, that's what mountain climbing does to you. Of course, these aren't real mountains, more like big hills. Real mountain climbers go straight up rock faces."

"No thanks, this will do me just fine." Then gazing out over the view, she gasped. "Oh, Peppy, the scenery here is breathtaking."

Not only was the green tropical splendor of the mountains before them, but they could see the dramatic southern side of Palmaltas as well. Steep cliffs dropped off into pounding surf with isolated little pink beaches dotted here and there. Beyond, the glimmering Caribbean gradually melted from turquoise into deep blue-violets. Slowly, Amy began to turn around, taking in all that she could see from their captivating vantage point. Eastward to her left in the distance was the military base but tall palm trees ringed the boundaries and they couldn't see beyond them. Somewhere below out of sight was the jeep. To the west, the mountains continued upwards where she could see clouds forming. Turning again she observed the peaceful northern shoreline. Each side of Palmaltas was a contrast to the other sides. Bougainvillea abounded everywhere—adding lovely reds, pinks, and violets to the various greens of the trees and shrubs. Depressing Bay City couldn't be seen, as it lay westward beyond the mountains.

Certainly their view, from whatever angle, was intoxicating. Once again she thought how her dream had come true of tropical bougainvillea and a brilliant, sun-speckled sea, added to which was the company of a sensual, enigmatic man. Unfortunately, the memory of Janice walking into the night with him intruded upon her reflections and an acute spasm jolted her heart.

"Let's eat," said Peppy bringing her out of her pensiveness into a more realistic frame of mind. Perhaps she couldn't deal with the memory of Peppy and Janice together but she could deal with food.

He opened his backpack and unfolded some plastic wrap that contained two, huge, pie-shaped pastries.

"What are those?" she asked.

"You mean you haven't eaten Palmaltas pizza yet?"

"You're kidding! That's pizza?"

"The best in the world. Remember pizza is Italian for pie and this is a meat pie. We're drinking bottled water. I don't know if anyone carries a canteen anymore, at least not here on the island." He handed her the "pizza" and a bottle.

"That's fine with me." She couldn't wait to bite into the pizza, not only because she was hungry, but also because she was curious. "Oh, this is delicious. What's in it?" she mumbled between bites.

"Baked shredded chicken and pork with various spices, topped with pepperoni, all baked between layers of a special island pastry."

"Goodness, it's heavenly. This is the best picnic lunch I've ever eaten."

Peppy just grinned and ate his also.

When they finished, she said, "My compliments to the cook." She assumed that he or Amos had made the pizza.

Peppy smiled again and said, "Yeah, it's great, isn't it? Johnny made it."

"Johnny?" she said, surprised.

"Sure, Johnny's a great cook. Okay, let's clean up. Give me your bottle and plastic wrap. I'll put them in this sack and store them in my backpack until we get back."

"Oh, an environmentalist. That's nice."

"Of course. Very few people come up here and the ones who do keep it clean. Luckily, the tourists haven't discovered the joys of Palmaltas hiking."

"Who does come up here besides you?"

"People who care," he replied mysteriously.

At times, she thought, Peppy would be very forthcoming then suddenly he would become uncommunicative. She hoped she was learning to heed those moments.

"We need to rest," he said, "and let our lunches settle. The facilities are over there." He pointed to some bushes behind a big rock.

"Facilities?" she asked foolishly, then blushed as she realized what he meant.

"Don't be embarrassed. Nature is what nature is. Some things can't be put off. Here, hand me your backpack."

She did so and was surprised to see that one of the miscellaneous items was a box of tissues, which he pulled out and handed to her, telling her to bury what she used. Meekly, she accepted it and went behind the bushes.

A while later as they rested, both of them reclining on the rock and Peppy chewing on a weed, Amy began to feel nervous while at the same time burning with desire for Peppy to hold her and kiss her in this serene environment.

To her surprise, he simply said, "Tell me about your family."

After all the time that they had spent together on the beach with Jeremy, he had never asked her anything personal. She had asked him as much as she dared about his life but he had never reciprocated. He had kissed her passionately, perhaps testing to see how far he could go with her and, at the same time, trying to make Janice jealous Friday night on the pier. Peppy had held her and embraced her but his interest in her had seemed to go no further than a physical one and not much of a physical one at that, she lamented.

But she answered him concisely because she loved her family very much. She told him about her parents, her siblings Tag and Polly, and about her career as a teacher. In fact, she assumed she had told him more than he had asked for and probably more than he had wanted to know.

"And what about you and your family?" she asked expectantly, longing to know more than what he had told her about Amos.

"I've told you about my parents and Amos," he replied tersely. "And I have a sister but, Amy, I don't want to talk about her. Maybe someday I'll tell you about her."

Terribly disappointed that he wouldn't open up to her as she had just done to him, she decided that Peppy talked when Peppy wanted to talk. Something traumatic had to have happened to turn this intelligent man into nothing more than a beachcomber. At least now she knew that he had both a brother and a sister but what had happened to make him so reticent about the sister and not about his brother? Would she ever learn the answer before he walked permanently off into the sunset with a beautiful island girl?

They were silent for a while and Amy wondered if he could hear her heart beating. He turned toward her and pulled her to him, enveloping his arms around her.

"Hmm, this is nice, isn't it?" he said in a laid-back manner.

"Yes, it is," she replied, yearning for something more than just being held

He jumped up, jarring her out of her melancholy. "Okay, let's pack up and get going."

She did as she was told wondering what was so momentous farther up the mountain that they couldn't linger a while in this spot.

She followed him onward and upward. The terrain became rockier with deep crevices and ravines and tricky underbrush. They were getting closer to the cloud cover and Amy realized she was getting chilly.

"Stop, Peppy," she shouted to him as he marched a few yards ahead. "I need to put on my jacket."

He stopped, sat on a rock, took a swig of water from a fresh bottle that he had removed from his backpack, and watched her as she undid her backpack to get out her jacket.

"You need to be very careful from now on. Step cautiously because there's a lot of moisture up here and these rocks can get very slippery."

Unfortunately, he didn't speak soon enough. Just as she reached into her backpack, she stepped backward a little, sliding over a slick surface. The backpack went flying through the air, and as she made a grab for it, she slipped, flying and tumbling down a ravine, landing in a bushy crevice that led deep into a hollow place in the mountainside.

She was stuck and as she tried to move, she found that she had twisted her right wrist. Whether it was sprained or broken she didn't know, but as she tried to lift herself out of an awkward position, a sharp pain shot through her arm and hand.

"Amy! Where are you? Are you all right?" yelled Peppy from somewhere above.

He couldn't be seen from where she had landed. Before she could answer, rain began falling, heavy rain.

Twelve

The rain, pouring down the ravine, soon created a thunderous waterfall. Amy immediately discovered that she was in danger of being washed even farther down to where she could hear water rushing like a river. She tried to snuggle back into the crevice hoping that she would be secure enough not to be washed away. The water created so much noise that she could no longer hear Peppy. Nor could she see anything either due to its density.

The slippery rocks were impossible to hold on to, so she grabbed the bush she had landed on with her good hand. The gushing water together with her grasp pulled it loose and she began to slip and slide away from the crevice. Holding her right arm folded against her chest, she grabbed outwards every which way with her left hand, but to no avail as her only accomplishment was the accumulation of cuts and bruises as she bounced downwards.

Suddenly she landed hard on a rocky outcrop and, rolling over on her stomach, she lay there spread out, panting and crying. She raised her head and saw another, bigger crevice, almost like a small cave in the wall of the ravine and slowly she inched toward it. As she reached it, she pulled herself inside with her left hand, none too soon because a mudslide came oozing downwards. Although it wasn't moving fast, there was no way that she could have withstood it if she hadn't reached the safety of her little warren.

Then, almost as fast as it began, the rain stopped and the mudslide subsided. The air was still. Not a sound could be heard. Where was Peppy? Had he tried to come after her and found himself caught in the onslaught of rushing water and mud?

Terrified and panicked, she cried out, "Peppy, where are you? Are you all right?"

From far above she heard him answer, "Amy, is that you?"

A moment's consternation overcame her. Who else would be yelling for him in this wilderness? But there was no time for sarcastic thoughts on her part. She had to get out of her predicament.

"Of course, it's me."

"Thank God! Are you all right?"

That's what she had asked him! "I-I'm not sure. I've hurt my right wrist and I'm stuck in a crevice-like little cave."

"Whatever you do, don't move until I reach you."

"But what about you? Did you get thrown down?"

"I'm fine. The rain started before I could get to where you fell. I held onto a tree and waited for the storm to let up. They usually don't last long around here."

"But how can you get me out of this mess?" she shouted. "There's been a mudslide."

"Don't worry," he shouted back. "Just stay put. Don't move. I'm going back to the jeep. Hopefully Amos has some rope in it."

"And if there isn't any?" She was getting hoarse from the shouting back and forth.

"Then I'll go back to the cabin for some. Hang on, Amy. Everything's going to be fine. I'll get you out of this mess. Trust me."

He sounded out of breath from yelling at her and she didn't want him to overexert himself. He still had a lot of hiking and climbing to do: going down, then returning up over slippery surfaces. Why or why didn't he put rope in their backpacks? Not enough room, she supposed, and probably too heavy. Besides, there was no telling where her backpack had landed. She was wet and freezing and wished desperately for the blanket that Peppy had packed.

"Amy?" he cried plaintively.

"Yes?" she moaned.

"You'll hold out for me, won't you?" He sounded sad and far away.

"Of course," she yelled back trying to sound cheerful. "Just get going, please."

If he answered anything, she didn't hear him. Silence descended upon her and there was nothing else to do but wait. At first, she relaxed cradling her wrist with her other arm, trying to get as comfortable as possible in her cramped quarters. But as the afternoon wore on, and the clouds darkened even more, panic slowly returned. What if it rained again? What if Peppy should get caught in a mudslide coming down for her and should fall all the way to the bottom of the ravine? What if he slipped and broke a leg climbing back from the jeep? They'd both be trapped on this mountain and nobody would know where they were. Or would Amos know, especially when he found Peppy and his jeep missing? Was Peppy in the habit of taking his jeep? Amos wouldn't arrive at the cabin until very late. Would he even notice that the jeep was missing or perhaps not care, assuming that Peppy might be bouncing around Bay City from one bar to another? What if they had to spend the night here, or even days, out of earshot of each other until the jeep was found? What if? What if? Her mind was reeling. Darkness fell and enveloped her as her thoughts and imagination continued out of control.

~ * ~

Pepe was furious with himself. He and Amy should have stayed on the rock where they had eaten their lunch. There was no reason for him to take her on to that cozy little nook in the rocks farther up the mountain. He had been too anxious to show it to her and ignored the opportunity that she tried to give him.

He made his way cautiously down the mountain. It took much longer than he thought it would but he knew that if he tried to hurry he might have a worse accident than Amy's. He hoped and prayed with all of his might that she would be all right until he returned. If there should be another mudslide that somehow caught her and dragged her down the mountain, he didn't know how he could ever live with himself. When at last he reached the jeep, he searched it from top to bottom. There was no rope. He jumped in and raced back to the cabin, knowing that there would be a group of friends there to help.

"Whew, bro, what happened to you?" asked Amos when he walked in the door. "You look like you've been rolling in mud."

Before replying he glanced around the room at the familiar faces. "I see that you are all here. Who did you get to stay at the concession?"

"One of my helpers volunteered to stay with the tourists," said Amos.

"Well, I hate to disrupt you but I need your help."

~ * ~

Suddenly, she heard voices far above her and saw lights bouncing off the walls of the ravine. Was she dreaming? She moved and hit her head on the roof of the rocky crevice. Unbelievably, she realized she must have fallen asleep but she was awake now and, yes, there really were voices and flashing lights.

"Help!" she cried out.

"Amy," yelled Peppy, "I'm coming down but keep talking, honey, so I can find you."

"But how can you get down in the dark? It's dangerous here, Peppy."

"Amos and some friends are up here. We've got rope and flashlights. I'm coming down with a rope around my waist. They're lowering me slowly. Just hold on a little longer, honey, and keep talking.

Honey? Peppy had never called her that before and now he had addressed her twice that way. A shiver ran through her body, not a cold one, but one that seared with torrid density. Peppy, with his strong physique, was coming to her rescue, and was doing it with kindness and concern. Most amazing was the realization that she had never doubted that he would try to rescue her. Janice or no Janice, she knew that Peppy would never abandon her.

"Amy, you're not talking." He sounded much closer.

"I-I'm over here in this crevice but I think you can pull me out easily."

Suddenly there he was, shining his flashlight onto her face.

"Okay, honey, easy does it. I know you've hurt your wrist so give me your good arm slowly. There, that's it. Now wrap your arm and legs around me. That's the way." With one of his arms around her waist and the other grasping the rope, he wrapped his legs around it, and yelled out, "Okay, men, pull us up. I've got her."

They pulled them slowly but, as Amy felt Peppy's masculine strength encircling her, she wanted that ascent up the ravine to last even longer. Although they were dangling precariously over a deep ravine, she felt safe and secure wrapped around his hardened, muscular body. His sensuality spread heat throughout her body, and for only a few brief moments they were cast together, lost in time and space. Much too soon, despite the slowness of the ascent, they reached the top of the ravine where Amos grabbed her and handed her over to, of all people, Eddie and Bert.

"Wha-what are you guys doing here?" she gasped as she scrambled onto firm soil.

"We were-uh-partying with Amos when Pepe found us. When he said you had had an accident, we knew we had to help," said Eddie.

"Oh, thank you, thank all of you so very much," she cried appreciatively.

"Nothing to it, Miss Amy," said Amos. "Every brother likes to help another brother rescue a damsel in distress."

"Well, distress certainly described my predicament," she said.

"Enough of this jabbering," said Peppy as Amos pulled him up. "I don't know about Amy, maybe she'd like to spend the night on this mountain, but I'd like to go home. Ready, men?"

They laughed and Amos said, "You first, brother. We're watching you all the way down to the jeep."

The others laughed, also, though Amy thought Amos meant he was watching Peppy so there wouldn't be any more accidents. But when Peppy suddenly picked her up and started carrying her down the mountain, Amos, Eddie, and Bert grinned and playfully punched each other. Whatever the innuendo might mean, her morale was boosted to new heights. Did Peppy's brother and friends think there was something romantic between them? But did they know about Janice?

"Peppy," she protested, "you must be exhausted. I can walk. My legs may be scratched and bruised but it's only my wrist that hurts. I'm okay, really."

"No, Amy honey, it's pitch dark among these trees, not even the flashlights can spot all the rocks and bushes and twigs that might send you flying again."

"Then-then let one of the others help me down."

"One of those lechers?" He winked. "Not on your life. Besides, you're light as a feather."

If ever there was anyone who was not a lecher, it was Amos nor did Bert and Eddie fit that description. Flirtatious at times, but never lechers. Then she heard snickering behind her and knew she was being teased again, a not unpleasant sensation.

However long that trek down the mountain took, like the rope ascension, it didn't last long enough for Amy. Again as a searing heat coursed through her body at Peppy's touch, she wanted to stay in the security of his arms forever. His strength and virility overpowered her senses and she relaxed, completely dependent upon and confident in his ability to carry her down the mountain.

Much too soon she found herself bundled into the backseat of the jeep between Eddie and Peppy. Bert sat up front with Amos who drove them back to the cabin.

Both Peppy and Amy were soaked and she desperately wanted to go back to the condo and shower, but the friendly warmth of the cabin beckoned her when they arrived.

She heard Bert ask Amos where Johnny was tonight.

"Out on the island, as usual," said Amos.

Would she ever meet Johnny, the islander who made great pizza, she wondered?

"Now, let me see your wrist," said Peppy. He moved it and twisted it gently, causing her to squirm and grimace a little. "Hurt much?" he asked.

"No, not too much."

"Good, then it's not broken. Amos, do you have a spandex wrap of any kind?"

"Yeah, brother, we always have stuff like that around. Tourists are always twisting limbs and such."

"Well, get me some."

Amos did so and Peppy wrapped her wrist for her.

"Now, I'm taking you home."

"In the jeep?" she asked rather idiotically.

"Well, my dear, I'm certainly not inclined to carrying you anywhere else tonight," he joked.

The others laughed and so did she.

When they reached the condo, Ossie was nowhere to be seen, presumably having gone off duty hours ago. A night watchman let them enter.

"Peppy," she mumbled, as they went up the elevator, "you really must be tired."

"Of course. Aren't you?"

"I mean, instead of wearing that hat outside, you put it on just before we came in." She wondered sleepily why he had it in his pocket in the first place.

"Is that so? The better to conceal you as I kiss you, my dear." He pulled her to him and pulled the brim over both their faces. As he began to kiss her, the door opened.

"There's no one around to see us at this hour, whatever hour it may be," she murmured.

"Maybe the night watchman has a hidden camera."

"Don't be silly. Besides, why would he care?"

Folding the hat and pushing it into a back pocket of his jeans, he walked her to her door, then grabbed her forcefully and began kissing her again. Her heart pounded and she melted into his arms.

"Oh, Amy," he sighed, releasing her, she felt, too soon. "I have never been so worried or so scared. I couldn't see or hear you down there. For all I knew you had been swept away in a flash flood or buried in mud."

"Yes, I was scared, too, for you more than for me."

"Why? I didn't fall down."

"I know that now but at the time I feared that you might have fallen also."

"Oh, Amy, Amy," he whispered huskily. He cupped her chin, kissed her forehead, and said, "Much as I want to stay, I think you need some rest, and believe me, I wouldn't let you rest." Then stepping back, gazing up and down at her, he added, "Besides, you're a muddy mess."

He tweaked her nose and disappeared into the elevator.

Standing there in front of her door, Amy trembled as passion swept over her. She desired Peppy, of that she was sure. Then she looked down.

"Oh goodness," she cried out. "I am a muddy mess!"

Not until she was snuggling into bed after a long shower did she realize that Peter Harris had not once encroached into her thoughts during her mountain adventure with Peppy. Was she really falling in love with a scruffy beachcomber? Could she compete with the likes of Janice, if indeed Janice was competition? After Peppy's behavior toward her today, she began to think that Janice, whether his lover or not, didn't matter. But should she give up on Peter so soon? Drowsiness and exhaustion overcame her and sleep postponed her perplexing dilemmas.

~ * ~

After a cold shower he dropped into bed pondering the day's events, certainly not the events he had planned. He had never been so scared. What if he had lost her in a stupid mudslide? Why hadn't he held her hand or kept her close to him at all times? Or better yet, not attempted to climb higher? He shuddered at how close he had come to losing her. If only he could have spent the night with her. They could have showered together and crawled into her big comfortable bed. He smiled to himself as he imagined what kind of bed it must be. But, he still had to be careful. He had to be completely sure.

Thirteen

Amy slept late the next morning and would have slept longer if Salty had not jumped up on her bed, purring loudly.

"Umm, you silly cat, can't I sleep in just once?" She snuggled down into the covers but to no avail as he walked over her as if she were some unnecessary lump and began purring into her ear and pawing her hair.

"All right already!" she shouted as she threw off her sheets and jumped out of bed. "Let's go see what you need, then I'll get ready for my day. It's my summer vacation," she grumbled, "and I let a cat dictate to me."

The phone rang soon after she had freshened Salty's water and put out some catfood.

"Hello."

"Amy? This is Lily. How are you doing? I tried to call you yesterday but there was no answer."

"Oh hi, Lily. No, I was out-uh-hiking-uh-sight seeing."

"Well, you must have been out very late. I gave up calling you at nine o'clock last night."

Amy's first reaction was that it was none of Lily's business where she was or when she came home. Lily had seemed nice enough the few times that she had seen her but she did belong to Palmaltas' social elite and Amy felt she wouldn't understand why she socialized with a fisherman. So, she kept her explanation to a minimum.

"Yes, I did stay out rather late. The Marisol always has beach parties in the evening and sometimes I drop in on them." A true enough statement except that last night she had been nowhere near the Marisol. Lily didn't need to know that, of course.

"Well, my dear, it's wonderful that you're so enterprising. Anyway, I'm calling to invite you to dinner Thursday night. I feel terrible for not having called you before now."

"Why, thank you, Lily. I would love to come. And don't apologize for anything. I understand. Where do you live? Is it near here?"

"Yes, actually everything in Palmaltas is close by but don't worry about transportation. Mart will come by for you."

"Oh, thank you. That will be great."

She told Amy the time for the party and after a little bit of chitchat about Donna and David, she hung up.

Taking a cup of coffee out onto the balcony, Amy sat and pondered her previous night's dilemma. She could still feel Peppy's kiss and embrace and hear his words ringing in her ears when he said she needed to rest and if he stayed he wouldn't let her. Her body tingled and burned and she felt alive, yes, alive, feminine, and desirable. It was a splendid feeling. Yesterday's adventure had invigorated her and pumped her full of self-confidence.

"Goodness, Salty, it's amazing what a mudslide can do for you."

The cat just sat and stared intently.

Then the image of the handsome, dashing Peter Harris superimposed the image of Peppy in her mind. Could she possibly have a chance with him also? But did she even want a chance with him? She had to face the fact that she had developed strong feelings for Peppy, but she also considered Donna's reasoning that a future with Peter far outweighed anything Peppy could offer. Or was that true? True love in a cabin with Peppy or a life of luxury in a mansion?

Then she shook herself. "Am I crazy, Salty? Both men are involved with other dazzling women. Who do I think I am that I can just roll in and steal the heart of either man? But don't I have to try? If I run from one or both of them, then I'll probably run from men the rest of my life. That would be Rick's legacy. No, no, I must try. At least I can do that."

"Me-ow."

"That's right. So, I'm getting off my duff and I'm going over to the Marisol for brunch. Maybe, just maybe, I'll see Peter Harris again. And if I don't, well there's the beach and Peppy." That was a thought that brought pangs of anticipation. As far as her feelings were concerned, Peppy was far ahead of Peter Harris.

But her newly acquired self-confidence in regard in attracting the attention of Peter Harris would have to wait for another day. Mr. Harris didn't appear.

Momentarily, she thought of asking the waiter if he had seen him, but she didn't want to appear too forward. He was probably used to women clamoring for information about his elusive employer.

After brunch and still brimming with enthusiasm and self-confidence, she found Peppy at his usual perch on the pier.

"My, but you seem very energetic after yesterday's muddy episode although you are a little late coming out," he said smiling.

"Yes, I feel great. I tried to sleep late but the cat wouldn't let me."

"Yeah," he said sensuously, "I wouldn't have let you either."

"Oh, Peppy." She laughed and hit him playfully on the shoulder.

Then inexplicably, at least to herself, she asked him if he would like to accompany her to Lily and Martin's dinner Thursday night. As soon as the words were out of her mouth, she wondered what had prompted her to do so. Lily and Martin, although nice and friendly people, more than likely wouldn't consider Peppy to be socially acceptable and she had refrained from telling Lily that she was with Peppy last night. Then she remembered Peppy's appearance Friday night and realized that he could be as presentable as anyone could if he chose to do so. Lily and Martin wouldn't have to know he was a beach bum fisherman. Perhaps she could pass him off as a tourist that she had met at the Marisol but that would be untrue and unfair to Peppy.

His reply, although rather expected, surprised her by his tone of gratitude and sincerity.

"Amy, that's very kind of you, but that kind of-uh-socializing doesn't interest me. I'm sure the invitation was meant for you alone. In fact, they may provide a spare man for you." There was a twinkle in his eyes, those beautiful blue eyes, which showed a side of Peppy that she had only glimpsed before.

"I certainly hope not!" she replied indignantly. "There is nothing I hate more than blind dates or people trying to fix me up with someone. I like to pick my own men." As soon as she said the last sentence she felt foolish, not only as if she were some kind of femme fatale who had the masculine world at her feet, but also remembering that Donna was trying to fix her up with Peter.

"Whew! Is that so?" he teased.

"Oh, I didn't mean to sound so pompous. It's just that blind dates for me have always been disastrous."

He put his arm around her, hugged her, and whispered into her ear, "I'm kind of glad to hear that although I can't understand how any date with you could be disastrous."

"Oh, Peppy, have you forgotten yesterday? You don't consider losing me to a mudslide a disaster?"

He laughed, and then said solicitously, "Now, let me look at you. You don't seem to be any the worse for it. How's your wrist?"

"Why, why," she sputtered, "I completely forgot about it."

"Then there must not be anything wrong with it."

"No," she said, flexing it. "It's a little stiff but there's no pain."

"That's great. Then you can hold a fishing rod."

"Oh you," she said, playfully hitting him again.

He grinned and they spent what was left of the morning fishing in companionable silence. Amy was happy, truly happy, and was looking forward to the afternoon and perhaps the evening in Peppy's company. A bond had been forged yesterday, she was sure, and her invitation to Lily's seemed to touch him. She felt that she had been forgiven for Friday night's mistake. At the moment, all she wanted was to be with Peppy.

Just before noon, Amos waved and beckoned to Peppy who reluctantly got up and walked over to the boating concession. A few minutes later, he came back and pecked her on the cheek.

"Something's come up, honey. I've got to go. You'll be here tomorrow?"

She nodded, full of disappointment yet elated at the kiss and the endearment of honey. As he walked away, past Amos up the beach, a sudden tinge of paranoia struck her. What if it was Janice who had called him away? She worked for Amos. Had she gotten a message to him somehow? She pushed her doubts aside. What did it matter? She had a special friendship with Peppy. She had to believe in that. So what if he did have other women? He was a free spirit and could have as many female friendships as he wanted. She shouldn't worry or care about any others. But she did care and it did matter.

All at once she remembered the two men at the beach party who had apparently scared away Peppy. Maybe it wasn't Janice at all who had called today for Peppy. Maybe something more sinister awaited him and Amos had come to forewarn him.

Oh, there was so much that she didn't know about Peppy. Thank goodness, she thought, he had turned down her invitation to Lily's party. Her imagination conjured up a scene of the two of them being followed to Lily and Mart's home by two Palmaltan policemen who would raid the party and arrest Peppy, embarrassing everyone. How silly, she told herself. Amos passed a message to his brother and she immediately concocted an idiotic scenario that probably had nothing to do with the real reason he was called away.

Disconsolate, she started to walk back across the beach to the condo. Peter, she thought to herself, maybe she should concentrate on him and her feelings for Peppy would dissipate. Reluctantly, she admitted to herself that was impossible.

"Hey, Amy, have you recovered from last night?"

Startled, she looked up to see Bert greeting her from his lifeguard tower.

"Yes-yes, I'm fine, thank you. How about you?"

"Hey! Couldn't be better. I wasn't the one who slid down a mountain."

"Yes." She laughed, suddenly feeling better, "that's true, but you did come to my rescue."

"Hey, I didn't do much."

"Well hey." She mimicked him. "I, nonetheless, appreciate your help and concern."

"Hey, no problem."

She waved to him and continued plodding back to the condo, where at the pool she encountered Eddie, Bert's counterpart.

"Hey," she said, anticipating his greeting. "Thanks for helping me last night."

"And hey to you, too," he said laughing. "I see you've been talking to Bert."

"Yes, he is full of hey. But really, I am grateful to you guys for going out to help me."

"Think nothing of it, Amy. I'm just glad you're all right. How's the wrist?"

"It's fine, just a momentary sprain or strain, I guess."

"That's great. Where are you going now? In the middle of the day?"

"Inside. Peppy had to leave and I didn't want to fish by myself."

He gave her a quizzical look and was silent for a few moments. She was afraid he might ask her about her relationship with Peppy and that was a subject she wanted to avoid. Instead, he invited her to spend some time at the pool.

"You know, Eddie, I think I will," she said, throwing her towel on a deck chair and plunging into the warm water. Not hungry due to her late brunch, she lounged and lazed around the pool until four o'clock when hunger pangs finally attacked her. Eddie had not had time to socialize with her because he had been occupied watching the kids of condo residents. But she didn't mind, it just felt good to have a friend nearby.

As she started to leave, Eddie yelled at her, "Come back more often, Amy."

"Thanks." She waved back. "I will."

~ * ~

He relaxed for a moment and smiled to himself. She had actually invited him to one of her social soirees. He was almost certain of her now and was she in for a surprise! This was going to be fun. He couldn't wait to tell Amos. Then he remembered what Amos had told him yesterday morning. That was something puzzling for him to ponder, something puzzling indeed. Maybe Amy needed a few more tests, after all.

~ * ~

After eating an early dinner on the balcony, Amy sat there and sipped white wine while the evening grew into night. Her one regret with Donna's condo was the lack of a western view and therefore she couldn't observe brilliant Caribbean sunsets.

"My, my," she said out loud to herself, "aren't I the spoiled one? A few weeks ago I would never have regretted missing sunsets. I was just so grateful to be here at any cost."

Salty meowed.

"Hey, guy," she said, adopting Bert's affectation, "I'm getting jaded with all this tropical opulence."

"Meow," he whined again.

"Yeah, you're right. I've got nothing to complain about, except that damn Peppy and the way he affects me. He's a beach bum for goodness sake. Why does whoever Janice is bother me so much? Why do I have to be so attracted to him? If I met Peter Harris formally, would my feelings for Peppy change? Wouldn't Donna be thrilled? Could Peter Harris take my mind off Peppy? Yet, Peter has Marla. Damn those gorgeous women, Marla and Janice. Oh, Salty, I'm terrible. I don't have the right to break up anyone's romance. I've had it done to me and I would never do it to anyone else. But those men: Peppy kissing me and spending time with me; Peter flirting with me; why are they pretending to be interested in me if they both have someone else? Oh, Salty, It's so unfair."

Seeming to sense her despondency, the cat leapt onto her lap and she hugged him affectionately as self-pitying tears ran down her cheeks. She could hear the bongo drums from Amos's nightly party. She wasn't completely alone but she felt that she was.

~ * ~

Wednesday morning Amy glanced at Donna's kitchen calendar and noted that the apartment cleaners were coming that day. She waited until they arrived then headed for the pier hoping to see Peppy. Luckily, he was there and he greeted her affectionately, raising her morale, although she knew she should be suspicious of his behavior. However, Amos interrupted them before they could get past their greetings.

"Hi, Amy, how's the wrist?"

"It's fine, Amos, and thanks for coming to my rescue Monday night."

"No problem. I'm just glad we got you out all right."

"Well, so am I." She laughed.

Then somewhat somberly, he turned to Peppy. "Say, bro, another problem."

"I'm on it," he said resigned to whatever fate awaited him. "Sorry, Amy, gotta go again." He pecked her on the cheek as he collected his fishing equipment. "Here, bro, take care of this stuff for me."

"Yeah, I always do," said Amos, winking at Amy.

They watched Peppy as he trekked away, not down the beach, but through the hotel. She assumed he was going to the bus stop, as the bus would certainly be faster than taking the beach route to wherever and whatever problem had arisen. She didn't know why but she felt he wasn't off to meet Janice and that thought gladdened her. He and Amos were acting much too serious for anything so trivial as an early morning lover's tryst for Peppy. But whatever the two of them were up to, Amos apparently wasn't going to enlighten her.

"Gotta get back to work, Amy. You gonna be okay?"

"Why, of course. I'll just hang around with Bert or Eddie."

"Good girl. See you later."

What a strange response, she thought, but yet it was a concerned response. A warm glow spread over her. How nice to have friends who cared for her, and masculine ones at that, she thought.

She walked back to the condo beach where Bert greeted her. "Hey, Amy, how about spending some time on my beach?"

"Hey, Bert, I'm going to do just that," she said, spreading her towel on the sand.

Refusing to ponder why Peppy had to leave, she made herself comfortable on Bert's beach instead of Eddie's pool. She had no intention of going back to the apartment until the cleaners had finished.

~ * ~

The message that he had just received irritated him no end. Now he would have to change course. Poor Amy would just have to wait a bit longer. He smiled at his own description: poor Amy. Then he thought of Amos who wanted him to get this part of the plan finished. Ah well, he thought, patience, patience. Right now he needed to get to Bay City and the Bay View Hotel.

~ * ~

Peppy didn't appear at all on Thursday, his absence causing her again to wonder what he could possibly be doing. Was he doing something for Amos? If so, what? Finding Amos too busy to visit and chat with her, she returned to the condo, just waving to Bert and Eddie as she passed them.

At least she had Lily's dinner party to look forward to. She would spend the day preparing for it. Lazily, Amy tried on dresses and experimented with various hairdos. Finally, she went to one of the shops below and bought a yellow linen sundress, cut low in front, and a matching jacket. It was expensive but she felt she had to do something drastic to bring her out of her doldrums. Next she bought pearl drop earrings to add just a tad of sophistication to the outfit. Last, she went to a beauty salon and had her hair done: one side swept back to meet a cascade of curls on the other side.

Later that afternoon she indulged in a perfumed bubble bath. Lounging in the soapy richness, she remembered Peppy's comment. Could he be right? Would Lily provide a male companion for her?

Palmaltas was full of handsome men. Peppy and Peter weren't the only ones. Suddenly exhilaration swept over her as she climbed out of the bath. She was going to a party where surely someone new would be waiting to meet her. Then the exhilaration drained away. Meeting someone new was the last thing she wanted.

Fourteen

Martin came by for her at seven-thirty. After getting into his Mercedes, of all things she thought, they drove across the road to, unbelievably, the Harris mansion. Her heart was pounding. Was he going to pick up the elusive Peter Harris? Would Lily and Martin have chosen him as a dinner companion for her? Certainly Donna and David would have done so. But Martin's next comments dispelled any expectation of being accompanied by the famous hotelier.

Pulling up in front of the mansion, a Mediterranean style home with red-tiled roof and ornate bars over the downstairs windows and balconies adjoining the ones upstairs, he commented, "We've got to tread very carefully tonight in front of Lisa."

"What on earth do you mean?" So, it was Lisa who was coming and not Peter.

"Lily invited both Peter and Lisa but Peter called this morning to say he didn't think he could come. At first Lisa was so happy to have her brother back that she forgave his disappearing escapade, but since his return he very seldom shows up for work at the hotel and she's very perturbed with him now. She's beside herself with worry and, if Peter doesn't show up, we want to help her keep her mind off him tonight and enjoy herself. And we want you to enjoy yourself, also," he added.

"But Peter may show up?" When he nodded yes, she said, "Don't worry, I'm sure I'll have a good time and it should be easy for me to avoid talking about her brother. I haven't met him, you know. I missed him Friday night but I did see him the other morning at the Marisol coffee shop."

"You did? That's odd. Well, here she comes. She must have seen us drive up. Lisa is divorced and rather the nervous type. I feel like I'm walking on eggshells when I'm around her."

Lisa Harris Rivera's arrival prevented Amy from asking Martin why he thought it odd for Peter to be in the coffee shop, if indeed that's what he meant. Her attention, however, immediately changed direction, and she focused on Peter's sister. Lisa was attractive of indeterminate age, probably late thirties. She was stylishly but modestly dressed in a cream-colored satin pantsuit. Her most noticeable feature was her hair, a garish, platinum blonde color and swept back into a severe bun. For some reason Amy had expected Lisa to be a brunette in keeping with most of the native Palmaltan women that she had seen. Then she remember that she was Peter's sister and wondered if she had brown hair like his and colored it for a more ostentatious effect.

Martin got out of the car and, as he ushered her into the back seat, introduced the two women. Lisa's remote sophistication made Amy feel awkward. Lisa was polite but not friendly. Amy could see how Lisa would dislike Marla but it hurt to think she might not like her either.

Martin turned the car toward the Palmaltas Hilton where, he explained to Amy, his and Lily's condo was situated nearby. The trip was very short and Martin kept the conversation going by simply making a few comments about the weather and the rainy season. Amy, of course, refrained from mentioning her first encounter with a Palmaltas downpour Monday afternoon. She shuddered to think what her two companions would make of her muddy adventure, not to mention her rescuers, although they were people she cared for.

Martin escorted them into the elevator, which went up to the penthouse, no less. Amy marveled at the friends that Donna had cultivated in the past two years. This was opulence at its best. While Donna's condo was decorated in vivid tropical colors, Martin and

Lily had decorated theirs in muted whites giving an aura of tasteful elegance.

"Oh, do come in," greeted Lily who was dressed in a low-cut satiny green jumpsuit, which brought out the richness of her natural tan. "Amy, I don't think you've met Petey."

Petey? Amy was astounded. Standing near the glass doors, which opened onto their balcony, was *the* Peter Harris whom she had seen at the Marisol coffee shop. So, he had decided to come after all. What would Peppy say if she told him that Lily had produced a male companion and that it was Peter, she wondered?

As Lily introduced them, Amy thought she heard an almost inaudible gasp from Lisa and Martin. Obviously, neither was too happy to see Peter, but for different reasons, Amy supposed. Lisa, would be upset with her brother for neglecting his business and Martin would have to tread even more carefully in the presence of both brother and sister.

Gathering her courage, Amy marched over to shake hands with Peter Harris, and said, "No, I haven't exactly met Mr. Harris although we exchanged nods the other morning."

"Please," he said, "call me Petey. I insist that everyone call me that."

How curious, she thought, since Donna had always referred to him as Peter but then maybe Petey was just a nickname used in addressing him.

"Very well, uh, Petey." How silly that name sounded for such a handsome, mature man. But hadn't she read somewhere that the very rich had nicknames that outsiders never understood? She remembered reading about a cereal heir who was always referred to in the society columns as Juicy-Poo although his given name was Jonathan. Only friends and family insiders would know why he was called that. At least Petey was a nickname miles above Juicy-Poo.

Her attention wandered to his attire. He was dressed casually in a white shirt, light tan sports jacket with matching pants. He was tieless, looking very comfortable and at ease and, in spite of the casualness of his attire, he exuded an air of sophistication. If a wealthy playboy wanted to be called Petey then so be it, she thought.

Lily, also, seemed to be comfortable and unaware of the discomfort that Peter's presence caused for Martin and Lisa. Amy, for one, decided to follow Lily's lead and try to enjoy herself. Whether Lily had invited Peter as a companion for her or to reconcile with his sister, she didn't care. At last, she had now formally met Mr. Peter Harris.

Out of nowhere came a momentary twinge of guilt as the spectra of Peppy flitted across her mind. He knew she was coming here tonight and that she would more than likely be paired with someone. But she had invited him and he had wisely turned her down. There was no reason to feel guilty, she tried to assure herself. Peppy was her friend and although she found him to be exciting and sensual, to say the least, she couldn't quite define his feelings for her. He kissed her passionately but always seemed to hold something back. Did he hold back because they were from two very different worlds?

Amy jerked her thoughts away from Peppy to Peter. Was she in his world? A question she had asked herself before. Never would she have thought so but Donna had escalated from middle-class Nebraska into the hierarchy of Palmaltas. Why couldn't she do it also? Stop it, she admonished herself, she must enjoy the evening and not worry about either Peppy or Peter.

Lily offered everyone cocktails and asked Peter to help her mix them. Lisa walked out onto the balcony alone, giving Martin time to apologize to Amy, although she thought an apology to Lisa was more in order. Personally, Amy was thrilled at the presence of Peter Harris.

"Believe me, Amy," he whispered, "I wasn't expecting him to be here. I can't imagine what prompted him to come."

He emphasized *him* with disdain and she wondered why since she thought he, David, and Peter were good friends. Then she remembered that Martin had replaced Peter as best man at Donna and David's wedding. Of course, she thought, Martin must have felt that Peter was some kind of masculine rival. She wondered if Martin had been told of Peter's new political conversion or if he knew the real reason that David was in the Caymans. Somehow she thought not on both counts. But she didn't care a flip for Martin's views of his guest and therefore played a wide-eyed innocence and kept the conversation light.

"Oh, Martin, I'm very happy to see Pet-er-Petey. That was one of Donna's goals, fixing me up with him."

"You've got to be joking."

Which had been her response, more or less, to Donna at first, but Amy's mind changed when she spotted Peter Harris at the Marisol. Or had it changed when she spied on Peppy walking away with Janice?

Lily and Peter interrupted them with the drinks, and Lily ushered them onto the balcony where they joined the very aloof Lisa. The dinner table had been set up out there and the atmosphere was lush, tropical, and romantic. Lily and Martin had a closer view of the Caribbean than did Donna. The waves splashing on shore were much louder here.

Peter flirted unabashedly with Amy and, fortified with heady drinks, she reveled in the attention. The only sour note was sullen Lisa. Why couldn't Lily have provided an escort for her, also, Amy wondered. Or had she invited someone who declined to come? That seemed very unlikely to Amy. Lisa was an attractive, wealthy heiress. Surely there would be plenty of men, especially tourists, who would jump at the chance to dine with her. But Lisa wasn't Amy's problem and she was determined to continue enjoying the evening.

Lily soon seated them and a young, attractive Palmaltan couple served lobster Thermidor with salad and crusty bread. While observing the servants, Amy wondered if they lived in Bay City or in Amos and Peppy's neighborhood of cabins. She also wondered if Lily herself had prepared the meal or if she had ordered it from one of the seafood restaurants on this end of the island, particularly La Concha Blanca.

The dinner conversation remained light dwelling on inconsequential matters such as weather and tourism. Amy would have loved to venture into more relevant topics, such as David and Peter's desire to improve the island, wondering how Lisa Harris Rivera felt about such things. But she had been warned not to discuss them with anyone, not even Peter's sister who might not yet know of them. And Martin and Lily were possibly ignorant of their friends' revolutionary plans, also.

The most awkward moment of the evening came when Lily said, "Lisa, you and your brother have such a strong resemblance, especially your natural hair color. Don't you think so, Petey?"

Amy was aghast at such rude behavior on Lily's part, as up to that moment she had been an impeccable hostess, but to cattily refer to

Lisa's dyed hair in that way was nothing more than insulting. Amy tried to picture Lisa with the natural brown hair of her brother and did indeed see a resemblance between brother and sister. But to point out that a guest, a socially prominent one at that, cosmetically altered her appearance made Amy wonder how trustworthy a friend like Lily could be.

Luckily, Martin changed the subject before Peter could reply. "Good grief, Lil, that's not important. Now, what's for dessert? You've outdone yourself with this meal, hon. So, what else did you cook up?"

Lily gave him a petulant glance then brightened at his compliment. One of Amy's questions was answered. Lily had prepared the repast.

"It's a surprise. Just wait." She rang a little bell and the male servant appeared to clear away the table. His female counterpart soon followed with chocolate mousse. Amy was impressed with Lily's cooking skills.

During the meal, Peter had been quite attentive to Lisa who had, for the most part, given him the cold shoulder. When she was younger, Amy had been used to sibling squabbles but they had diminished as they grew older. Perhaps wealth presented different family values but she thought Lisa was unnecessarily harsh with her handsome brother.

After the mousse remains had been cleared away, they returned inside where Martin served small glasses of brandy. Amy barely sipped hers when she found it much too strong for her taste and she knew she had already had too much to drink.

Lily came to the rescue with cups of espresso.

After the coffee, Lisa asked Martin if he would mind taking her home.

"I'd be glad to," he said, "and you, Amy, are you ready?"

Before she could reply, Peter chimed in with an invitation.

"Maybe you'd like to walk back with me, Amy. I'm staying at the Marisol right now," he said as he stared at Lisa.

Amy wondered how they could be so alienated that they couldn't stay in the same mansion together in their own rooms. Then she was sure that her previous notion for the reason for tonight's gathering was correct. Good-hearted Lily, not untrustworthy Lily, was trying to reconcile the two siblings while at the same time trying to pair her with Peter. She recalled a comment by Lily the night of the wedding rehearsal, that Donna wanted her to meet Lisa. And now, in one evening, she had met both Peter and Lisa. Perhaps Lily's hair comment had not meant to be catty at all, just a way to remind them of their family similarities, although she thought Lily could have found a more suitable way than that one.

"You're staying next door to the Marisol in Donna Risot's condo, aren't you?" he inquired.

"Yes, but she's Donna Díaz now."

"Ah yes, the great wedding. Sorry I couldn't have been there." This was the first mention or allusion to Peter's disappearance that had been made all evening and Amy was surprised at the tinge of sarcasm in his voice. David Díaz was one of his best friends, yet he was making light of not attending because of a self-imposed exile. Perhaps she was putting too much into words and his expression. Clearly, there were many things that she didn't know about Peter Harris and should not be judgmental.

"As to walking me back, yes, that would be very refreshing."

Lily beamed but Martin scowled. Her intuition that there was some kind of masculine rivalry between Martin and Peter seemed well founded. Martin, a married man, seemed to resent that she would let his friend Peter, a bachelor, accompany her home.

The evening was cool and pleasant as they ambled toward Donna's condo. The conversation was friendly and aimless until Amy tentatively mentioned Marla, wondering what he thought of Lily inviting her instead of his fiancée.

"Palmaltas is a lovely island with lovely people," she said. "And newcomers such as Marla Hunter seem to flock here as well." She almost laughed at her own ridiculous statement but she was very curious at what Peter might say about Marla while with another woman.

Before he answered, a rather mischievous smile crept across his face. "Ah yes, Marla. A beautiful woman. I admire her a great deal." His tone was strangely affectionate yet remote. Shouldn't a man about to be married refer to his intended with more than admiration?

Nonetheless, a sharp pang of jealousy swept through her. Marla and Janice were two beautiful women who continued to interrupt her potential romances, although to be truthful, it was she who desired to interrupt theirs. And she had brought up the subject of Marla, not the other way around. Perhaps that was why he answered as he did.

Peter turned his focus on her, dismissing further conversation of Marla. "So, Amy, how do you like Palmaltas?"

"I love it," she said and plunged into a praiseworthy commentary on the exquisite scenery of the island. She wanted to talk about the plight of ordinary Palmaltan citizens but didn't want to spoil the light camaraderie they were beginning to share. Perhaps, if she were lucky, at another time they might have an added opportunity. She could do nothing but hope.

When they reached the condo, Ossie opened the door for them, coldly staring at Peter and then at her. Peter, on his part, seemed oblivious to the doorman and nonchalantly escorted her to the elevator. Perhaps Ossie had no great appreciation for Peter Harris, but Amy felt hurt because he had always been friendly to her. His attitude was especially odd considering his comment Monday morning unless, of course, his comment about her charming Peter had been made facetiously. Oh, how she wanted to shout out to the world that Peter Harris was a good man, intent on helping the plight of his people, but she didn't even dare discuss his plans with the man himself, not until they knew each other better.

Peter rode up the elevator with her and escorted her to her door. She had known Peppy for weeks before he escorted her home and then it was only after a harrowing experience. But her first formal encounter with Peter brought him to her door.

As she groped in her purse for the key he grabbed her and kissed her hungrily and forcefully. So unexpected was this move that she momentarily succumbed to his embrace, but then she remembered his smile when she had mentioned Marla and she pushed him back. Besides, she thought, with his playboy reputation, he probably expected females to swoon in his arms. If she was going to capture the heart of Peter Harris then she had to show a modicum of self-respect and self-control. He must consider her worth pursuing.

In a casual manner, he asked, "How about a nightcap, Amy?"

Still stunned by his amorous advance, she declined. "No, Pete-er-Petey. Not-not tonight. I have had enough to drink this evening and if I offered coffee, then the caffeine would keep us-uh-at least me up all night. Another time, perhaps."

He grinned roguishly, apparently not in the least bothered by her loss of composure. "Staying up wouldn't be so bad, but no, you're right. I certainly don't want to push you. As you say, another time."

He reached down and kissed her again, a brief but strong kiss.

"I hope to see you again soon. Good-night, Amy." He bowed and turned toward the elevator.

Inside the apartment, with the door locked for the night, she stood leaning against it, panting. A dinner party with Peter Harris, walking in the moonlight with him, being kissed by him: if only she could tell Donna. She would be ecstatic.

As Amy lay in bed she played Peter's kissing scenario over and over in her mind. But as she began to drift off to sleep, Peppy's face superimposed Peter's and her body burned with desire.

Suddenly she sat upright, shaking off the approaching waves of sleep and dreams. Salty jumped on the bed at her sudden movement.

"Oh, Salty, what is the matter with me? My common sense says to go for Peter Harris with whom I would have security and luxury. But my heart, soul, and body are crying out for Peppy. And worst of all, after his behavior tonight I don't like Peter very much in spite of his desire to help his people. What have I done? I can't let myself fall in love with a scruffy beach bum. Or then again, why can't I?"

"Meow," was his answering word of wisdom. But what did it mean?

<h1 style="text-align:center">Fifteen</h1>

Friday and Saturday Amy lolled on the beach pondering her feelings for Peppy and Peter Harris. Peppy didn't show up either day and she forced herself to concentrate on Peter. She tried to convince herself that she wasn't falling in love with Peppy. It was a sexual, physical attraction, nothing more, she assured herself. He obviously didn't feel as strongly as she did or he would be combing the beach, the condo, the Marisol looking for her. Instead, he let days go by without an appearance. After all, he was only a beachcomber, what else could he possibly have to do? And that was a question she avoided as she again worried that Peppy might be involved with something illegal. But it was Amos who had called him away on the days that he did appear. Would Amos be involved in something clandestine also?

Amos was too busy to talk, being inundated with tourists clamoring for his attention, but he always managed a friendly wave, for which she was grateful. She felt abandoned, although she knew she could join Bert and Eddie anytime she needed human conversation, albeit rather juvenile conversation. She did call Lily to thank her for a lovely dinner. Lily said she was pleased to hear from her but Amy thought that she sounded occupied and in a hurry, the busy socialite perhaps.

She forced herself to concentrate on Peter Harris. Should she see him again, to see if some magic might be possible between them? Donna would urge her to do so. When and if she did see him, she wouldn't mention Marla. The more she thought about the two of them, the more she convinced herself that his reaction to Marla's name Thursday night had been less an affectionate one than a polite one. How could he really love Marla while kissing her and asking for a nightcap?

Both Donna and Lily seemed to think that she and Peter would make a great couple. Amy didn't know Lily very well but she trusted Donna implicitly. Yes, Donna had said he was a playboy. He had certainly acted like one Thursday night but he had used self-restraint with her. Perhaps that meant he had been testing her, to see if she would succumb to his fame and fortune or if she would practice some self-restraint herself. She hoped that she had passed that little test.

Then she became angry with herself. Why should she have to pass anyone's test? She was who she was and had nothing to be ashamed of. Peter Harris should look at her just as David Díaz had looked at Donna.

For two days Amy avoided going back to the Marisol coffee shop because she didn't want Peter to think she was chasing him. That idea also angered her. If she wanted to have an occasional breakfast there then she shouldn't let him intimidate her. Besides, where else was she going to find him and decide for herself just how friendly she wanted to be with him? True, he knew where she lived and could contact her anytime he chose. But maybe, just maybe, despite his comment that he hoped to see her again, her behavior had convinced him that she wasn't worth pursuing.

Her mind was a jumble. Had she passed some sort of test with Peter or had she put him off? Why did male and female relationships have to be so childishly complicated, she wondered? There was only one way to find out how Peter Harris felt about her and more important, how she felt about him. Perhaps more casual encounters at the Marisol would do the trick. The summer was passing and she didn't have time for patience. Peppy seemed to have abandoned her and the pain that caused her was immense. She doubted that Peter could arouse the feelings that Peppy did but she had to give him a chance or so she tried to convince herself.

Sunday morning Amy left by the front door where she encountered Ossie chatting with Daniel, who was as amiable as ever.

"Hi, guys," she greeted them. "What an easy life you lead, just hanging around here." She was joking, of course, which Daniel seemed to understand but Ossie just looked away, saying nothing.

"Maybe so." Daniel laughed. "But as soon as my clients who are guests of condo residents show up, I'll be busy carting them around the island, through Bay City to Black Water Cove."

"Yes, you will be busy." She sincerely wanted Ossie to acknowledge her, but he walked away to talk to a groundskeeper who was tending a flower garden. Apparently her appearance Thursday night with Peter Harris still annoyed him and he didn't want to fraternize with anyone connected with the higher echelon of Palmaltas society. But that idea was ludicrous. Ossie dealt with society people all day, the residents of the condo, and he was paid to be friendly. She knew Daniel didn't care much for Peter and obviously Ossie cared even less.

Since there was nothing she could do about their attitude, at least for now, she proceeded on to the Marisol, thinking how wonderful it would be when Peter's true feelings about his country were finally revealed. So, if Ossie were angry because she had been with Peter, then sometime in the future she was sure he would change his mind.

With that upbeat reasoning, she entered the Marisol coffee shop.

To her dismay, not Peter but Marla was sitting at a table by a window with a view of the beach and the sea beyond. Brazenly, Amy approached her.

"Why hello, Marla, do you mind if I join you?"

She looked up, startled, not recognizing Amy at first.

"Oh, uh-you're-uh-I'm sorry but I don't remember your name. Aren't you that friend of Donna Risot's?" Her tone was more patronizing than apologetic.

"Díaz. She's Díaz now."

"Yes, of course. The wedding. Maid of honor."

She still had not responded to Amy's self-invitation so she repeated it. "May I?" and sat down anyway.

She replied, rather dubious, "Yes-yes, of course."

Deciding to plunge ahead with her newly found courage, Amy said, "You must be thrilled to have Peter back now."

"Of course," she replied in a mild but confident manner, "but I knew he'd be back."

"So have you set a date for a wedding?" Amy was almost appalled at her own audacity, finding this woman much more intimidating than Peter himself.

Her look indicated that this was none of her business. Amy acknowledged to herself that it wasn't but Marla answered nonetheless after a brief pause.

"No, no we haven't. Peter has to get some business matters straightened out." Her voice trailed off, indicating either boredom at having to converse with Amy or that she was preoccupied with another matter entirely.

"Oh, of course," Amy said brightly as she realized and enjoyed how much her presence was irritating her. "He had a lot to get caught up on due to his prolonged absence."

Marla's answer rather surprised her. "No, not necessarily. Things were fairly well taken care of here but new matters always arise and Peter is the man in charge.

She sipped her coffee and stared out the window. Only the waiter asking for Amy's order, which was coffee and a cinnamon roll, broke their silence.

"I hope you get a lot of exercise," Marla said unexpectedly.

"Why? What do you mean?"

"The cinnamon rolls here are loaded with fat and sugar."

"Well maybe, but that's what I'm in the mood for."

"As for myself," she continued, ignoring Amy's comment, "my breakfast consists only of decaf, fruit, cereal, and skim milk."

Amy smiled more to herself than to Marla. Here she was discussing breakfast with the fiancée of Peter Harris, a woman that she was contemplating to replace. The entire situation was ridiculous, she thought.

"Well yes," Amy said, "that is healthy but I intend to swim off today's calories. Usually I just have cereal, also, but I do like my caffeine," she babbled on only to be interrupted by a male voice, a familiar one.

"My, but Palmaltas and the Marisol are truly blessed. Such two lovely ladies adorning our coffee shop."

Both women turned and looked up into the mischievous gleam in the eyes of Peter Harris himself.

"Oh, Petey, you're always full of..." Marla hesitated and looking at Amy, finished her sentence. "...compliments."

Amy felt sure that she was going to say something else not nearly so nice. She was amazed that the uppity Marla called him Petey also but perhaps she would be the one to call him that more than anyone else.

Obviously knowing and not caring what she had intended to say, he laughed and said, "May I join you?"

"Do we have a choice?" Marla responded tersely.

Suddenly, this engaged couple made Amy feel very uncomfortable. Their repartee was friendly enough, at least Peter's was, but Marla's had an edgy tone. Were they really in love? She had expected Peter to greet his fiancée with a kiss or a peck on the cheek but all he had done was compliment both of them. Was it her presence that had held him back? Did she have a chance after all?

"And so," he said, turning to Amy, "have you recovered from the other evening?"

"Why-why..." She blushed. "There was nothing to recover from. I had a very pleasant evening."

"What evening are you talking about?" Marla demanded.

"Thursday night, wasn't it?" he asked Amy rhetorically and continued, "We had dinner with Lily and Martin. Your future sister-in-law was there, too."

"Oh lord, thank goodness I wasn't invited. That must have been an entertaining evening. Lisa can be such a drag. How did you get along with her?"

"She ignored me. I was polite to her," he said laughing.

At that moment Amy felt sorry for Lisa Harris Rivera. Referring to her as Peter just did indicated that he was not only teasing Marla but was being sarcastic regarding his own sister. It was apparent that he was aware that the two women didn't get along and his loyalty seemed to be more with his fiancée than with Lisa. Marla's personality was much too dominant for it to be otherwise. How could Peter be so attracted to a woman like that?

Then she thought that if she could get along with Lisa and attract Peter at the same time how much happier the Harris family would be. She mentally kicked herself. There was no way she could pull off something like that and deep down she knew she didn't want to do so.

As Marla arose so did Peter.

"Come, Petey, there are some things I'd like to discuss with you." She turned and walked away, ignoring Amy in the process.

He hesitated, all smiles and charm, and said to Amy, "I'll get your breakfast check and I'll call you later."

His next move was the most surprising of all to Amy. He bent down and kissed her on the cheek, something not even Marla had rated.

Stunned, she smiled meekly and watched him follow Marla out of the coffee shop. He didn't stop to pay either Marla's or her bill but, after all, he was Peter Harris the owner of the hotel. The bills were either automatically applied to his account or dropped altogether, she assumed.

Did Peter's action mean that she did have a chance? Or was this just simply the way a man of his class acted? Wasn't the way Peter was treating Marla the way Rick had treated her? Carrying on with another woman behind his fiancée's back? Knowing her sympathy should lie with Marla, Amy just somehow couldn't dredge up any for her.

Another woman had wanted Rick and now she was flirting with Peter. Was it the idea of doing something clandestine against Marla that made her want to pursue Peter? Which did she want most, the pursuit or the man himself? Could she possibly be that mercenary, even to a woman like Marla?

Confidence had returned to Amy and she wanted to know if she could actually win the heart of Peter Harris, infamous playboy, secret revolutionary. Whether she should make an attempt or not, deep down inside of her she wanted to know if she were capable of such a seduction.

Another thought popped into her mind. Why did Peter tell Marla today about the party? Hadn't they been together this weekend? Or perhaps he had had no intentions of telling her at all until he saw Marla with her and decided to be nonchalant about the whole thing.

Then, as always, Peppy's face appeared in her mind, but this time a sad face, one she had not seen before. Shaking the image away, she ate her breakfast.

A while later, Amy walked out to the beach, waved at Amos, and looked around for Peppy, curious as to how she would feel when she saw him.

But he was nowhere to be seen and didn't appear at all that day.

~ * ~

Another Monday morning. Another day at the beach. Exactly a week ago, Amy had anticipated a beach date with Peppy and it had turned out to be a mountain climbing and almost disastrous adventure. What would this Monday or even this week bring? Could anything top the excitement of last week?

Despite all these occurrences and the friends she had made, she still felt alone, so very alone. She had met two handsome, sensual, enigmatic men. Both had embraced and kissed her but she was still insecure as to their true feelings or intentions toward her. She tried to convince herself that it was she who had the choice. Would she choose Peter or Peppy? But that wasn't the case at all. It was more like she was waiting to see who would win her first, while all the time she knew both men were involved with other women. Perhaps she was just a little sideshow for both of them, the naïve tourist hoping for a summer romance.

She skipped a Marisol breakfast and headed straight for the beach, deciding to play hard-to-get for Mr. Peter Harris. She figured she didn't have a chance if she made the Marisol her camping around. If Peter were really interested in her then he should come looking for her.

She arrived early, not expecting to see Peppy at that time anyway. Her feelings toward him were confused. She missed him terribly but obviously he didn't feel the same way about her. Should she concentrate solely on Peter and slowly phase Peppy out of her life? Or was it the other way around? Was he phasing her out of his?

When she reached the end of the pier, she stood staring dreamily out to sea with an ache in her heart that she didn't want to admit. Peppy, how had she let Peppy enter her soul? If by some chance she ended up with Peter, would Peppy be hurt? Or had Peppy already hurt her with his absence from the beach and walking away into the night with Janice?

Without warning someone grabbed her from behind, clasping her back to his chest, his arms encircling her. Trapped in a muscular vise, the odor of fresh soap wafted around her as someone nuzzled her ear.

Sixteen

She struggled but he held her tight. "Peppy, is that you and what are you doing?" she gasped, heart pounding.

Gradually, he released her and turned her around. "Giving you a bear hug. I haven't seen you for a few days."

"Well, that wasn't my fault," she said with petulance.

"No, that's true, but I've missed you."

"Oh really? And where-where have you been?"

"Busy."

"That's what, not where, and not much of a what, either."

"Well, aren't we the nosy little busybody," he said laughing, pulling her close again, this time to kiss her properly.

With all her doubts she knew she should resist but she couldn't. It felt so good to be in his arms and to be kissed by him. Peppy so obviously took her for granted, she thought, that he assumed she would readily, eagerly succumb to his advances and what was worse was that she desperately wanted to do so. How could she stop both Peppy and her emotions from going out of control?

"What's the matter?" he asked, pulling her down to sit beside him on the edge of the pier.

Now, she knew, was the time to bring her doubts to the forefront but she was a coward, afraid that he wouldn't tell her anything, polarizing them even more, or even more afraid of what she might learn. How could she tell Peppy of her doubts after such a passionate greeting and one to which she had responded in like matter? She must have done something, her expression, perhaps, because she could see that he sensed something was amiss. She dared not ask him the questions that perplexed and worried her without appearing to be suspicious and critical, questions that kept circling inside her mind. What did he mean by busy? Why wouldn't he tell her? Could he possibly be involved in drug trafficking? What was his involvement with Janice? Was Amos part of this busy life and was he really the good guy that she had pictured him to be? She didn't dare ask any of these things. She would either be making a fool of herself or learning something that might be dangerous to her.

Since she had remained silent, he quietly asked another question.

"Did something happen the other night?"

"The other night?" she repeated, confused.

"Uh-huh, your friends' dinner party."

"Oh, I guess you could say that," she replied rather despondently. Apparently, she realized, Peppy was going to have an easier time prying answers out of her than she had with him.

"So, what happened?" he asked gently, making her feel a little foolish and even guilty, although there was little reason for guilt considering all her doubts concerning him, but nonetheless she felt that way.

"Peter Harris was there."

"Oh was he now?" he said.

"Are you surprised? You shouldn't be. You yourself said that Lily would probably have a male companion for me."

"So it was just the four of you? Lily and her husband, you and this-uh-Peter?"

"No, there was an additional guest, Peter's sister Lisa Harris Rivera."

"What?" He seemed genuinely taken aback.

"Peppy, why are you acting this way? You knew I was going to that party. Peter and his sister are friends of Lily and Martin."

"Well," he said slowly, "I'm just surprised that Peter and his sister were at the same party."

"Why would you say that? What do you know about them, other than Peter is Amos' boss?"

He eyed her with suspicion. "Everyone on Palmaltas knows of them. Some say they look very much alike. Do you think so?"

"There's a family resemblance but Lisa obviously dyes her hair so she won't look like Peter. I got the impression, and Martin certainly indicated this, that she's rather put out with Peter right now."

"She's dyed her hair? To what color?"

Suddenly Amy laughed.

"What's so funny?" he asked.

"That you're acting like a nosy gossip, wanting to know all the tidbits of my social evening with Palmaltas' richest people."

He lightened up a bit and grinned. "So, humor me. What color did she dye it?"

"Platinum blonde, a color straight out of old movies."

"How do you know it was dyed?"

"Oh, get real, Peppy! You men! Always falling for fake blondes. Anyway, Lily made the comment that Lisa and Peter had the same color of hair. And Peter has brown hair."

"Hmm, that makes sense. How did you feel about meeting this Peter Harris?"

Oh dear, she thought, how was she going to approach this turn in the conversation? She had to act with caution.

Evading his direct question, she said, "There was one thing that struck me really funny about him."

"What was that?"

"Everyone calls him Petey. And he insisted that I call him that also."

Suddenly Peppy rolled back on the pier laughing so hard that he had to clutch his stomach.

"Well really, Peppy, it is amusing but not that hilarious. Even his fiancée calls him that."

He shot straight up. "How would you know that?"

"Because I joined Marla for breakfast at the Marisol yesterday."

"You did what?"

She laughed. "I know. I'm getting a little too brazen for my own good. I invited myself. She was none too pleased to have me."

"This is getting good. Go on."

"Peter came in and she called him Petey. Then they left."

"Is that a fact? Well, well, well."

He was silent for a few minutes before he continued, "You just never know about rich folks, do you? I mean Petey isn't the most masculine of nicknames." He started to laugh again.

"Oh, come on. Look at you. What about Peppy? Isn't that a little silly?"

He was still laughing. "Oh, Amy, you are a dear. Pepe-Pe-Pe, Spanish for Joe, remember? No one considers Joe a silly name or unmasculine. Only you and little Jerry call me Peppy."

"Yeah, I guess you're right." She knew it was time to tell him that Peter Harris seemed to be interested in her and might call her. But before she could find a way to tell him without hurting his feelings, he pulled a surprise on her.

"Well, now that you've had your evening with the high and mighty, how about an evening with some real people?"

"What on earth do you mean?"

"Amos is giving a beach party tonight."

"He does every night for the tourists."

"No, not tonight. Johnny's taking over for him. Occasionally Amos likes to go home and cut loose with his friends. It'll be fun, a real Palmaltas beach party with the natives and not tourists, except you, if you'll come.

There was a pleading in his eyes and she knew she couldn't say no nor could she tell him that she might become involved with Peter Harris. Besides, she wanted to go to Amos's party with Peppy. Was she ever going to remove herself from this dilemma of choosing between two men? Or did she really even have a dilemma? Another night would be Peter's. Did she have to choose, especially if she left at summer's end? Just go home with tales of two romances? Then what? But she wanted to stay just as Donna had done. Peppy, sexy and sensual, represented a world that seemed exciting and adventurous and not quite safe. Peter, handsome and charming, represented wealth and security, yet that was what she had thought about Rick. Whatever happened or decision she reached, the summer was proving to be quite intriguing.

She accepted Peppy's invitation.

"Great," he said, "Amos will come by for you around seven when Johnny relieves him. I'll be at the cabin getting things ready and waiting for you."

He kissed her on the cheek and walked over to Amos' concession to talk to him for a while. Suddenly they laughed uproariously and then Peppy walked inside the hotel.

Was he taking the bus back to the cabin, she wondered? Why was he leaving so early to get ready for a night party? So many questions and so many doubts. But she knew one thing, she was looking forward to the party.

So much for phasing Peppy out of her life.

~ * ~

A little after eight o'clock that evening, Amos knocked on her door.

"Are jeans appropriate?" she asked.

"Perfect," he said as happy-go-lucky and as handsome as ever. She wondered why he wasn't married. Amos was, by far, the handsomest man she had seen on Palmaltas. All of the men she had met had been handsome, from Bert and Eddie the young lifeguards, to Daniel the chauffeur, Ossie the doorman, Peppy her enigmatic beachcomber, and, of course, the charming and dashing Peter Harris, hotel tycoon. What a list! And in a contest for good looks and charisma, Amos would win, hands down. So why hadn't some island girl or some enterprising female tourist captured his heart?

"Are we walking?" she asked.

"No, Johnny brought the jeep for us."

"You know, I've never met Johnny."

"You haven't?" he seemed genuinely surprised. "That's strange. I thought you had. Well, you will sooner or later."

He escorted her down the elevator and out the front door where another doorman was working. Ossie's night off, she supposed.

As Amos drove the short distance to the cabin, he commented, "Pepe tells me that you've met Petey Harris."

"Yes, but don't tell me that you call him that also?"

"Not exactly, at least not to his face. Then I address him as Mr. Harris. Petey's a silly name, don't you think?"

"Yes, I thought so for such a distinguished man. Is that what you two were laughing about when Peppy left me this morning? Discussing Peter's nickname?"

"Oh, you saw us laughing, huh? Yeah, that's why we were laughing." He laughed again.

"Tell me, Amos, how do you feel about Peter Harris? Do you like him?"

He took his time in answering. "It's hard to say," he said at last. "I don't think I should talk about my boss."

"Oh, of course." But that response was enough to let Amy know he didn't think much of him. How she wished that she could tell Amos and Peppy and even Ossie that Peter was now working along with David Díaz to overthrow the current government of Palmaltas. But she had promised Donna and she knew, sooner or later, that Peter's true colors would shine through. Her personal problem wasn't concerned with the colors of Peter's politics but with the true colors of his heart and his attitude toward women.

They arrived at the cabin where loud, boisterous music could be heard coming from not only the beach but from inside the cabin as well. The party was in full swing and had begun without them.

Peppy greeted them, gave Amy a hug and kiss and led her around the cabin to the beach and the party. Peppy's affectionate welcome ignited a warm glow, which spread all over her and she eagerly anticipated the festivities.

"This music doesn't sound quite like the calypso of Amos' parties," she said to Peppy.

"It's reggae with a Palmaltan adaptation," he said. "Calypso appeals more to the older tourists at the hotel and that's why Amos gives parties with a calypso background. Reggae, which comes from Jamaica, appeals more to our friends. We Palmaltans just like to mix things up a bit."

"Well, it sounds great, whatever kind of music it is."

"The music you hear coming form the cabin is a tape of the Boogie Brown Band, one of the best reggae bands in the world. Basie Clinton Fearon, the bandleader, is a personal friend of Amos. The people out here on the beach like to play along with his music."

"How did Amos meet him?"

"Basie and his keyboardist Barbara Kennedy met Amos years ago when they came to Palmaltas for a gig. Every time Basie makes a new tape, he sends one to Amos."

"They sound like nice people."

"Indeed they are and now let me introduce you to some more nice people."

A big fire was blazing. Several young men, including Bert and Eddie, were tapping bongos and playing various musical instruments while others were dancing, drinking, and eating. There were a few women who Amy soon learned were married and accompanied by their husbands. She seemed to be the only single woman there and everyone treated her as Peppy's special girl. Miss Janice was nowhere in sight and she felt exhilarated by the attention and atmosphere. Never had she attended a party like this.

All of a sudden, Peppy whirled her into the dancing and she attempted to wriggle and writhe to the rhythm just as he did. After several dances Peppy gave her a drink that he called Cuba Libre, which turned out to be rum and cola, to loosen her up he said. Soon any remaining inhibitions disappeared into the night.

Peppy was sensuous and surprisingly energetic and she happily succumbed to his charm. He gyrated around her then she did the same around him, both of them laughing all the time. Finally, she collapsed into his arms, exhausted.

"Clam bake time," he said.

"What?" She gasped, panting.

"Hot clams. I'll get you some."

"This is a clambake? I've always dreamed of attending one."

"Your dreams are my commands, Madame," he said rakishly as he settled her into a folding chair then stepped away toward the fire.

An older man sat down beside her.

"I'm glad you told Pepe about being with Petey Harris," he said.

His voice was familiar but his comment unnerved her. She turned to get a better look at him through the flickering firelight. Then she laughed. He was Ossie, out of uniform.

"He asked me if I'd seen you with him and I replied yes. Then I asked how he knew and he said you'd told him."

"Oh, I'm glad you understand," she said. "I was afraid that you had misinterpreted everything."

"No, no. I haven't misinterpreted anything. He isn't our favorite person on this end of the island. Luckily Pepe thought the whole thing was funny."

"Oh, because he's called Petey. Did you know he was called that?"

"Huh? Yes, of course. Those of us who work at the condo get together with employees at the Marisol during breaks and lunchtime. They've told us all about Petey."

His tone sounded sarcastic to Amy but before she could come to Peter's defense, Peppy returned, hands full of two plates of clams. Ossie smiled at Peppy and gave him his chair then sauntered away.

"You know, Peppy, I've never thought of clam bakes as being a Caribbean thing."

He laughed and said, "I don't see why not but these clams are imported. Uh, Amos gets them cheap from the Marisol."

"You're kidding!"

Before he could respond, Daniel, accompanied by a beautiful young woman who Amy supposed was his wife, brought up two canvas chairs and unfolded them.

"Miss Amy," he said, "this is my wife Aleji. Do you mind if we join you and Pepe?"

"Oh, please do."

The canvas chairs weren't very sturdy and Amy clumsily balanced her plate on her lap while Peppy showed her how to remove the clams from their shells. Aleji offered her homemade, lemon-butter dip for them.

As they sat there, laughing, talking, and eating, Amy subconsciously observed the fire and the dark sea beyond. The loneliness of this morning had dissipated and was now replaced by a warm fellowship that she had experienced only at the holiday family gatherings on the farm in Nebraska. All of the revelers had settled down to eat and talk, also. The music had been turned down low and the happy murmur of conversation rippled over it. Many guests whom she didn't know wandered over to them, presumably to meet her, flattering her to no end.

As all good evenings must come to an end, this one did shortly after midnight. Amos, Peppy, and a few remaining friends cleaned up the beach and took everything into the cabin. Peppy and Amy said goodnight to Amos.

Peppy drove her back to the condo. The short drive was quiet and peaceful. Only once did Peppy say anything. Reaching over and squeezing her knee softly, he asked, "Did you have a good time?"

"Oh, Peppy." She sighed. "You know I did."

He smiled, driving on and saying nothing more.

At her door he pulled her into his arms, wrapping them around her forcefully. He kissed her slowly, then urgently. Her heart pounded and she didn't want the moment to ever end. He was firm, strong, and tender, his lips pressing, his tongue searching. She had surrendered to his caresses the moment he touched her and knew, at that moment, that she would do anything that he desired.

Finally, he released her, pushing her back as if that were the most painful act of his life. He said simply, in the sweetest, kindest voice, "Thank you, Amy, thank you."

He opened her door, her heart pounding even more in anticipation of what might happen next, but all he did was usher her inside and kiss her gently and briefly. Then he retreated back out of the door and headed in the direction of the elevator.

After she had closed the door, she sank into one of the sofas, weak-kneed from Peppy's ardent passion yet confused as to why he had left her. She couldn't understand why Peppy would reach a certain point with her then pull back. Yes, he was treating her with respect but he was arousing her passion level to a height that she had never experienced before, leaving her burning and unfulfilled. Unexpectedly, the image of Janice leaped into her mind. Was Peppy now, at this moment, heading for her welcoming arms?

"Oh, stop it," she said out loud. "I must consider only how Peppy treats me. Where are you, Salty?" she called out, looking for the one being in which she could confide.

"Meow," he said as he jumped into her lap, purring and rubbing her chin.

"That's right, Salty, he treats me like a fragile princess despite those wonderful bear hugs. And Peter-Petey, what am I going to do about him? Peppy's friends make fun of him but they wouldn't if they knew what I know. Oh, Salty, do I have a chance with either one of them? And if I did, which should I choose: a beach cabin or a lofty mansion?"

No answer, just purring.

Did she really have any choice? Two other women seemed to be way ahead of her. Her dilemma had not changed and was continuing.

~ * ~

Going down in the elevator he thought that perhaps he was the most stupid man in the universe. He realized that he could have had her for the taking. She did seem to be all that he wanted in a woman but he had come this far and now was not the time to rush his plans and perhaps ruin everything. Arriving at the ground floor, he walked out of the building into the fresh warm night, anticipating another cold shower.

Seventeen

The next morning, feeling lazy yet happy, Amy sauntered down to the little kitchen where she made a pot of coffee, all the while talking to Salty, who answered once in a while with a bored meow.

"I know, boy, you couldn't care less about my suddenly exciting social life. I just wish that you had some words of wisdom that I could understand."

The doorbell interrupted this little plea.

"My goodness, who could be here at this hour of the morning?" she exclaimed.

She opened the door to, of all people, Peppy!

"Hmm, so this is how you look so early in the morning," he said roguishly.

"What?" Glancing down at her attire, she hastily pulled together the sides of her white satin robe, which had hung loose over a blue silk nightshirt.

"May I come in?"

"Of-of course." She stumbled, quite flustered. "Would you like some coffee?"

"That would be nice."

"I've been sitting on the balcony. Go on out there, make yourself comfortable, and I'll get the coffee. How do you like yours?"

"Black, and thanks."

"That's the way I like mine, too."

In the kitchen she poured the coffee into two big mugs and carried them out to the balcony. They sat for a few minutes in companionable silence, just sipping their coffee.

As they gazed out upon the sun rising over the sea, the mewing of seagulls could be heard in the distance while the fresh, morning fragrance of salt air and tropical blossoms drifted in with a light breeze. This was closer to paradise than Amy had ever dreamed possible, especially now with Peppy sitting next to her.

"Aren't you going to ask me?" he said, breaking the silence.

"Ask you what?"

"Why I'm here."

"Oh." Suddenly she laughed.

"What's so funny?"

"I hadn't even thought about it. This is the first time you've been here. Inside, I mean, and at this time of the day. Yet this seems so natural for us to be out here sipping coffee..." Her words trailed away.

He grinned. "Yes, this is-uh-rather nice."

"So why are you here?"

"Amos is lending me one of his glass-bottom boats Thursday. Hotel occupancy is low this week and he anticipates slow business. So, are you ready for that boat ride you were promised earlier?"

"Oh, Peppy, how fabulous! I would love to go. Oh, thank you."

"That's great. I'll come by for you around seven. That won't be too early, will it?"

"Oh no, of course not. I'm usually an early riser. I'm just slow this morning because of-of last night."

He smiled. "You had a good time then?"

"You know I did. I thoroughly enjoyed the entire evening. What shall I wear on the boat ride?"

He laughed. "Women, always worrying about their clothes. Just wear something light. I'll take care of everything else that we'll need."

"Will you be at the beach today and tomorrow?"

"No, I-I've got things to attend to. Just you be ready at seven Thursday morning."

"I will be."

"Fine, so Amy, my love, I'll see you then. No, you don't have to see me out, although I'd love to see that robe slip off when you stand up."

Speechless, knowing her cheeks must be glowing red, she clutched her robe around her. Then some common sense returned.

"Are you crazy, Peppy? You've seen me in a bikini more often than anything else. My nightshirt covers a lot more of me than a bikini does."

Not responding to her slight indignation, he grinned and stood up. Bending over, he kissed the tip of her nose, and said, "I don't dare go any further than that. You're quite a temptation, Miss Amy."

He turned and walked out of the apartment.

She sat there, flaming hot. "Oh, Salty, what have I done? Should I discourage his advances? Yet I don't want to. But what will I do when Peter Harris calls? If he calls, that is. Well, I can't sit around waiting for him. If Peppy invites me on exciting dates, then how can I refuse? This summer isn't going to last forever and I can't afford to miss any opportunities to have fun."

However, she did sit around the condo for a couple of days. After Peppy had left she tried to convince herself that she had to be tired from all her excitement. Tumbling down a mountainside, meeting Peter Harris at Lily's get-together, partying on the beach, all of which should mean that she needed to stay in and rest. But she wasn't tired. She was exhilarated. There really was no need to go to the beach. Peppy wouldn't be there. Her tan had bronzed enough. She carefully applied sunscreen everyday but she had turned darker anyway. She didn't want to overdo it and invite a later bout of skin cancer.

But all procrastination aside, she knew deep down within her subconscious that she was staying put because she hoped that Peter Harris might call. If he asked her out for Thursday she would proudly decline, saying she had another engagement. There was no need for him to know with whom, although she doubted that he knew Peppy, the brother of one of his employees.

Her imagination was running wild and she was enjoying it. After she had turned him down for Thursday she could picture Peter asking her out for Friday or Saturday and then perhaps she would accept. She refused to feel guilty about hypothetically two-timing Peppy who, more than likely, would once again disappear from the beach scene, probably doing something illicit with drugs or two-timing her with Janice. Of course, he might be doing something legitimate such as undercover police work. It was the specter of Janice that kept her wishing for Peter's call.

Then she remembered that a few moments ago Peppy had called her his love. Had he meant it? Or was that just his habit with all women? Last night's memories came flooding over her. All of his friends had accepted her as his woman or at least that was the way their actions had seemed. Would he have tried to fool not only her but them as well if Janice were in the picture?

"Oh damn, damn, Salty. I'm so confused. Why must I have these feelings for Peppy? I want Peter Harris to call. Yes, I really do." Deep down she knew she said that more to convince herself than anything else.

Jumping up, she ran upstairs to shower and dress and to put aside thoughts of both men. When she came back downstairs, she resolved to keep her mind busy by reading the novel she had started weeks ago. Determined to forget both men for two days, she delved into the book and immediately found herself engrossed with the exciting adventures of an archaeologist who became embroiled in the mysteries and mystique of ancient worlds, a far cry from Amy's Palmaltan world.

So for two days she read and told herself that she wasn't waiting for Peter's call, which was just as well because he didn't call.

~ * ~

Wednesday night Pepe walked with Amos down the beach to the cabin.

"Looking forward to tomorrow, bro?"

He grinned. "It's a break that I need. Just you keep an eye on things."

"Don't worry. Sooner or later we'll catch those two traitors in action."

"The Bay View continues to be their meeting place."

"Yeah, but he's supposed to be there."

"But why would she be there?"

Amos laughed. "You know perfectly well why she was there."

"I know, I know, and you have heard them conspiring but we need proof, legal proof."

"Just you have a good time tomorrow. By the way, I'm scheduled to take out a boat tomorrow also."

"What? Couldn't you get someone else to do it? I want you to keep an eye out for either or both of them."

"Most of my workers have this week off since this is a slow week for the hotel. I do have one group that wants to go out tomorrow. I doubt that anything momentous will happen and even if it did, I might not be aware of it anyway."

"Yeah, you're right. I just want everything straightened out fast so I can lead a normal life."

Amos burst out laughing. "Pepe, you don't even know what a normal life is."

He gave him a tired look. "Maybe you're right but I'm ready to find out."

~ * ~

Thursday morning Peppy was punctual at seven o'clock. He was dressed in his usual beach attire. Amy had chosen a halter-top and shorts to wear over her bikini with sandals on her feet.

"Would you like some coffee?" she offered.

"No time for it. I like to get an early start when I go out in one of the boats. Besides, I've got a big thermos full enough for both of us."

"Okay, fine. Sounds good to me."

When they approached Amos and his concession, Amy noticed some clouds building up over the eastern horizon.

"Do you think we'll run into those clouds?"

Peppy stared eastward and said, "I imagine the sun will burn them off as it gets higher in the sky although the rainy season will be in force soon. What's the matter? Are you remembering our muddy adventure?" He nudged her playfully.

"Yes, but those clouds last week began over the mountains, not over the sea."

"Trust me, there's nothing to worry about. If a squall comes up, we head back. Those clouds have been appearing for several days and they always dissipate by midmorning."

"Oh, I'm not worried, just curious, I guess." If Peppy said not to worry, then she wouldn't. The sky was clear over their part of Palmaltas. A beautiful day was dawning and beckoning them to the emerald sea.

Amos greeted them, friendly as ever. He helped Peppy push the little glass-bottom boat into the water and they each took one of Amy's arms and lifted her into it, laughing as they did so.

Peppy had already outfitted the boat with a picnic basket, plenty of drinking water, and fuel for the motor. A canopy covered two-thirds of the boat where passengers sat. The glass bottom, below the canopy, immediately caught her attention.

"I can see you're going to have a hard time keeping Amy's head up," joked Amos. "She's going to be like all of my regular customers with eyes turned downwards."

Peppy laughed. "That's okay, one of the reasons I'm taking her out."

Amy was so busy studying the shallow water below that she didn't consider that there might be other reasons.

Just before they shoved off, Amos said, "Be sure and keep in touch."

"Aye, aye, sir." Peppy laughed.

"Why did he say that?" Amy asked.

"No one should go out to sea without communicating once in a while with the shore or in this case with me since I will be out also," said Amos.

"But surely we're not going that far," she said.

"Far or close, Amos wants to know where we are," said Peppy. "It's his boat. And Amos likes to play it safe."

"Well," she joked, pretending to be indignant, "I hope he cares about us, too."

They all laughed as Amos pushed them farther out. Peppy started the engine, which putted to life and they were off on their adventure.

The sun did indeed appear to burn off the distant clouds and Amy was grateful for the protection of the canopy. Peppy, however, was seated at the wheel in bright sunlight, his silver hair glistening, his muscular arms shining as if polished in bronze. He wore a short-sleeved, white shirt above khaki cut-offs, and sneakers without socks, always the eternal, irrepressible beach bum.

Occasionally, he would turn off the motor and they would float aimlessly as he pointed out the various sea-life abounding below. Schools of exotic tropical fish dashed here and there and even a Portuguese man-of-war drifted by. There was plant life, also, rising and swaying from the depths of the water. Peppy seemed to be amused by her naïve enthusiasm but she didn't care. This was an exalting day and she wanted to make the most of it, no matter that she was as giddy as any amateur tourist. Besides, that's what she was, she reminded herself. What else could Peppy expect from a Nebraska schoolteacher?

"When we return," he explained as they floated, rising and falling by the gentle motion of the sea with the motor still off, "I'll circle Palmaltas. It's a quite a view, both below the sea and above."

"Oh, Peppy, how marvelous. This is so exciting."

He grinned, possibly because of her enraptured naïveté, but she hoped that he was just happy and enjoying her company. Apparently she was right because he drew her up to his seat in front of the wheel and set her on his lap, his arms encircling her. She felt giddy with excitement at the thought of being alone with Peppy, floating on the Caribbean, no less.

Feeling his strength encircling her, a burning, tingling sensation raced through her body. It was the most exhilarating sensation that she had ever felt. She knew that if he tried to go any further with her, that she would be powerless to resist him. In fact, she wished that at that moment he would do more than hold her tightly. She wanted to be ravished by Peppy here and now. She didn't know how she was going to contain herself if this was all he was going to do.

He leaned forward and kissed her on the cheek, his hot breath sending shock waves through her soul. She turned and, surprising even herself, kissed him full on the mouth.

"Ah," he murmured, "you want more, do you?"

"Oh, Peppy, yes, I do want more," she replied breathlessly, clinging to him as if she were in danger of being torn away from him.

He turned off the motor, letting the boat drift in the waves. He picked her up and carried her back to one of the cushioned seats under the canopy.

Her first thought was that she knew she was at his mercy, a wildly deliriously wonderful thought. Her second thought was that she knew Peppy was her friend and that he wouldn't hurt her. Her third thought was to stop thinking, which she did as she allowed him to kiss her without any resistance on her part.

"Are you sure?" he whispered in her ear.

"Yes, please."

Grinning his irrepressible grin, he began to pull off her top while she feverishly tried to unbutton his shirt.

"Take it easy," he said. "Remember anticipation is better than realization."

"You must be kidding," she said as she burned with anticipation.

He laughed. "Yes, I'm kidding."

He pulled off what tidbits of clothing she had on. Not giving her time to finish unbuttoning his shirt, he whisked it off but let her unzip his cut-offs. She reached inside, almost swooning at the touch. He quickly removed the last vestiges of his clothing and the two of them stared into the eyes of the other.

Then, with half closed eyes, she watched as his eyes seemed to roam over her entire body making her burn even more. What was he waiting for, she wondered.

She pulled him down on top of her. "Please, Peppy, please now," she begged.

He grinned and slowly began to kiss her beginning with her eyes, moving downward, brushing his lips over her taut nipples, her flat tummy, until he reached the utmost point of her desire, licking her into a frenzy.

Then just as abruptly, he raised himself, reached under the seat, opened a drawer, and hastily pulled out a condom.

"Oh," she moaned. "I forgot about that. How did you know that was there?"

"My good brother Amos is always prepared. No telling what some of his tourists want to do on the other side of the island."

"Good grief," she whispered as he began to make love to her, thrusting with the motion of the waves, lifting and thrusting, lifting and thrusting, until she cried out with orgasmic pleasure. Surely, she thought to herself, that no ocean ride in history could ever match this one. They rode the sea waves of fierce ardor and passion until both were satiated.

Amy couldn't believe that she had acquiesced to Peppy so easily but she didn't regret it for a moment. At that moment in time there was nothing that she wanted more than to spend her life with Peppy making love to her.

For his part, he looked down on her, winked, and stood up, a little wobbly at first.

"Look what you've done to me, woman," he said. "I can't even walk straight."

She laughed and said, "Maybe it's just the waves."

"Uh-huh," he said, slipping on his clothes.

In a lackadaisical mood she did the same, not in the least modest in front of him. Both clothed, they ambled back to the prow and Peppy sat down at the wheel. Amy was in a dreamy mood, at first not noticing the changing atmosphere.

He started the motor and they progressed slowly toward the eastern horizon where now she could see clouds building up again and she wondered when they would turn back. As the clouds grew larger, Peppy suddenly turned on the radio and called Amos, motioning for her to go back to one of the benches under the canopy.

"Hey, bro," he said into the transmitter, "got any weather reports for us?" There was silence for a few minutes, then, "Damn right. I'm heading back."

"Wha-what's wrong?" she asked.

"Amos says there may be possible squalls out here. He keeps in touch with weather stations on Palmaltas and Jamaica. He's turning back with his group of tourists."

"Do you mean Amos is at sea right now? I thought that was why we had the boat today because he didn't have many customers."

Peppy laughed. "Did you think we had the sea all to ourselves? Amos owns several boats and has employees who take them out. Today, he had only one boatload and took it out himself. So, yes, he's out but closer to shore than we are."

Without warning, a fierce wind blew up whipping the canopy cover. Peppy started to turn the boat as rapidly billowing clouds let loose a torrent of rain.

"Damn!" he shouted. "I can't believe I let us get caught like this."

"That's okay. I don't mind getting wet," she said, trying to reassure him, shouting back over the rain and now howling wind.

"Oh, you're going to get wet all right. That canopy is shelter form the sun, not from a squall. Hold on."

His words were barely audible above the noise of the wind, rain, and lapping waves. Amy clung to the back of the bench she was sitting on as the small craft bounced up and down over the rising sea.

As soon as Peppy had turned the boat toward Palmaltas, he started to turn it back again toward the east.

"What are you doing?" she cried.

"We're too far out. I'm heading for the island. It's closer. That's where we were going to picnic anyway."

She could see him mouth the words more than she could hear them. Worry and concern were etched all over his face and she knew she shouldn't try to communicate with him until they had landed. He had plenty to do, keeping the awkward craft upright and on course. She felt helpless but she knew Peppy was more than capable for both of them.

The sky was dark, visibility was limited, but she knew the boat was equipped with a compass and whatever else modern technology could provide and that Peppy knew where they were going.

Abruptly, almost like magic, they were out of the squall and a little green-topped island rose before them.

"We made it." Peppy laughed, pointing to the beach they were fast approaching.

She heard a scraping sound and Peppy jumped out of the boat and pulled it ashore, tying it down to some poles sticking out of the sand.

The rain had stopped but the sun was still hidden by gray clouds.

As Amy carefully stood up, Peppy held out his hand to help her step off the little craft.

"I'm afraid our picnic basket is soaked. It took quite a beating," she said.

"The inside is waterproof. The contents should be okay, not that I'm thinking of food right now."

Laughing, he picked her up, swinging her in his arms, then gently lowered her to the wet sand and not so gently rolled on top of her, kissing her passionately.

Thinking that a handsome, powerful man on a deserted island was ravenously kissing and hopefully about to make love to her again sent her into another rapturous mood. Life couldn't get any better than this.

"Ahem," came a deep, husky feminine voice. Peppy jumped up, leaving Amy lying in the sand, panting.

Looking up Amy saw him hugging a beautiful, raven-haired, dark-skinned woman. Janice!

Eighteen

Uncontrollable jealousy raged through Amy as Peppy abandoned her to lie flustered and confused in the sand while he embraced and kissed Janice. This was almost more than she could endure. And to think that he had planned to picnic here, not only with her but with Janice, also!

Perhaps observing her consternation, he reached down and pulled her up, laughing as he did so, an act that did nothing to improve Amy's mood.

"Amy, finally, you get to meet Janni, my sister-in-law."

Speechless, yes, and flabbergasted barely described her feelings, not to mention the flood of relief that swept over her."

"But-but," she sputtered, "I thought your name was Janice."

"Janis," she said, spelling her name out in that melodic, husky voice, and pronouncing it *zhah-nees*. "But everyone calls me Janni."

"But-but," Amy repeated, turning to Peppy, "do you have another brother besides Amos?"

"No," he said, puzzled, "why do you ask?"

"Because you just said Janice-Janni is your sister-in-law."

"She's Amos' wife. Wouldn't you know my brother would catch the most beautiful girl on Palmaltas? They run the boat concession together. He, usually there and she, usually here. Although sometimes they trade places or Janni comes over to help out like Monday night for our party."

Now that Amy knew what her name really was, she could differentiate Peppy's subtle accent of Janni, which he pronounced *zhah-nee*, from Johnny. This was Johnny, she suddenly realized, Jeremy's Johnny.

"Amos is married? I-I thought you were both bachelors." And Amy silently pleaded that Peppy was still one.

They both laughed and Janni said, "Just what did Amos do to make you think that?"

"Nothing, not a thing. I-I never saw him with anyone, so I assumed..." She let the words die away.

"Well, I'm glad to know he behaves himself," said Janni.

"Come on, Janni," said Peppy, "you know you've never worried about him. He adores you."

"But, Janni," Amy said, "why do you sub for him at the concession so he can give parties? Don't you want to go to them, too?"

Janni gave Peppy a funny look. "I hardly ever do that, just special occasions like Monday night."

"Why was Monday so special?" Amy asked innocently.

Peppy nudged Janni who said, "If it wasn't so special then maybe I was conned."

Peppy interrupted, saying, "Come on, you two. Let's get up to the cabin. I think another squall is coming up."

Janni raced across the wet sand to a narrow path, which led between rows of well-tended flowers to a tiny cabin perched on the side of a small hill. The island itself was minuscule consisting of several small hills covered more by tall bushes than short trees. At high tide Amy could imagine that a lot of it would be underwater, which would explain why the cabin was built so far above the beach.

Peppy grabbed her hand and pulled her along as he raced behind Janni to the shelter. They soon reached the cabin porch and all three turned to look out at the gray, roiling sea, which again was being pounded by torrents of rain. Shaking the water off them, they laughed and commented on how lucky they were to be ashore.

Janni opened the door and invited them to enter.

"Oh, this is so cozy," Amy said as she looked around the room. There was a kitchenette to her left with a large window, which opened onto the porch. For now it was closed with big wooden shutters. There were no panes of glass.

Noticing her stare, Janni said, "When Amos brings the tourists here I open the shutters and serve drinks and sandwiches to them. They either stay out on the porch or return to the beach for sunbathing and snorkeling. They never come inside. There are portable restrooms for them behind the cabin. We, however, have all the amenities, as you can see. The little kitchen, the sitting and sleeping areas are compact but comfortable for one or two people staying in a one-room cabin." Her voice, although deep and husky, had the lilting melodic quality associated with the English-speaking populace of the Caribbean.

"And," she continued, "our bathroom is just off the sleeping area and is more elaborate than what we offer the tourists. By the looks of you, Amy, I would say you need a shower and a change of clothes."

"Thank you, Janni, I am drenched but I don't have any other clothes."

"I have something I'm sure you can wear," she said as she led Amy to her closet next to the bathroom. She was much taller than Amy who couldn't imagine her clothes fitting her, but the ever-practical Janni quickly solved that dilemma. "Here," she said, "shorts and a white shirt should do nicely. You can roll up the sleeves and tie the shirt around your waist if it's too long."

A little while later, Amy emerged dry, comfortable and grateful for Janni's hospitality. The knowledge that she wasn't involved with Peppy produced a relief that she couldn't believe was possible. But that relief also made her realize how out of control her feelings for Peppy were. She wanted him, hungered for him, and she didn't regret their sexual interlude on the boat. But how did he really feel about her? Was she just a tourist interlude for him or did he feel the way she felt? She had to know.

Pushing aside her questions for the moment, she stepped out on the porch where she found Peppy and Janni ensconced in old-fashioned rocking chairs. The squall had deteriorated into a steady rain. Peppy was smoking a pipe and Amy accidentally giggled at the peaceful, rather rural scene before her. Janni wasn't his lover or his sister. She was his sister-in-law. She giggled again at that thought.

He turned and looked up at her.

"Here, come join us, Amy. We have another rocker. The tourists seem to like them. You can't imagine how many people just want to sit and rock, sip a drink, and stare out at the sea. What's so funny? Why are you grinning like that?"

"Oh nothing, exactly. You and Janni look at this moment so domesticated, yet I can't imagine anyone less domestic than you, Peppy, and Janni doesn't quite fit the role, either."

Janni didn't respond, but Peppy, in a slightly indignant yet teasing sort of way, said, "I'll have you know that the wife of my brother Amos is a most conscientious homemaker. Just because she's a ravishing beauty doesn't signify that she's incapable of keeping a mean house."

Janni kicked him playfully, but still said nothing.

"Oh, I'm sorry," apologized Amy. "It's just that, oh, I don't know. Just forget what I said."

"It's okay, Amy," said Janni eventually. "This is the way many islanders live, sitting on a porch in the evenings after the day's work is done, relaxing and gossiping with friends and family, grateful to live in such a beautiful part of the world. But I can see why you thought Pepe looked out of place. He looks out of place anywhere."

"Not so, not so," he said, laughing. "I look perfectly in place on a Palmaltas beach, don't I, Amy?"

"Yes, you certainly do. The professional beachcomber. But I never expected to see you sitting in a rocking chair, smoking a pipe. You never smoked at the beach or on the pier."

"No, this is the only place where I want to pick up my pipe. In fact, I keep it here."

Suddenly, Amy wondered if this was where Peppy went when he didn't show up on the beach. He seemed to be completely at home here. If so, then Amos must have complete confidence in him to let him stay with his beautiful wife. She wondered why Peppy didn't stay here all the time and let Janni spend more time with Amos. Peppy could easily pass out refreshments to the tourists. Surely that wouldn't put too much of a strain on his beachcombing skills. But didn't Peppy once tell her that he hardly ever came here? Just how much of the things that Peppy had told her could she believe?

"Janni," Amy asked, "do you spend a lot of nights alone on this island?"

"Well yes, during high tourist season, as we call it. After Amos and his clients leave, I clean and close up things. And once in a while I take my own boat back to Palmaltas. Sometimes if I get all my chores done early, I even go back with them."

"Is your boat a motor boat?"

"Yes, of course."

So, Amy thought, that explained why Amos' cabin was so neat and tidy. And Janni, who was most definitely not a man named Johnny, was the one who had made the pizzas that Peppy and she had shared on their ill-fated hiking trip. A strikingly beautiful woman who could cook, manage a household, and help run a tourist business, Janni was indeed quite a surprise.

But if Amos and Janni lived together in the cabin, except during the tourist season, where did Peppy live or at least spend his nights? The island seemed the most logical place yet Peppy had given the illusion that he lived with Amos in the cabin. Perhaps he did when Janni was here on the island.

"However," said Janni, interrupting Amy's thoughts, "Amos sometimes spends a night or two here, and I go back with the tourists. But for the most part at this time of year, I stay alone, which doesn't bother me although I do miss Amos. But evenings alone can provide peace and quiet for the soul."

"Do you and Amos own this island?" asked Amy innocently.

There was sudden silence as Peppy and Janni exchanged furtive glances.

Peppy responded for her. "Technically, the island belongs to Palmaltas but the Marisol owners have leased it."

"So, in a way Peter Harris is your landlord," Amy said.

This innocent remark produced an unlady-like cackle from Janni.

Peppy took his time in responding. "Let's just say that your Pe-tey Harris would like to expand development here but it's just not feasible due to the high tides."

Janni continued to laugh.

"Luckily," added Peppy, "a board of directors among others, keeps your Pe-tey Harris in check."

"He's not my Petey," Amy retorted, angry at his sarcastic use of Peter's nickname. She wondered if perhaps Peppy was just a little jealous of Peter. Someday they would learn of Peter's desire to help improve Palmaltas and would change their opinions of him.

Quickly changing the subject, she said, "I hate to bring this up, but I'm hungry. Were you able to salvage the picnic basket?"

"Yes, I went down for it while you were changing and luckily it was still intact."

"How did your clothes get dry so fast?" Amy asked.

"I changed into some of Amos' clothes while you were showering. His stuff is pretty much like mine. Janni came out on the porch, if you're wondering and worried about us being modest."

Amy knew he was teasing her again, but she blushed anyway.

"Now, about that food," he said. "Janni has plenty of supplies but I fixed quite a repast for us beforehand and I had planned for us to eat on a little beach on the other side of the island. But the squall took care of all that."

"So I'll set out what you fixed," said Janni.

"I'll help you," said Amy who jumped up and went in with her. Janni opened the shutters and peering out, they could see Peppy in his chair, not smoking, but talking on a portable radio.

"He's trying to call Amos to see if he got back all right."

"Trying?"

"Yes, Amos hasn't answered yet so we assume that he's back at the Marisol and has walked out of earshot of the radio."

"But wouldn't Amos be worried about us? And try to call us?"

"Yes, but the tourists are his first responsibility. Oh look. Peppy is talking to someone now. It must be Amos."

Confident that Amos was fine, she calmly opened the picnic basket and found sandwiches, fresh fruit, and a bottle of champagne.

"Do you think we should drink this now or later?"

Amy laughed. "Oh, let's drink it now. Peppy can pop the cork."

Janni asked Amy to bring three tumblers from a small cabinet. As they walked out on the porch, Peppy turned off the radio.

"Well, what did you learn?" Janni asked.

"They returned safely and he's relieved that we got here in time and that you're okay."

She smiled. "Anything else?"

"The squalls bypassed Palmaltas altogether and his tourist group is having a ball telling all and asunder about their narrow escape from a storm at sea."

"Tourists can be so silly," commented a serious-faced Janni. "Amos would never endanger them."

"Of course not, but everybody's safe so let's eat," he said. Janni handed him the champagne and, with a bit of effort, popped the cork.

They laughed, relaxed, and began to eat Peppy's lunch. Perhaps this wasn't the way that he had planned for them to eat it but Amy thought it was much more comfortable sitting on the porch of the cabin than down on a wet beach. It was a most enjoyable meal with the three of them sitting there in rockers on the little porch eating chicken and cheese sandwiches and drinking champagne, though it seemed out of place.

"You know, this is rather confusing, Peppy," said Amy after taking a sip of her champagne.

"What is?" he asked.

"You fixed a picnic lunch although you knew Janni would be here with plenty of food. As you said, you and I were going to eat on a little beach but Janni would have seen us and probably have come down to investigate, anyway. Why not just eat some of her sandwiches and drink her beer instead of going to all that trouble of making lunch yourself?"

"Yes, dear brother-in-law, I was wondering that myself," said Janni.

"I did it because I didn't want to interfere with you, Janni, when you handed out refreshments to Amos' tourists."

"My word, Peppy," exclaimed Amy. "You, Mr. Considerate Beach Guy, bringing champagne on a picnic. I'm impressed."

Janni laughed melodiously. "Yes, I'm impressed, also. My, my, quite a little picnic you had planned."

"Well, I did have an ulterior motive, also. I had planned to ask Amos to do your duties for a while so you could join us, Janni. I thought it was high time that you and Amy met and that we should celebrate in style."

"Well," said Janni, smiling, "we'll never know if you're just saying that to appease me. But yes, Amy, I'm glad that we've now met formally."

"Yes, so am I." Amy didn't add how relieved she was to know the true relationship between Janni and Peppy.

The small group fell into a companionable silence.

On a sunny day Amy could imagine how spectacular the view would be, as she glanced at the gray clouds and sea, the wet sand, and the exotic, but momentarily drooping flowers. Janni was indeed a woman of many talents to be able to care for all of this and cater to the whims of Amos' tourists, also, she thought.

After they had finished their little meal, Peppy said he was going to call Amos again for the latest weather reports to make sure that it was safe for them to return.

"Do you want to go back with us, Janni?" he asked. "I'd feel safer going back in your boat. That canopy on ours took quite a beating."

"Yes, I think we should all go back as soon as possible. I don't particularly want to be here if another squall should come during high tide."

"How about the glass bottom?" Amy asked. "Did the storm affect it?"

Peppy laughed. "No, it's plexiglass, very durable."

Peppy called Amos and listened with a glum face.

As he disconnected, he said, "Amos says for us to stay put. Weather reports call for more squalls in this area throughout the afternoon and night. He says there's no reason to rush back and chance running into another one. If it was just me by myself, I'd go back but not with two lovely women dependent on me."

"I've never been dependent on you, Pepe," said Janni, playfully. "But we'll do what Amos says. You're not in any hurry to get back, are you, Amy?"

"No, not at all. But-but won't we be in danger if a squall hits us during high tide?" She wondered when high tide was but felt silly asking about it.

"Not if we keep a close watch out and head for higher ground if the water rises too high," she said.

Amy shuddered but made no reply. She didn't want them to think she was scared or worried. After all, Janni had spent many nights alone on this little island.

Amy helped Janni put things away in the kitchen, not that there was much to do. She rinsed out her clothes and hung them on the porch although with the high humidity, Amy knew they had little chance of drying.

The temperature had fallen somewhat due to the rain but she felt hot and sticky nonetheless. Maybe it was the anticipation that more excitement was yet to come if they indeed did have to abandon the cabin in the middle of the night for higher ground.

"Won't the boats be washed away if the island floods?" she asked Janni.

"They're securely moored. We've never lost a boat yet. Luckily no one has ever been here during hurricanes because we always had sufficient warning about them. The squalls aren't quite so dangerous. But if we should lose the boats, Amos will come to our rescue. No one is ever really stranded here."

The rain let up during the afternoon but they could see the billowing, lead-colored clouds and churning sea to the west and knew they didn't want to chance running through such a mess.

Peppy led Amy on a soggy walking tour over the little island on paths that tourists had trodden well. Had the weather been different, she would have been enthralled by the excursion but the sloshing trek to the highest hill or mound was pure misery. The view would have been entrancing on a sunny, clear day, but now everything was coated in a dull, wet gray.

The dreariness didn't stop Peppy from hugging and caressing her as they stood atop that windy hill with occasional gusts of moisture sputtering on their faces. Amy knew she shouldn't have cared about the weather once she was in his arms, but something about the atmosphere filled her with a premonition that not all was well.

"What's the matter?" he asked as he affectionately brushed wet strands of hair out of her face.

"I don't know, Peppy, I feel like something's going to happen."

"Hey, honey, don't worry. We're safe enough. The tide has never reached the cabin yet." Then he pulled her into the safe haven of his arms and kissed her lovingly.

But her premonition wouldn't go away.

"Hey, lover people," yelled Janni from below on the porch of the cabin. "Soup's on. Come get it while it's hot."

"What is it about you women?" joked Peppy. "Always wanting food at the most inopportune times."

Amy laughed but was happy to retreat to the security of the cabin although surely being on the hilltop with Peppy was just as safe. Perhaps the grayness and the wetness were causing the atmosphere to become claustrophobic and stifling.

After an evening meal of a delicious seafood soup consisting of shrimp, crabmeat, and vegetables served with hot crusty bread, Peppy returned to the porch with the radio while the two women cleaned up. When everything was put away, Janni retired to the bathroom and Amy decided to join Peppy.

As she approached the door, she could overhear his part of the conversation. What she heard caused her to stop short, hitting her like a bolt of lightning.

Nineteen

"What do you mean? He changed the delivery? So, that's how he was doing it. Well damn Pe-tey! At least we've got the bastard where we want him." Peppy paused apparently listening to Amos on the other end. "He hasn't figured out our relationship, has he?" Another pause. "Well, that's something." Pause. "What? You're sure the stuff is going to the Bay View? So, we were right all along." He paused for a long time. At last he said with disgust, "No, you're not going to kill him because I want that pleasure."

Amy stepped back from the door in a daze. Was this what her premonition had been about? And had her previous paranoid mental ramblings been correct? That Peppy and even the innocent-appearing Amos were really drug traffickers? And if that were not bad enough, they were actually plotting to kill Peter Harris! What else could Peppy have meant by "delivery" and "stuff" if not drugs?

Peter had somehow found out and changed the destination of the shipment, putting himself in grave danger. Did he change the destination so that he could intercept it without repercussions from the authorities or other drug dealers? If only there was some way in which she could warn him. But even if she did, somehow, get hold of

Peppy's radio, would she know how to use it? She had never seen a radio like this one. She had no idea which button to push, or whom to call. Was there a way to call information, she wondered? Peter was staying at the Marisol not the Harris mansion and considering what she had just heard, he might even be at the Bay View Hotel in Bay City. If she did succeed in locating him, would he believe her?

Then the gravity of the situation really hit her. Her friends, her dear friends Peppy and Amos, who seemed so kind, so concerned, so jovial, might possibly be devious, cutthroat dealers in illicit drugs. What about their other friends? The party Monday night, was that the special occasion that made Janni take over for Amos? And the reason that Peppy nudged her not to talk about it? Had drug dealing gone on before Amy's eyes and she had not seen it? Daniel, Ossie, Bert, Eddie? Were they involved? She sank onto the small sofa and buried her face in her hands. And, she had let Peppy make love to her! Peppy, a possible murderer! What was she going to do? How could she extricate herself from this situation? For one thing, she had to continue to play the cool, little innocent schoolteacher. Unexpectedly, Janni gave her a way out.

"Amy," she said as she left the bathroom. "What's wrong? Are you sick?"

Amy looked up, feigning a pained expression, which wasn't hard to do under the circumstances. "Yes, yes, I-I'm so sorry but I think I am."

"Oh no, I hope it wasn't my cooking."

"I-I don't know. The squall. The boat ride. I don't know. I feel queasy."

"Then you must go to bed. Maybe all you need is a good rest."

She had had plenty of rest the past two days but she was only too glad to escape to a welcoming bed and pretend to sleep. Real sleep was out of the question with two possible criminals around. To think of Peppy that way was breaking her heart and terrifying her at the same time. No matter how badly her feelings had run amok, she had to maintain a clear head and a cool demeanor.

"But there's only one bed. What about you and Peppy?"

"We have spare sleeping bags and can sleep in them. Come on, let's get you to bed."

"I-I think I can manage, thank you." Stumbling into the bathroom, Amy almost threw up from fear and taut nerves. The noises she made, authentic enough, must have been very convincing as Janni was very solicitous when she came out. Janni turned down the bed covers and Amy crawled into the bed without removing the skimpy clothes that Janni had lent her.

Janni turned down the light and joined Peppy on the porch. Amy could hear the murmuring of their voices and supposed they were discussing not only her illness but Peppy's call to Amos as well. Although she wished that she could eavesdrop on them, she didn't dare leave her bed, which was a good thing because Peppy soon came in and bent over her. In fear, she gazed up at him, trembling.

"Amy, honey, what's wrong?"

He sounded so caring, but was he really, she wondered?

"I-I don't feel so well," she said in a voice so weak that she must have sounded like a small girl.

"Is it your stomach? Something you ate?"

"Yes, it-it's my stomach but I don't know why."

He sat on the bed, pulled back the covers, and gently lifted her into his arms. She was still trembling, even more so, but oh it felt so good to be in his arms. She shook herself. No matter how her body gave in to Peppy, her mind had to remain focused.

"My goodness, you're shivering. I hope you don't have a fever." He hugged her carefully and softly kissed her then released her into the security of her covers. "Get a good night's sleep, honey, and let me know if you need anything. Janni keeps a pretty good medicine cabinet for the tourists, you know. Do you want me to get you something or at least see what she has?"

"No, no," Amy gasped. The last thing she wanted was to take one of Janni's pills or anything from her medicine cabinet.

"All right then. Try to get some sleep," he said tenderly as he bent down to kiss her forehead.

He returned to the porch, presumably, Amy thought, to resume his conversation with Janni. Sleep? That was the last thing Amy was going to do.

~ * ~

He and Janni sat quietly in their respective rockers on the porch. He broke the silence and said, "I wonder what's wrong with Amy."

"I don't know. She seemed just fine and then without warning she said she was sick. You and I aren't sick and we all ate the same thing."

"I think it's about time I ended this part of my plan."

"Well, I should say so. It's gone on far too long."

"But I had to be sure."

"And are you now?"

"Oh yes, after this afternoon on the boat, I'm sure."

"That sounds mysterious."

He laughed.

~ * ~

She awoke with a start. How could she have fallen asleep, she wondered. Glancing around the darkened room, she spied both Peppy and Janni asleep in their respective sleeping bags on a little rug in front of the sofa. As her eyes became adjusted to the dark, she spotted the radio on a little table by the door. Was it possible? Could she actually do it?

Cautiously, she crept out of her bed and tiptoed past the lightly snoring twosome. As she reached the door, she grabbed the radio, and sneaked outside, closing the door without a creak.

Luckily, the rain had stopped and only a light wind was blowing as she walked off the porch and away from the house up the path toward the hilltop. She didn't want to go too far but far enough not to be overheard.

Looking at the radio, not having a clue what buttons to punch, she wondered if she needed some kind of code for Palmaltas. Was she already within the area? Desperate, she began to punch.

"What the hell are you doing?"

Nearly jumping out of her skin, Amy turned to see a stern Peppy standing right behind her. The night was dark but she could see his face well enough.

"I-I couldn't sleep. I was curious. I've never used a portable radio and just wanted to see how it worked. I-I wasn't going to call anyone, honest."

"Amy, Amy, you're delirious." He rubbed her forehead. "You're perspiring. That fever is doing things to your mind. Come on, honey, let's go back to bed."

He took the radio away from her, picked her up, and carried her back to the cabin where he tucked her into bed. He pulled up a chair and sat down, Amy assumed, to watch over her.

Were they playing games with each other, she wondered? She, trying to be sick and helpless? Peppy, oh so caring and oh so solicitous? Were they fooling each other?

He grasped her hand and stroked it. Amy moaned, not acting this time, as his touch and his strength sent a burning electric current cruising through her body. What was she going to do? How could she let a-a criminal affect her this way?

With wind and rain pounding the little cabin again and Peppy sitting next to her, she knew that she was headed for a night without sleep. And the tide? Another worry. Inexplicably she began to feel drowsy.

~ * ~

He sat there looking at her. What on earth had happened to her to cause her to act this way? She didn't feel feverish now, thank goodness. Her behavior worried him. Why was she acting as if she were in some kind of delirium? Oh, Amy, Amy, he moaned to himself. Then he thought of all the things he had to do tomorrow. Poor Amos. Well, he would take care of those problems but for now he had Amy to worry about. It all had to end and soon.

~ * ~

The squawking of the radio wakened all three of them. Despite her worry, fear, and suspicions, Amy had slept fairly well. Perhaps, she thought, the easiest way to fall asleep was to try not to sleep.

She hunkered down in bed to listen as Peppy spoke into the radio and discussed, she assumed with Amos, their return trip. He ended with a stern threat, once again sending fear throughout her soul.

"Don't worry, bro. I'll take care of Pe-tey at the right time. Leave him to me. I'll see you later."

He turned to Janni, replacing his austere demeanor with a jovial one as if threatening the life of another human being was a trivial matter.

"So, what's the plan?" asked Janni.

Which plan was she referring to, Amy wondered. Their return or doing away with Peter? His answer was a relief, albeit a temporary one.

"The squalls have moved away and are dispersing. The prediction for today is sunny and calm winds. Amos wants you to stay put. His tourists from yesterday are already clamoring to come out here."

"How about you and Amy?" she asked. "Do you still want my boat?"

"I don't think so. I'm going to check on ours now while you rustle up some breakfast. Thank goodness the tide wasn't much higher than normal last night. In fact, I think we were pretty lucky, just a few gusts of wind and rain hit us."

Amy's mind was churning. She would go back alone with Peppy. But what difference would that make? Janni was obviously in on the drug deals and the plot to do away with Peter. But why had Peppy threatened to take care of Peter when he knew she must be listening? He couldn't have expected her to sleep through the squawking of the radio. Of course, he didn't think she would understand what he was talking about. He didn't know that she had overheard him yesterday being more explicit. Whether Amy returned with both of them or just Peppy, would she be in any danger? Surely not, if she continued to act like the naïve little tourist. But if Peppy cut off the motor as he did yesterday and they drifted about, would she be able to resist his advances, if he made any? Remembering how easily she had succumbed to his advances, even encouraging them, made her feel weak. She would have to continue her act and insist on getting back as soon as possible. Then when she landed on the Marisol beach she would scamper away, out of harm's reach and try to find a way to notify Peter of the danger he was in.

As if her thoughts had reminded him of her presence, he turned and walked over to the bed.

"How are you feeling this morning, Amy?"

"Not-not much better," she lied.

He sat down beside her and took one of her hands and held it. "Would you prefer that we wait a while before leaving? I really would like to set off as soon as possible. Or do you want to stay with Janni until Amos gets here?"

If Peter had not been in danger, Amy would have much preferred to wait for Amos and the safety of the tourists but she had to go back with Peppy, pretended ailment or not.

"No, I want to leave as soon as possible, also." She sat up and added, "I think maybe now that I'm sitting that I feel better."

"I think I need to get you to a doctor," he said. "You just haven't been yourself since after dinner last night."

"Don't be silly. I'll be all right. Go check on the boat while I get dressed."

He bent over and pecked her on the cheek then walked out. Her clothes were still damp but she put them on anyway. They would dry soon enough in the bright sunshine.

Janni fixed tasty omelets and Amy momentarily gave up pretending she was sick in order to eat one. She knew she was going to need strength from all the nourishment she could get.

"Hey," said Peppy on returning, "you're definitely on the mend."

"How's the boat?" she asked, steering the conversation away from herself.

"It's in pretty good shape. The canopy is a mess and Amos will have to put up a new one. You may get sunburned on the way back."

"Oh, I'll be okay."

"I've got some sunscreen that I keep on hand for the tourists," said Janni. "You can borrow some but you look tan enough. I don't think you'll burn but since you're not feeling well, the hot sun beating down on you might make you worse."

"Thanks, Janni, I will put some on before we leave, just to be safe.

And, she thought, such concern from two people involved in planning a murder!

They set off shortly after breakfast. Amy hoped that Peppy would make a beeline for the Marisol and not dawdle around to show her the underwater sights or attempt to make love to her. For the most part he did seem to be heading back at a rapid pace, until at one point he slowed down and asked her to come sit with him as he steered. Not wanting to make him suspicious, she did so, wondering how she could extricate herself if he tried to repeat yesterday's zealous exercise.

He put his arm around her and they sat back on the cushions and watched the sea glide by. Had she not heard his threatening phone call, she would have been deliriously happy awaiting another round of love-making but sadly she was nervous, scared, and jumpy. Unfortunately, he noticed her tenseness.

"What's the matter, Amy? Are you getting queasy again?"

Grateful for the suggestion, she answered in the affirmative.

"Then go lie on one of the benches. Here, put one of Amos' hats over your face." He reached under his cushion and pulled out a cap.

Amy lay down with the cap over her face. She could feel the sun beating down on her, the reverberation of the motor, and could smell the salty sea. She dozed off only to be wakened by Peppy yelling at Amos as he and his group passed them. She contemplated how innocent, how harmless those two brothers seemed. How could Donna have been so wrong about Amos? Why hadn't David known about Amos' involvement with drugs? Fleeting thoughts as she dozed off again.

The boat had stopped, so had the motor. Amy jumped up expecting to be on the Marisol beach.

They were still at sea.

"Wha-what's happened?"

"Don't you remember? Yesterday I promised you that on our return trip I would circle Palmaltas so you could see the island from all angles and observe the sea life that abounds around here. I was just waiting for you to wake up, hoping that you would feel better."

"Oh no, Peppy, please. Just take me on into shore. I really want to go home."

"You still feel that bad?" He got up and came over to her, concerned and solicitous, once again.

If this was an act, she thought, then it was a very good one. Now knowing that he wasn't involved romantically with Janice-Janni, she wondered how he really felt about her, especially considering the time that they had spent together this summer and yesterday's passionate interlude. If she hadn't known of his intentions toward Peter, she would be anticipating more of those interludes. Peppy's act was all too convincing but now she had to put a lot of distance between them, leaving her with a sadness that she found almost too much to bear.

Unfortunately, Peppy wasn't distancing himself from her. He embraced her and began to kiss her. Terrified, not only for her own sexual feelings that he aroused, but also from the illogical fear that he might just push her overboard if she resisted, she gently pushed him away. She knew she had to proceed very carefully.

"Please, Peppy, I-I'm not well. Do you know how embarrassed I would be if I-I-uh-I threw up on you?"

He looked at her, she thought, with an unbearably hurt expression.

"Are you sure, Amy? This is a very strange illness of yours. You ate a hearty breakfast and I thought you were better."

He stared at her for a few minutes longer, then got up and started the motor.

Her thoughts were rampant and turbulent. Desperately, she wanted to get back to Palmaltas to warn Peter and to get away from Peppy. But would Peter believe her? Would she be able to find him in time? If only Donna would return. She'd know what to do. Lily? Would Lily believe her? Would she help her find Peter? But how was she going to put off Peppy? Would he continue to be concerned about her and come looking for her?

Suddenly, she knew what she had to do. When they landed she was going to tell Peppy the truth, or part of it anyway.

Palmaltas was getting closer and closer. Peppy swung out and she thought for a moment that he was heading away from the Marisol, then abruptly he swung back toward the beach. He had to follow the currents, she supposed, or maybe there were hidden rocks. Knowing nothing about the ways of the sea, she could only guess.

They put-putted close to shore then, as he killed the motor, he jumped out and pulled the craft to its mooring beside Amos' concession.

As he helped her out, he said, "I'll walk you to the condo."

"No, Peppy, please." Then gathering her strength, she said, "I-I heard you talking last night on the radio to Amos."

"So?"

"So-uh-so, I heard you tell him that you would take care of Peter Harris."

The beginning of a wry grin appeared on his face, sending shock waves riveting down her spine.

"Oh please, Peppy," she gushed, afraid that she wouldn't have the courage to make her plea. "Please don't do it."

"Do what? What do you think we were talking about?"

"Peppy, I know! I know what you've been doing. The drugs and all, but please, please don't kill Peter Harris!"

His mouth fell open in astonishment, the grin disappearing. She turned and ran as fast as she could.

He stood there, furious, watching her run away from him. This had to end. Enough was enough. He stormed up the beach, ready to smash anyone who got in his way.

Twenty

Although the condo was only a short distance from the Marisol beach, Amy felt that she had been running forever when, at last, she stumbled into the elevator. Reaching the apartment, she unlocked the door and jumped inside quickly locking it again. She stood gasping for air, not able to move or think. Without warning, her momentary paralysis was replaced by panic. What should she do now? Call Lily? No matter whether Lily believed her or not, she had to try.

There was no answer as she let the phone ring and ring. Next she called the Marisol. The switchboard operator put her through.

"The office of Peter Harris," announced his secretary.

"Please, please, I have to talk to Mr. Harris. It-it's an emergency."

"Who is calling, please?" She sounded so calm, so efficient.

"Amy Andrews."

"Just a moment. He just walked in the office."

The moments passed, her heart beating rapidly, praying that Peter-Petey would answer.

"Hello," came a noncommittal voice.

Had he forgotten her already, she wondered?

"Peter, this is Amy," she babbled. "Do you remember me? Thursday night? Lily's dinner party? The coffee shop with Marla?"

"Umm, how are you, Amy?"

"Please, Peter-uh-Petey, I've just learned something you must take seriously. It's life and death."

"How melodramatic. Please tell me."

"There's a plot to kill you."

Silence, then, "How do you know this and who are you talking about?"

"I-I overheard a certain beachcomber. I don't think you know him but he's the brother of one of your employees. Anyway, I heard him tell his brother that he was going to kill you because of what you were going to do about a shipment of what I think is drugs."

More silence. "And what are the names of these brothers?"

"Peppy-uh-Joseph, actually, and Amos Soto. Amos runs a boating concession on your beach."

"Well, well, well. Thank you, Amy. Don't upset yourself anymore with this. I'll take care of the problem. Now, I have a question for you."

"Yes, anything."

"We're having a dance here tomorrow night. Would you please accompany me?"

Flabbergasted and infuriated that a man facing possible death would even consider a frivolous social event, Amy said, "Absolutely not! Here I am trying to save your life and you, an engaged man, want to use me to two-time your fiancée. I respect you, Peter, uh, Petey, for wanting to help the people of your island but your attitude towards women is despicable."

"Then you are turning down my invitation?"

"Good grief, yes, I'm turning it down. No matter what my friend Donna thinks of you, I think you are abominable. Now please focus on the danger you are in."

"Indeed I will. Thank you for your trouble and concern. Perhaps we will run into each other sometime and you will tell me how you learned of this-this plot." He hung up.

Amy was dumbfounded. She had tried to save the life of a man who seemed to be more interested in a social engagement than a dangerous situation. The more she thought about their conversation, the more puzzled she became. He had spoken in a calm, business-like voice with no surprise, no emotion, nothing like the friendly Petey of Thursday night or Sunday morning. Was it because he already knew about the plot or because he thought she was crazy? But if he thought her to be crazy, then why did he invite her to a dance? What about Marla? Was that relationship over? Even if it was, it was no concern of hers. She knew now above all that she had no interest in Peter Harris. She had tried to like him and had almost convinced herself that she did because of his desire to improve his people. But his behavior had convinced her that he was not what she wanted in a man.

Convincing herself that she had done all that she could to save Peter's life, she stayed in the condo the rest of the day, praying and hoping not only for Peter's safety but that Peppy wouldn't attempt to follow through on his plan. Surely Peter could look out for himself now that he'd been warned and Peppy would think twice before trying to kill him knowing that she would possibly accuse him.

But the worst part of all of this was how she felt about Peppy. She couldn't turn off those feelings.

"No, no, no, Salty! I can't feel this way about Peppy, not if he's going to try and kill someone. Not if he's involved with the drug trade on Palmaltas. But how could my Peppy be so mercenary? My lazy, lackadaisical, sensual Peppy? How did I let him take advantage of me like that? Okay, Salty, I know what you're thinking. I was ripe for the plucking. And I suppose that you are amazed that he waited so long to do it. But doesn't that mean that he cares for me?"

Salty rubbed his head against her leg and sauntered into the kitchen.

The next morning, after a restless and turbulent night, Amy turned on both the TV and radio, appliances that she had ignored all summer, in hopes that no Palmaltas murder was being reported. There was nothing of the sort, just local talk shows and weather, glib, happy, chatty stuff. Much relieved, she informed Salty that she was going to have brunch at the Marisol.

"I don't want to ever see Peter Harris again but I do want to make sure he's still alive. I'll go over to the coffee shop and ask the waiter if Mr. Harris is working today."

Determined to ascertain that he was indeed still alive and that Peppy wasn't yet a murderer, she set forth for the Marisol, hoping that she wouldn't run into Peter. But whether she did or not, it didn't matter, she realized. She had nothing to fear from him.

As soon as she was seated, she heard a ruckus coming form the coffee shop entrance. At least she wouldn't have to ask the waiter about Mr. Harris. She saw Peter and Amos having a loud argument.

My goodness, she thought, had her information caused Peter to seek out Amos? But Amos seemed to be the angrier and more threatening of the two men. Poor Peter just cowered and stepped back from the onslaught of words and menacing looks. Never had Amy seen the amiable Amos appear so ferocious.

At that moment, she knew she had had enough. She had run away from Peppy yesterday but today she was determined to have a confrontation. He wouldn't hurt her in front of the Marisol beach crowd. In fact, she doubted if Peppy could ever physically hurt her. He had risked a lot to rescue her from the mudslide and they had bonded during their beach time together, not to mention making love on the boat. She couldn't believe that he would lift a finger against her even if she had betrayed him to Peter Harris. Peppy might be a criminal but he was a man with feelings. He had cared for Jeremy and he had cared for her. She had to believe that much.

As Peter and Amos took their fight into one of the hotel offices, Amy slipped out of the coffee shop, forgetting about breakfast. Her next problem was how to find Peppy. If he wasn't on the beach or the pier, then she was going to take the bus down to Amos and Janni's cabin in hope of finding him there. And if he wasn't? She wouldn't let her mind go any further.

She stormed out onto the beach full of determination and spotted him immediately standing on the pier without his fishing gear, just staring out to sea.

He turned and saw her approach. "Well," he said, "aren't you afraid that I, a would-be murderer, will throw you to the sharks?"

Trying hard to ignore his sarcasm, she pleaded, "Peppy, please listen to reason. I know deep down you're a good man. Please don't make your life worse than it is. Drug trafficking is one thing, but murder?"

"And just where did you come up with drug trafficking?"

His eyes were twinkling and she began to have doubts.

"I-I heard you talking to Amos about Peter stopping a shipment of drugs."

"I don't remember saying drugs."

"Well, I-I assumed."

"That's it, Amy. You assumed. Oh yes, we were talking about drugs but not the way you assumed. It's your Pe-tey who is bringing in illegal drugs with the medical supplies for the tourists and using the Bay View Hotel as the front for his operation. Saying I would kill him was just a figure of speech."

"What? Peter who is a man fighting for his country is also a drug dealer? You're joking!"

"No, Miss Amy Ann, I am not. You silly, silly girl. So, you weren't sick on the island. You were terrified. Of me. Don't you know I wouldn't hurt you for all the drugs or money or anything in this world?"

He pulled her into his arms and began to kiss her, embracing her so tightly that she couldn't breathe. A sudden happiness rushed through her along with the electricity, the excitement that his touch always brought. She believed him. Oh yes, she believed him with all of her heart.

She pushed herself back. "Oh, what have I done? Amos! Poor Amos!"

"What do you mean?"

"I told Peter that you and Amos were involved with drugs and that you were going to kill him. He and Amos are fighting now."

"Is that so? Well, Amos can take care of himself."

"But, but Peppy, it's not fair. Peter must have confronted Amos and he became fighting mad. Oh, this is all my fault."

Much to her consternation, Peppy burst out laughing. "Oh, Amy, don't worry. Amos will-uh-straighten it out."

"But I said terrible things. What if Peter fires Amos?"

"And I said, don't worry."

He embraced her again, holding her close and firm. If only the world could stop and she could stay in his arms forever, because now she knew for certain what she had refused to admit to herself during the past forty-eight hours. She loved Peppy, whether he was a notorious drug dealer, murderer, or beach bum.

She pushed herself back again.

"Now what?" he asked.

"Oh, Peppy, I love you but…" Her words died away.

"But?"

"But I don't understand what's going on. Peter Harris wants to save his island yet you claim that he is a drug dealer in one of his own hotels. How do you know this?"

"Let's just say that Amos told me and Amos doesn't lie. He has access to what's going on around here. Besides, Ossie and I have seen your Pe-tey at the Bay View involved in conduct not becoming a patriot."

"But Donna swore that he had changed."

He smiled. "Don't worry about Donna. I'm sure she'll understand when she learns the whole truth and then she'll explain it to you."

"Why can't you just explain it to me?"

"Because I don't want to talk about it anymore. There is something else more important for us to do."

"Oh, what?"

"Would you go out with me tonight? A real, formal date?"

Amy burst out laughing.

"And why is that so funny? You stood me up once before, remember?"

"No, no that's not why I'm laughing. Yesterday when I tried to warn Mr. Harris of his impending danger, instead of taking me seriously, he invited me to a dance for tonight."

"And you accepted?"

"Absolutely not! I was furious. He didn't take me seriously regarding the threat on his life and even worse he was two-timing his fiancée. I can't figure out why Donna likes him so much and why she thinks we're suited for each other."

"Why is that funny enough to make you laugh at my invitation?"

"Oh, I don't know. Just the thought of both of you asking me out for the same night, I guess, and neither one of you taking me seriously."

"I'm taking you seriously, Amy. Believe me. So, what is your answer?"

She smiled. "Of course, Peppy, I would love to go out with you."

"Great! Will you meet me in the cocktail lounge of the Marisol at eight o'clock?"

"Well yes, but why can't you pick me up at the apartment?"

He grinned, a very mischievous grin. "Humor me, Amy, please."

With reluctance and disappointment, she agreed.

He gave her a hug, turned, and walked away.

Stunned, Amy stood by the edge of the pier, shaking. Despite all the embraces, kisses, and the passionate lovemaking on the boat, Peppy had never told her his true feelings. He had never said that he loved her. She walked back to the apartment where once again she began a one-sided conversation with Salty.

"What an idiot I am. Why did I have to tell Peppy that I loved him? His only reciprocation was to ask me for a date and then inform me that he will meet me somewhere instead of coming by for me. I don't know what's going to happen with this friendship or whatever it is, Salty, but one of these days I'm going to let Mr. Peppy Soto have it full blast."

~ * ~

Walking away from Amy and not crushing her in his arms and kissing her over and over had been hard to do but he knew that he had done the right thing. His plans for her would soon be fulfilled. He could wait a short while longer. He smiled. At least now he was sure of her. In the meantime he had work to do. A lot of work.

~ * ~

Amy couldn't put thoughts about Peppy and Peter out of her mind. Doubts came crowding into her mind. Why had Peppy told Amos that he would take care of Peter, figure of speech or not? Did Peppy and Peter even know each other? Somehow she found that unlikely although Peppy had said that he and Ossie had seen Peter at the Bay

View. When and why did that happen? Why should Peppy care so much about Peter's alleged drug dealing? Was Peppy dependent on Amos and Janni's business? Was Peppy just leading her in circles, trying to make her think he and Amos were impeccable and that Peter was the guilty one? Or, and suddenly another thought occurred to her, something that she wished could be true, that Peppy could really be an undercover agent. But undercover for what or for whom? Oh, she wished, if only whatever Peppy was doing was legitimate.

She spent the rest of the day moping around the condo, wailing her misgivings to an uninterested Salty. Peter Harris had cowered before Amos' verbal onslaught. Surely that would result in Amos' dismissal. Or did Amos, along with Peppy, have some kind of underworld ties that could threaten Peter or were both brothers undercover drug agents who suspected poor Peter of all people? The Peter Harris who had been presented to her, the Peter Harris who was Donna's friend, the Peter Harris who was an undercover revolutionary, couldn't possibly be that merciless. What was the truth?

Peppy's insistence that they meet at the cocktail lounge left her bitterly disappointed. Of course, she had walked over to the Marisol almost daily, usually from the back entrance of the condo via the beach, and a few times she had left from the front entrance and had traversed the short distance of the grounds in front of both establishments. But for a formal date, especially one with Peppy, she felt that he should escort her. Would Peter have treated Marla the same way?

Then she remembered the night of Peter's return party. Marla had made an entrance first. Marla and Peter represented two monumental egos. But Amy was the antithesis of Marla as was Peppy of Peter. The last thing she wanted to do was make an entrance, especially in a cocktail lounge.

That evening she chose a dark violet, clinging, silk dress and brown sandals with two-inch heels. She brushed her dark hair forward over her head, then flipped it backward to give it more fullness. Addressing herself in the mirror, she said out loud, "For a Nebraska schoolteacher, I look damn sexy. Peppy had better appreciate me."

Then a sharp pain stabbed her heart as she wondered if he was as innocent as he claimed. Her mind reeled with the irrational possibilities that had plagued her all day.

"Meow."

"Oh, Salty," she cried, bending down to pet him, "you're the only male around here who understands. But I'll tell you one thing, I'll never again tell a man I love him until he tells me first. With all the doubts and suspicions that I have about Peppy, the worst is wondering if I have humiliated myself to a man who was just conning me all along."

Tears began to form and she hurriedly brushed them away lest they ruin her make-up. Keeping her head held high, she prepared to walk alone over to the Marisol.

As she left the condo, Ossie complimented her. "You look lovely tonight, Miss Amy."

She thanked him as more sharp pains pierced her. Ossie was a friend of Amos and Peppy. He had been at the "special occasion" party that Janni had sacrificed for so that Amos could attend. And what was that "special occasion"? Would she ever learn the truth?

The cocktail lounge was dark and she hesitated in the doorway. She had never entered one without a companion. A waiter approached and asked if she'd like to sit at the bar or at a table. Glancing around, she decided that the barstools looked uncomfortable and even unladylike, not that she particularly thought of herself that way. On the other hand, deep cushiony chairs that surrounded low, round wooden tables looked discreet and comfortable. She chose one in a corner, which gave an overall view of the lounge.

After ordering a daiquiri, she surveyed the few other occupants. To her astonishment, she recognized a tall, dark handsome man attired in a tuxedo chatting with the bartender.

Her mouth threw open in astonishment. He was Amos! Amos in a tuxedo!

At that moment he turned and Amy held her breath, hoping he wouldn't spot her, but he did, grinning and waving, before he turned back to resume his conversation. She exhaled, relieved that he wasn't going to reproach her for accusing him of a terrible crime to his boss.

But what was he doing here dressed like that? Peppy had been right about one thing. Amos could take care of himself. If he had been fired, he wouldn't be standing here now, dressed like that, having a friendly discourse with a Marisol bartender.

The waiter brought her drink, refusing payment, stating her bill had been paid. Since Amos was the only person in the lounge who knew her, she assumed he was her benefactor. The other male patrons were accompanied by wives or girlfriends. Had Peppy not told Amos that she was the accuser? Was he being his usual friendly self through ignorance? But why the tuxedo? Why wasn't he out on the beach, entertaining his tourists?

To her immense relief, he soon left, waving and grinning again, without approaching her. Had he not been dressed so formally or been in a fight instigated by her with Peter, she would have considered his behavior perfectly normal.

With Amos' departure Amy felt terribly alone, although unreasonably so. After all, she had wanted him to leave. Where was Peppy? What if he stood her up tonight just the way she had stood him up on the pier?

She decided not to think about what Peppy might or might not do and turned her thoughts to Peter Harris. She hoped that Peter did desire to help his people and that Peppy had been wrong about the drug dealing. Nor did she understand his treatment of women. He had been a flirtatious rogue at Lily's party and she had enjoyed the attention, but flirting with her under Marla's nose at the coffee shop and inviting her to a dance made her quite suspicious of his motives. Then there was his behavior in front of Amos this morning that did nothing to impress her. He was the boss and should have been more forceful yet Amos clearly had emerged the winner in that boisterous tête-à-tête. But Donna and David admired Peter. What did they know that she hadn't been able to discern the few times that she had seen him? Of course, she was jumping to conclusions. None of it was her business anyway.

As she glanced down at her empty glass she realized, now that Amos had left, she would have to pay for her next drink. Not that she couldn't afford it, she just felt foolish and awkward paying for drinks she didn't want while waiting for a date that she wasn't so sure would appear.

"May I order you another drink?" asked a familiar voice.

She looked up and stared into the smiling face of Peppy! A Peppy who was clean-shaven and also dressed in a tuxedo!

"Peppy!" she gasped. "You look wonderful!"

"Why thank you, milady," he said as he slipped into the chair next to hers.

"I-I'm so glad you came."

"Why, did you doubt me? Believe me, I wouldn't have missed this date for the world."

"Oh, Peppy," she moaned. "Do-do you think Peter Harris knows who you are, that is, if he should walk in here and see you? Especially since I told him that you were going to kill him?"

"I don't give a damn about your Pe-tey. And why should you be concerned about him at all? I'm the one you love."

Oh, she cried silently to herself, why had she ever told him that? Why had Peppy insisted that she meet him here? Did he expect Peter to show up? Was he going to take care of Peter tonight, in front of her?

"Peppy," she said sternly, "why did you tell me to come here tonight?"

Nonchalantly, Peppy glanced around the lounge, so handsome and immaculately dressed. Polished. That was the word, she thought. Her scruffy beachcomber had been transformed into a polished sophisticate!

"All in due time, my dear, all in due time. Don't you like it here?"

"It's fine. But what do you have planned? Are we going to eat?"

At that moment a wild apparition appeared in the doorway, fuming and shooting sparks, figuratively speaking, in all directions.

"Oh my gosh," whispered Amy.

"What's wrong?" asked Peppy who had his back to the door.

"There's someone who's not very happy."

Peppy turned around to see a furious Marla making a beeline for them.

"You bastard!" she snarled and slapped Peppy full on the face, then turned and walked haughtily out of the room.

"My word! Why did she do that? How could she know you? Oh, Peppy, did you do something after all to Peter?" Amy was almost in as much turmoil as Marla had been.

Peppy interrupted her, laughing, in spite of Marla's stinging blow. "I haven't done anything to Pe-tey. Yet. Come on, let's go to the party."

"But-but," sputtered Amy.

"But-but nothing. I know you love me, so quit worrying about Pe-tey. There's a beautiful dance in the ballroom waiting for us."

"But you can't go!"

"And why not? Is there something wrong with my attire?"

"Of course not. You look-uh-fabulous but that's the dance that Peter invited me to. I can't go with someone else after turning him down."

He laughed again, arose, and pulled her up. "Don't worry about it, Miss Amy Ann. Let's make an entrance."

And what an entrance they made, much to Amy's chagrin. The ballroom was packed with people: media photographers, reporters, and Peter's friends who, she knew, were expecting to see Peter Harris.

A huge banner that streamed across the room flabbergasted her, proclaiming in bold letters:

CONGRATULATIONS, PETER AND AMY!

But instead of entering with Peter, she had entered with Peppy! The room went wild, cameras flashing, even applause. Applause? Why applause, she wondered?

"Oh, Peppy," she cried, "what have we done?" Then she thought of the nerve of Peter Harris to think that she would become engaged to him just because he was who he was. Or did he consider marrying her, if that's what the banner meant, a reward for saving him from Peppy?

"Mr. Harris," shouted a member of the press, "when did you dump Marla?"

"Mr. Harris?" Amy exclaimed, turning to see if Peter had followed them into the room. There was no one behind them.

"Congratulations, darling," said Lily as she hugged her then turned to kiss Peppy on the cheek!

"Good work, old man," said Martin, shaking his hand.

To Amy the world had gone mad. What had Peppy done to Peter to make Peter's friends congratulate him? Then she spotted Amos across the room with an elegantly attired Janni, both of whom were smiling and laughing. Amy was in a room turned upside down, a notion reinforced by more familiar voices behind her.

She turned to see Donna, David, and Jeremy enter the room. When, she wondered, had they arrived from the Caymans?

"Well, honey," said Donna, "you did it. I knew you could."

"I-I did what?" she said, bewildered as ever as she hugged her and Jeremy.

"Why, you did just what I wanted you to do. You landed Peter Harris, Palmaltas' most eligible bachelor."

"No, no, I didn't! Maybe he told you that, but-but it's not true. My gosh, is that why you're here? Oh, Donna, there's been a terrible mistake."

Jeremy tugged at Amy's dress. "Amy, Amy," he cried happily, "are you really going to marry Peppy?"

"What?" she exclaimed, dizzy with all the confusion.

"Yes, old buddy," said Peppy, scooping the boy up in his arms. "She most surely is."

Standing there with her mouth open, not knowing what to say, Amy finally gasped, "But what about Peter?"

Amos stepped up and said, "You mean you haven't figured it out? My good bro Pepe is Peter Harris."

Twenty-one

Amos' statement, which was heard apparently only by those standing next to them, mainly Donna, David, and Jeremy, left Amy dazed and in shock. But no one gave her time to recover as the guests pressed forward to congratulate them. The evening became a blur as Peppy-Peter's masculine friends insisted on dancing with her and she was whirled about numb with incomprehension.

For a brief moment, Donna pulled Amy aside, both friends brimming with questions for the other.

"Amy," she said, "Jeremy insists that Peter is Peppy, his beach pal. How can that be? He, and later you, met Peppy while Peter was still in exile."

"Oh, Donna, I don't understand anything at all. Peppy and Amos claimed to be brothers but how could Peter and Amos be brothers? And what are you doing here? When did you arrive? Why didn't you come to your condo?"

"Peter called us this morning. I don't know how long this dance-party had been planned but it was apparent that it's been very recent since he decided to turn it into an engagement party. He sent a private plane for us and ensconced us in his mansion. He wanted to keep the whole thing a secret as a surprise for you. Well, from the look on your face, I can tell his plan worked. But we've got to get together soon, very soon, so you can tell me how you managed to reel in the biggest catch on Palmaltas after all, and on your own without my help. But one thing I must know right now. I just don't get this Peppy business and how is Amos involved?"

"Donna, I-I'm as confused as you are, more so probably. The Peter Harris I met was someone else."

"What?" she exclaimed, astounded.

"Yes, the man who I thought was the real Peter Harris is handsome and somewhat charming but to be honest I don't care for him. Everyone calls him Petey."

Donna's response wasn't what Amy expected. She burst out laughing. "You little twit! That's P.T., initials for Philip Terrence, Peter's obnoxious cousin. Can't you tell the difference in the sounds?"

"I thought everyone was speaking the local island accent or intonation."

"Good grief! I cannot believe that you mistook P.T. for Peter."

Before Amy could press her for more information, David whisked Donna away to dance.

Amy just stood there, more stunned than ever. Before she could regain her composure, Lisa Harris Rivera, who had just entered the ballroom, approached her. All at once she remembered the comment that Lily had made at her party about Peter and Lisa having the same color of hair. Now that she knew Peppy was Peter and not P.T., she could see that Lisa's platinum hair was as natural as her brother's.

"My dear," she said, "I am so relieved to learn that it is you who will be joining our family. Not only does Peter sing your praises but so do your wonderful friends, Donna and David Díaz. I've listened to them all afternoon." She gave Amy a light hug and kissed her cheek then disappeared into the crowd where a moment later Amy glimpsed her trying to ignore Amos.

Amos? Was Amos really the brother of Peter Harris and therefore of Lisa Harris Rivera? Or had Amos and Peppy-Peter simply been playing an elaborate joke on her? If so, why? Peppy was obviously

Peter Harris. All of the people in this room couldn't be involved in trying to fool her. They all recognized him as Peter, not Peppy. What had happened to Marla? She was furious with Peter but that was understandable considering that this party wasn't for her.

Amy's perplexed musings were interrupted as she was once again claimed by some obscure friend of Peppy-Peter's. Oh, what was she supposed to call him, she asked herself, as she was swept about the dance floor.

Suddenly someone tapped her partner's shoulder and said, "The rest of the dances belong to me."

She stared up into the scintillating blue eyes of Peppy who grasped her around the waist and pulled her close to him. A very slow musical number was playing and he crushed her body to his, swaying slowly to the rhythm. A warmth, a heat, that only the proximity of Peppy could induce, swept over her. The music slowed even more and Peppy wrapped his arms around her, brushing his lips against her hair. For the moment, at least, she felt that they were the only ones in the room, swaying in each other's arms. All at once the music changed and a Latin rhythm exploded, a sexy Latin rhythm. Peppy jumped back and began to writhe to the beat. He winked at her and led her into the steps. She caught on quickly and soon they were immersed into what Amy assumed was the rumba although she knew it could be any Latin dance. It didn't matter, though. They twisted and turned and moved to the beat. If she had thought the warmth she had felt earlier was as aroused as she could get, this dance put that feeling to shame.

Without warning Peppy pulled her close and led her to a side door where, unbelievably, they managed to sneak away from the festivities. With his arm around her, he led her out to their favorite perch, the end of the pier. Taking her into his arms, he began to kiss her, ardently, feverishly. Was this really going to be the rest of her life, she wondered? Living in the strong comfort of Peppy-Peter's arms? If this were a dream, she prayed that it never end.

But she had to wake up. No matter the sexual heat that she felt, she pushed Peppy back. She wanted answers. She was furious at the prolonged deception.

"All right, Mr. Peppy Peter Harris, whoever the hell you are, what has been going on? Why the masquerade? Are you and Amos really brothers?"

She pounded his chest demanding answers yet at the same time all she wanted was to melt back into his arms and stay there.

"Okay, okay," he said, giving her a roguish grin. "However, I must say that you've made the past few weeks most enjoyable."

"What? You've been having fun at my expense?" she cried out, indignant. Suddenly, she felt like such a fool and had the urge to run away and hide in embarrassment. But she had to have some answers.

"It wasn't meant to be," he stated, more soberly this time.

He tried to pull her to him but she would have none of it, no matter how much she really wanted him to hold her.

"Come on, Peppy, I have to know everything."

"You will, Amy, in due time. After all we have the rest of our lives together to talk about our courtship." He began to pull her into his arms but she pushed him away.

"Courtship? Is that what you call this-this masquerade?"

"Honey, this is a night for celebrating. Let's not argue. Let's savor the moment."

"You can't be serious! I don't understand a thing that has happened. You, Peppy the beachcomber, are really Peter Harris, playboy hotel tycoon. You have played an elaborate joke on me all summer long."

"It wasn't meant to be that way, honey. There are circumstances that you don't understand."

"Well, why don't you explain those circumstances to me?"

"Because, as I said, we have the rest of our lives to discuss them. To be honest I had not planned for the disguise to last as long as it did but, other circumstances aside, I wanted to be sure about you."

"What? You were testing me?"

"Honey, I have known a lot of women in my life and have even thought I loved some of them but they all seemed to be after my money and social position more than me."

"And you thought that I was after your money, too? I didn't even know you had money, Peppy."

"No, but you thought Peter Harris did and, admit it, you were intrigued by him."

"The person that I thought was Peter turned out to be your cousin and to be honest, I didn't really like him."

He laughed, infuriating her more. "When did you find out who P.T. was?"

"Donna just told me."

"Oh, Amy, Amy, let's not argue," he said quietly.

"Oh no, you aren't getting off so easy."

"Is that so?" he said with a roguish grin.

She looked at him with fire in her eyes. She realized that he wasn't taking her seriously and expected her now to fall into his arms, complete with forgiveness for all that he had put her through.

"Yes, that's so," she said with defiance.

"Oh, Amy," he moaned, "please don't take it so hard. We had fun, didn't we?"

"Fun? Fun? Here you were putting me through the ropes, trying to figure out if I was good enough for you! Well, Mr. Big Shot Billionaire Pretend Beachcomber-Fisherman, maybe I had the same thoughts about you. I have a past, too, you know, and perhaps I needed reassurance before I could trust you. No, don't come one step closer until you realize that I am a human being with feelings and that above all I must be able to completely have faith in the man I love. Then and only then will I consider your proposal, if that's what tonight's party was all about. You took me for granted, the homely little schoolteacher who you obviously thought would sigh and fall into your arms, grateful to be there. This has been too much for me to take in one night. If you love me, and I haven't heard any words to that effect, then you will kindly think about what I've said."

She turned and walked away, hoping against hope that he would come after her and beg her to stay with him. But he didn't come and when she reached the condo entrance, she glanced back and saw him still standing on the pier. Tears began to stream down her face. Now, what was she going to say to Donna? Oh, if only she had some place private to go to, someplace where she could sort out her feelings. Damn that Peppy anyway! He was everything that she could possibly ever want in a man and more. Had she ruined all of her chances with him? Was he that spoiled that he thought any woman he wanted would be overwhelmed with gratitude and do as he wanted? She was furious at the way she had been tricked all summer, just so he could be sure of her!

~ * ~

Standing on the pier and watching her stomp through the sand to the condo sent pains of anguish through him. What had he done? Had he gone too far with his little game to see if Amy really loved him? No woman had ever talked to him like that. Maybe he had deserved her tongue-lashing. Hell yes, he deserved it. At least he could admit that much to himself. Now, how was he going to get on her good side and convince her that he loved her and cherished her as he had no other woman and that above all she could trust him to eternity? What did she mean that she had a past, also? What had happened in Amy's life to make her say that? And why hadn't he considered that she might just be a tad upset with his masquerade? Just like the other women he had known, he had expected her to fall into his arms grateful to be there. Yes, he grimly admitted, he was definitely full of himself. She had certainly put him in his place. Now, he had to find a way to get out of it.

~ * ~

Amy wasn't ready to go inside the condo. The party was still in full swing and she imagined that the condo would be empty except for Salty. She wondered how long Donna and David would keep Jeremy at the party. She stood in the shadows and looked back at the pier where Peppy was standing, looking in her direction. Peppy? He wasn't Peppy after all. And it was Peppy with whom she had fallen in love, not Peter Harris. Peppy didn't exist. He was just a character that Peter had created. But why? Just to test her? That didn't make sense. Yet he had taken Daniel's place that first day when she arrived.

She watched him walk away from the pier but he didn't go back to the party. He walked to the shadows between the Marisol and the condo and disappeared. Perhaps he was going back to the mansion.

She sat down on the steps in front of the door that led to the back elevator. She was tired, emotionally tired, and her mind suddenly felt numb.

She had no idea how long she sat there before at last she got up and started to open the back door. Looking back one more time, she noticed that the party seemed to be over.

"Well, it should be," she muttered. "The party honorees left a long time ago."

She entered the elevator and went up, wondering if Donna, David, and Jeremy were back. She knocked on the door and walked in not waiting for an answer. Donna looked up from the sofa with an expression of amazement.

"What?" she exclaimed. "I didn't expect to see you tonight. I assumed you would spend the night in the mansion being ravished by the sexiest single man on the island."

Amy gave her a look of exasperation, not knowing how she was going to tell Donna what had happened.

Donna, however, seemed to notice her expression and said, "Honey, what's wrong? What happened?"

"Nothing happened, that's what. I'm still more confused than ever."

"I can understand that. My mind is reeling I can tell you. Amos and Janni have spent the evening explaining some of what has been going on to Lisa and me. It seems that David knew part of it as well. Amazing how these men can keep secrets."

Amy sank into the sofa cushion. "Well, would you mind enlightening me? I would kind of like to know what has been going on also. Peppy, I mean Peter, wouldn't tell me anything except that he was testing me."

"What? Why wouldn't he tell you the whole story?"

"I don't know, Donna. He said we had the rest of our lives to talk about it but that confused and upset me more."

Amy then told Donna exactly what she had said to Peter and how she had walked away from him.

"Do you remember when I arrived that someone besides Daniel met me at the airport?"

"Uh, yes. Oh my goodness, don't tell me that was Peter? Right under our noses?"

"Yep, and he was Jeremy's little friend Peppy, also right under your nose so to speak, except whenever you accompanied Jeremy to the beach he performed a disappearing act."

Donna just sat there staring at her not saying a word. Amy expected her to be angry with her but her response completely surprised her.

Donna, after a few moments of silence, said, "And to think it was all my fault that you and Peter didn't arrive together at his return party."

"Now that's another thing I don't understand. I was supposed to have met him at the pier but he arrived in a limousine."

"The way Janni explained it tonight was that Peter was going to meet you at the pier, walk you between the condo and the Marisol, across to the mansion, and get into the waiting limousine. You and he were going to make a spectacular entrance and Marla would retreat to the States. Only you didn't show up so he left, furious at you, thinking that you were more impressed with our rich friends than with him. However, when he couldn't find you at the party and I told him that you had left for another date, he felt somewhat relieved. He continued his act with Marla that night but didn't leave with her."

"Now that is something I don't understand. Didn't he have any feelings for Marla? That was rather a shabby way to treat a fiancée."

"There's a lot that I still don't know but I think that Peter somehow found out that she was a gold digger, just as I had suspected all along."

"Well, she was very angry tonight. She walked into the lounge and slapped Pep-Peter."

"Wow, I wish that I could have seen that. I thought I saw her and P.T. leaving with some very stern men tonight but I didn't pay much attention to them. I was more interested in you and Peter. Anyway, as I was saying, Peter sneaked out that night and saw you on the pier. He decided to give you another chance and asked for another date."

"And I saw him walk off into the night with Janni, his sister-in-law who I thought was his real girl friend."

Donna burst out laughing. "Yeah, Janni said that this has been a comedy of errors all along."

"It hasn't been a comedy for me. After what I said tonight, Pep-Peter may never speak to me again."

"Oh, Amy, I'm so sorry. I should never have insisted that you break your date with your beach friend. What a terrible buttinsky I've been. You are obviously able to pick and choose your own men. And you had chosen the right one, after all, and he was the same one that I had chosen. Well, I'll make it up to you if it's the last thing I'll ever do."

"You mean you're not mad at me for giving Peppy-Peter a piece of my mind tonight?"

"No, my dear, you did exactly what you should have done. As much as I adore Peter I realize that even he needed to be taken down a notch or two. No, don't you worry, everything's going to turn out just fine. Just wait and see."

"Well, wait is what I'm going to do. Although I still don't know everything that happened and why he did what he did, I have to sort out my emotions. I have to make sure that he loves me and respects me. To be honest I feel as if I've been treated as a little nitwit without an ounce of sense. And considering how I acted on that little island I'm beginning to wonder if maybe that's true."

Donna hooted. "At least you're honest about that yet that's Peter's fault for carrying on his masquerade for so long. But yes, you did let your imagination get the better of you."

"So Janni told you about my behavior on the island? Sheesh, how embarrassing."

"Trust me, in years to come you will laugh at it, too."

"Somehow, I doubt that. In spite of everything I love Peppy-uh-Peter. Oh, how am I ever going to accept him as someone else?"

"You don't have to accept him as someone else. You along with Amos and Janni know the real Peter."

"But haven't I ruined everything? What if he's so angry at what I said tonight that he never forgives me?"

"Never forgive you? Are you serious? That man went to a lot of trouble to fool you, a stupid thing to have done, mind you, but at least it shows how much he cares for you. No, Amy Ann, don't worry. Mr. Peter Harris is coming to the end of his philandering days."

Amy shrugged, gave a little half smile, hugged her and went up to bed. She couldn't sleep wondering how she was going to patch things up with Peppy. Peppy! Peppy who was really Peter. Her entire time in Palmaltas had been spectacular enough but tonight's events had become mind-boggling. Would Donna really take care of things with Peppy or would she make things worse? How would Peppy feel about her interfering? Perhaps in the morning she should tell Donna not to say anything to him and let the two of them work out their problems, that is, if Peppy still wanted to be with her. She tossed and turned, thinking one thing then reversing her thoughts. She finally fell into a restless sleep.

~ * ~

He started to walk toward the mansion just as he had done on the night that Amy had stood him up but he wasn't in the mood to face Lisa. Instead, he walked out to the front of the Marisol and followed the sidewalk that led past the hotel toward the cabins across from the airport. He wanted to see Amos and Janni so he turned in the direction of their cabin. He felt sure that they would understand his dilemma and would commiserate with him. When he arrived, the cabin was dark. Realizing that they were still at the party, he took off his jacket, tie, shoes and socks and rolled up his pant legs. With an air of despondence he walked down the beach to the shoreline and waded a mile or so in the lapping waves.

Finally, he turned back, hoping they would be home by now. He found them sitting on the back porch sipping drinks.

"Hey, bro, what goes?" asked Amos. "Where's your sand princess? When we saw bits of your tuxedo attire draped here, we figured the two of you just wanted to be alone out on the beach somewhere."

"She is just a bit peeved with me at the moment, maybe forever."

To his surprise Janni laughed. "And why would that be, dear brother-in-law? Because you ran a scam on her all summer long?"

He gave her a regretful look. "Yeah, you might say that. How did you know that was the reason?"

"Because I would be just a bit upset with you, too, if it were me."

"Yeah, I guess you would," he said despondently.

Janni laughed again.

"And just why do you think this is so funny?"

"Because, Pepe dear, this year two women have brought down the infamous skirt chaser Peter Harris."

"And just how do you figure that?"

"Marla came here with the intent of marrying you and acquiring all of your money and you almost fell for it. And when you finally did find the love of your life, you became just too confident, too cocky."

"Damn! I came here expecting to find a bit of sympathy and all I get is ridicule."

"Amy loves you, Pepe," said Amos. "Give her time. Besides, you have time now. The charade is over. Right after you and Amy left the party, P.T. and Marla were handed over to the Americans. Their drug dealing between here and the States went beyond greed into the realms of stupidity."

"I never thought that you would be able to hide in plain sight," said Janni. "But I will give it to you. You pulled it off even fooling Amos' friends except Ossie who knew what you were doing."

"My friends didn't know that Peter Harris was my brother," said Amos.

"I know," said Janni. "Some of your undercover stuff was kind of silly, though."

"What do you mean?" asked Pepe.

"Breaking and entering your own office to see if you could find evidence of what you suspected P.T. of doing."

"Yeah," said Amos, "that was dumb. Hiding out on the beach was one thing but to go up to your office, even after hours, just wasn't necessary. P.T. may not have been the brightest relative in the world but he wouldn't leave a paper trail for anyone such as your secretary to find."

"Okay, okay," said Pepe. "We all know what happened. No need to rehash it. P.T. and Marla are gone. We are going to work behind the scenes for David."

"And you are going to marry Amy," said Janni.

"And all of us will live happily ever after," joked Amos.

"I wonder," said Pepe.

Twenty-two

The next morning Amy awoke, showered, and dressed with a resolve to convince Donna not to say anything to Peppy. She smiled grimly at herself in the mirror. She had to stop thinking and saying Peppy. He was Peter and she probably would never see him as Peppy again with no more meetings on the pier or the beach. Instead, he would be the immaculate businessman that she had thought P.T. was. P.T.? Why hadn't she put two and two together? Both Lily and Donna had mentioned him and she had just let him fly right out of her mind. So, Peppy was no more. Could she love him as Peter? Would she even get the chance to find out?

She walked downstairs and found David and Jeremy out on the balcony eating breakfast.

"Where's Donna?" she asked.

"She had some errands to do," said David.

"So early?" gasped Amy, wondering if Donna might already be interfering on her behalf with Peter.

"We're going back to the Caymans, Amy. I still haven't finished the work I started there. We came back yesterday just for the party. That was quite a shindig, I must say."

"Yes, I guess so, in more ways than one. Did Donna tell you what happened between Peter and me?"

"To a certain extent. You and Peter are going to have some tall tales to tell your grandchildren."

"Grandchildren?" she blurted, almost crying. "What a thought, that's really stretching it! He hasn't proposed to me and if he does there's something he still hasn't told me."

Jeremy interrupted, having listened wide-eyed, to the two adults. "Peppy told me he was going to marry you, Amy."

She smiled at her little friend. "You do know that his real name is Peter, don't you, Jeremy?"

"Yeah, I think that's funny. Peppy isn't poor. He's rich."

"I guess you just never know about people," she said wistfully.

David gave her a stern look. "I think you're overplaying the melodrama, Amy. Sure, Peter went to great extremes in courting you but he had to know if you were the real thing."

"And I certainly had to know if he were the real thing, also. But there is so much that I don't understand. Can't you tell me why Pep-Peter did what he did? I mean, the whole story. He said there were other circumstances."

"Well, maybe I can help out not only from what Amos and Janni told us last night but also from what I had already learned from Peter."

Amy gave him a wan, little smile. "Okay, David, let me have it."

"The story begins with two little brothers, the sons of Peter Harris, American hotel magnate, who married a Palmaltan. He had two children by her, Peter Joseph and Lisa. He also had a mistress and had a son by her, Peter Amos, who kept his mother's maiden name of Soto. When the boys played together they went by their middle names, except that Joseph naturally became Pepe."

"Oh," gasped Amy. "That explains a lot."

"Uh-huh, it does indeed. Neither Peter's mother, a woman who devoted the rest of her life to religion, nor his sister Lisa accepted Amos. But Peter not only played with Amos when they were children, he also became his best friend. As they grew older, Peter would go to the cabin, dress comfortable like Amos, and drink a few beers. Most of the time he was too busy to get away from the hotel but when he did, he became the Pepe of his childhood. However, Peter Harris, Sr., had a brother who was his partner. That brother had a son named Philip Terrence, always known as P.T. However, P.T.'s father died young and Peter, Sr. took over the entire Harris hotel empire, which includes the Marisol and Bay View here on Palmaltas. When he died, Peter became CEO of the holdings here in Palmaltas and Amos became a silent stockholder in the two hotels and the ones in the States. Apparently, Amos is just as wealthy as Peter. P.T. was just low-level management and recently was brought to Palmaltas to prove that he was capable of running the family businesses in the States."

"But why do Amos and Janni live in that cabin and continue to work out of a boat concession if they are so wealthy?"

"My dear Amy, Amos loves that cabin. It was his mother's. Don't shed tears for him. Besides he wants to run the concession and the boat rides. Even before he knew about me and my plans for Palmaltas, Amos had decided to live and work like any Palmaltan. He didn't want to be considered as a society elite even though he has just as many qualifications as anyone else. No, when all Palmaltans are free, then and only then will Amos change, although I doubt if he will do so. He's a very happy man."

"Oh, how wonderful and admirable. And what about P.T.? I gather that Peppy and Amos do not care much for him, especially since he seems to be involved with drugs."

David laughed. "No one cares for that meddling jackass. He was the one who brought Marla to seduce Peter."

"What?"

"Marla came as a tourist to the hotel posing as an accomplished businesswoman who had been a model and now ran an agency. But it was all a front to impress Peter, who fell hard for her. But Amos kept seeing them together on the beach where they thought they were hidden from Peter and could talk freely. That idiot P.T. didn't know Amos was his cousin and talked right in front of him. Amos listened to their conversations and relayed them to Peter."

"But what about the drugs? Where do they come in?" In spite of being emotionally drained, Amy was intrigued by the Harris saga.

"P.T. and Marla wanted a piece of that action and thought that Palmaltas would be the perfect place to begin. Little did they know that the government runs the drug trafficking here. I'm sure that had Amos and Peter not caught on to what they were doing, the government would have thrown P.T. and Marla to the sharks, literally."

Amy sat up, jolted, but before she could say anything, David continued.

"It seems that Peter's masquerade started as a dare when one afternoon several months ago, Amos and Peter were lounging in front of the cabin and Ossie came by."

"Ossie was involved in this?"

"Not exactly. Ossie knew their father and family history. His family used to live near Amos and his mother. Anyway, he's one of the few people on this island who knew that Pepe was also Peter. No one was trying to keep a secret but as Peter grew older he became more Peter than Pepe. Anyway that afternoon, Amos, Ossie, and Peter were swapping yarns and sipping beers when some younger guys, including Bert and Eddie, passed by on the beach. Amos called them over and introduced Pepe his brother and offered them some beer. They joined them and had a good old time. When they left, Ossie said that those boys didn't have a clue that Pepe was *the* Peter Harris. They had accepted him completely as Amos' half-brother, a drifter or something. After Ossie left, Amos became serious and told about overhearing the latest conversation between Marla and P.T. There was no doubt that they were conspiring to get Peter to marry Marla so she could eventually divorce him and take him for a cleaning and P.T. also mentioned their plan for smuggling in drugs. Anyway, Amos said that Ossie had just given him an idea, that he bet that Peter could just change into his clothes and hang out on the Marisol beach and nobody would recognize him. Peter was very skeptical but Amos said that he needed to disappear for a while to see how Marla and P.T. handled the situation. They also needed to get proof of the drug smuggling. Amos dared him to become Pepe the beachcomber."

"So the disguise originated to catch Marla and P.T. and not to fool me?"

"Exactly! It seems that Peter was annoyed at Donna's attempts at matchmaking you two. He decided to use his Peppy attire to see if you really were the saint that Donna described."

"Oh, if only Donna hadn't interfered."

"I disagree."

"What? You approve of what she did? Even the return party where she caused me to cancel my date with Peppy?"

"I agree that she went overboard with that but I'm glad that she tried to convince Peter that her friend Amy was a better catch than Marla, although he already had his suspicions about Marla before you arrived. You fell in love with Peppy and he fell in love with you. That was what Donna wanted. It's all worked out."

"No, it hasn't."

"Well, time will tell."

"But, David, when you found out later that Peter was here all the time, even during the wedding, weren't you mad at him?"

He paused for a moment. "I think the way he and Amos went about spying on P.T. and Marla was not the best way to catch them. It was very amateurish to say the least but I have forgiven him for standing me up as best man at my wedding."

"When are you returning to the Caymans?" Amy asked, changing the subject.

"This afternoon."

"So soon?" Suddenly she wondered if Donna would have time to see Peter but surely that would be best if she didn't. If she and Peter Harris were to have a life together then it was up to the two of them to straighten out their problems and not rely on someone else. If! Why were there so many ifs in the world?

David stood up and said, "Come on Jeremy, let's get this show on the road. You and I have a lot to do this morning."

"I'm ready, David," he said, looking at his stepfather with great admiration as he pushed away from the table.

Amy felt a surge of happiness for the little boy. She loved him dearly. Suddenly a picture formed in her mind's eye of Jeremy and Peppy sitting side by side, each with a fishing pole dangling over the end of the pier. Peppy loved Jeremy, too, and that perhaps was the first thing that had endeared him to her. She waved to them as they left, wondering what it was that they had to do.

She felt lonely all of a sudden. What was she going to do after they left? Would she see Peter? Should she go down to the Marisol beach and talk to Amos? Should she just wait and see if Peter contacted her? She smiled at herself when she remembered that just a short while ago she had sat here in the apartment hoping that "Petey" would call her. She could feel her face burning in embarrassment at the mistake she had made.

~ * ~

Amy spent the morning on the balcony soliloquizing with Salty. "Oh, when is Donna coming back, Salty? What errands could she possibly have to run?"

The cat rubbed his head back and forth against her sandaled foot and purred.

"Well, you're not much help this morning. I need answers. Should I wait for Peter to come to me and apologize? And what if he has so much masculine pride that he won't do so? Look at what he put me through. Donna thinks he went to a lot of trouble to make sure I was *the one* for him and therefore shouldn't worry about him. But I don't really know him as Peter. What if he has a double personality? How could the Peppy that I knew be the Peter who fell for Marla?"

She looked down at the cat as if she were expecting an answer.

"Okay, so you think I'm getting carried away again just like I did on the island. Perhaps I am. But this waiting is killing me. What if he makes me wait a day or two or even a week? I'll go stark raving mad. I can't go home because I have to stay and take care of you." She smiled to herself at that thought.

"But if he makes me wait an eternity, what am I going to do in the meantime? Hang out with Bert and Eddie? I guess there could be worse fates."

Salty jumped into her lap and rubbed her chin.

She laughed and said, "That tickles, Salty, you little rascal. But do you know what makes me mad? I'm supposed to make Peter wait and here I am waiting on him to make the first move. What if he's in the same conundrum as I am or so mad at me for having the audacity to tell him off that he expects me to come crawling back to him?"

"Meow."

"Well, finally, you said something. But do you have any advice for me at all? One thing is for sure, I am not going to crawl back to him. So, that settles it. Mr. Peter Harris, the so-called most eligible bachelor on Palmaltas, is going to have to come to me and if he doesn't then at the end of the summer or whenever the Díaz family returns it's goodbye, Palmaltas, and good riddance, Mr. Harris."

She knew she was on the brink of tears because she couldn't bear to think that there was a possibility that she might not see Peter again. Surely anyone who had performed such a masquerade just for her benefit wouldn't give up just because she had spoken her mind. Her thoughts reeled back and forth until Donna, David, and Jeremy came back.

Donna bounced out to the balcony and greeted Amy. "Well, kiddo, we're off in a few minutes. We're going back in Peter's plane. Take good care of Salty and you be a good girl," she said with a twinkle in her eye.

"What? You're leaving now? Will you see Peter before you leave?"

"He arranged everything for us and there's no reason for him to see us off."

"Oh," Amy said, meekly, now realizing that she and Peter would have to settle their problems themselves without outside interference.

Donna gave her a big hug, as did Jeremy and David. Gathering their bags and wishing her and Salty well, they left.

Now Amy felt stricken. She was more alone than ever. She roused herself and decided that she had to do something. She couldn't sit around and mope. She went upstairs and changed into her bikini. Grabbing her beach towel and her beach bag, she went down the elevator, and passed the pool area waving to Eddie as she did so. She proceeded to the beach where she put down her towel and stretched out on it.

"Hey, Miss Amy, I see that you're still here at the condo," said Bert.

She glanced up at the handsome young man and said, "Hey, Bert, yes I am. I'll be here until the Díaz family finishes their business in the Caymans. I'm still condo and cat sitting."

"Is that so? Well, congratulations on your engagement. I guess you were really surprised," he said, squatting down beside her.

She shot up. "What? You know about last night?"

He laughed. "Yeah, all of Amos' friends knew about it."

"Well, I imagine he didn't tell you what happened. He may not know himself. So far, Peppy-er-Peter and I are not engaged."

"Oh, I'm so sorry, I guess I misunderstood. I thought last night was an engagement party."

"Don't worry, there was a lot of misunderstanding last night."

"And don't you worry, Miss Amy," he said standing up and starting to walk away. "I'm sure it will all work out the way you want it to work."

She lay back down, covered her eyes with her bag, and let the sun beat down on her body. If only Bert's prediction would come true.

~ * ~

From his office window he gazed down at her lying on the beach in the sun. She was so beautiful, so delectable. How had he spent most of the summer with her without devouring her? Their time together on the beach, even their lovemaking on the boat, had barely been a warm-up to what he really wanted to do to her. Well, now he had to do what he had to do. He could only hope that he had made the right decision.

Twenty-three

"Hmm, what have we here?" said a familiar voice.

She shuddered at the sound, a pleasant and thrilling shudder. Slowly she removed the bag and looked up. It was the face of Peppy!

"Why-why are you dressed like that? I would have thought you would be all business-like from now on."

He laughed. "Yes, I did go to work this morning in a suit but I saw you out here from my office window. So, I walked over to the mansion and changed."

"Why? Did you think I wouldn't speak to Peter Harris? Just to Peppy?"

"No, I think I was just nostalgic for the old days."

She burst out laughing in spite of herself. "The old days? Like last week?"

"Exactly. Do you think we can manage it, Amy?"

"Manage what?" she asked, daring to hope.

"No, wait a minute. I'm getting ahead of myself. Don't answer my question. Let's buy lunch at the cantina and take it out onto the pier. Let's not get ahead of ourselves."

Disappointed that their conversation wasn't going the way she wanted, she agreed to his request nonetheless. She got up, gathered her things, and walked with him to the cantina. He bought their lunches and they walked over to the pier, waving at Amos in the distance. They sat and ate in silence.

When they finished, Peppy said seriously, "Now, Amy, is the time for a serious question and a serious answer."

She waited expectantly. "Okay," she replied simply.

"Will you have a date with me tonight, a formal date, dressed as you were last night or something similar?"

She felt like saying something witty such as who was coming for her, Peppy or Peter, but his mood was so serious that she decided that now wasn't the time for frivolity. "Yes, I will. Where will we meet?"

He smiled. "Don't be silly. I'll pick you up at your own door at seven o'clock for dinner." He reached over and kissed her lightly on the cheek. Then he got up and gathered their lunch leftovers and walked away.

She couldn't believe that he had gone to the trouble of putting on his Peppy attire just to ask her for a formal date. She sat there on the pier for a while gazing out to sea, inhaling the salty air, letting the sun beat down on her, and listening to the mewing of the sea gulls. She was almost afraid to even think what this date request might mean. He was so inscrutable at times, well, almost all of the time, that she never knew what to expect. Would tonight be the night that ended the waiting, one way or the other? The peck on the cheek had not been very encouraging. She almost dreaded the upcoming date. He had said he was nostalgic for the Peppy days here on the beach. That must have meant, she thought, that Peppy would be gone forever. Wearily, she arose and walked slowly back to the condo. She was going to outdo herself tonight. If she was going to face rejection from Peter Harris then she would do it in style. She thought back to the demands that she had made last night and how she had expected him to try to understand her. Perhaps she had demanded too much for a man like Peter Harris. Well, at least the waiting would be over but she still had the summer to spend alone with a cat.

~ * ~

He stood at her door, hesitating to knock, wondering if what he was doing was the right thing. Amy had turned out to be unpredictable and he had no idea what her reaction was going to be tonight. But, he had to get this over with. Waiting wouldn't accomplish anything. He knocked.

The door opened and the vision that stood there overwhelmed him. She was dressed in a pale lavender dress that emphasized her tan, her figure, and her big brown eyes. Her shiny dark brown hair flowed over her bare shoulders framing her face in loveliness. He inhaled deeply.

~ * ~

She stood looking at him, just as handsome as he had been last night although his attire wasn't as formal. There was nothing that she wanted more than to be with him but she dreaded that the evening might prove to be other than what she desired.

"Come in," she said softly.

"Just for a few minutes. We have a reservation at the Marisol dining room."

Suddenly she laughed. "And why would the owner of the Marisol need a reservation?"

He smiled and said, "I'm just trying to be a regular guy going out with a regular girl."

"Oh, is that so? Well, in that case, let's go."

They went down the elevator in silence. At the door they exchanged pleasantries with Ossie then walked over to the Marisol. Once they were seated in the dining room in a private corner by a window that had a view of the Marisol gardens beyond, he ordered the house wine for them.

"Since it's the house wine and my house, I know that it's a good wine," he said.

"I'm sure it is," she said, wondering if their conversation was going to be as inane as this all evening. Surely, he wasn't as nervous as she was.

The waiter brought the menu and she told him to order for both of them since he knew what the specialties were. He ordered soup, salad, broiled lobster with drawn butter, and lime mousse. They ate in silence, once in a while exclaiming how good the meal was. Amy was getting increasingly nervous. This wasn't the way she wanted the most romantic meal she could have ever dreamed of to go. She knew Peppy well enough to be comfortable in his presence. But this wasn't Peppy, she told herself. This was Peter.

Finally the meal was over and he suggested a walk around the grounds. They left by a side door and were immediately engulfed by a warm breeze and the fragrances of tropical flowers. Amy found herself walking side-by-side, arm-in-arm, with the man she loved into a tropical paradise. She had never visited this part of the Marisol grounds before.

"It's lovely here," she said.

"Yes, it is. My mother planned these gardens and Lisa manages them now."

"How wonderful." How she wished she could say something stimulating and exciting. However, at the mentioning of Lisa a thought did occur to her.

"At the party I thought I saw Lisa snubbing Amos yet Donna said that Amos and Janni explained everything to her and David and Lisa. What kind of relationship does Lisa have with Amos?"

"Up until now, they didn't have one. When I disappeared, Lisa could and should have gone to Amos for help and support but she was too stubborn to do so. For that reason I left her in the cold as to what I was doing. She didn't like P.T. anymore than anyone else did but she supported him for a while. Then when I returned she was mad at all of us."

"I guess that explains her behavior at Lily's party. And don't tease me about my confusion with her dyed hair."

He gave a nervous laugh. "I wouldn't dream of it. It's a natural color that we both inherited from our paternal American grandmother and we are both well-known for the color of our hair. I always wore my hair much longer than it is now. When I became Pepe to spy on P.T. and Marla, Janni cut it very short so it wouldn't look so platinum."

"But does Lisa accept Amos now?"

"She's beginning to come around. At least she listened to Amos and Janni. She's not a bad sort, really, just needs pushes in the right direction once in a while."

They walked through the gardens in silence then turned back and ambled toward the beach.

~ * ~

He felt very nervous. The meal had been pleasant but she had been too formal although he was pleased that she had inquired about Lisa and Amos. How was he ever going to get through this? What was her reaction going to be? Never had he imagined that he would be in this kind of situation. Well, maybe he deserved it. But he couldn't prolong this anymore. He had to do it.

~ * ~

Reaching the beach, he stopped and turned her toward him. He gazed down into her eyes and she wondered, heart pounding, what he was going to do, kiss her or tell her that it was all over? The waiting ended. He pulled her to him and began to kiss and caress her. But she did what she had to do. She pushed him away.

"What do you think you're doing?" she asked.

"You mean you don't know? I-I know about your past, Amy. Donna told me about Rick this morning. I understand why you have behaved the way you did and I hope that you will understand my behavior also."

"Donna? You saw her? She told you?"

"Yes, and now I want to know if you will marry me."

She stood there, breathless, almost afraid to speak. Gathering her strength, she said, "Then please do it properly."

He moaned and fell to his knees. "Miss Amethyst Andrews, will you marry me?"

"That depends," she said stoically as he moaned again. "Will I marry Peppy or Peter J. Harris?"

"Both of us and you may call me whatever you want."

"And if I should call you Peppy in front of your upper-echelon friends?"

"They will just think it's a cute affectation on your part. So, is that a yes?" He started to get up.

"Hold on," she demanded, pushing him back. "There's something else you haven't told me and I can't marry you until you do."

A wry grin spread across his face as he stood up and took her into his arms. "Of course, and I've wanted to say it for a very long time. Amy, I love you and I always will."

She melted into the strong protection of his arms, intending to stay there forever.

Meet Tricia Lee

Tricia Lee is a native Oklahoman who has lived in the Southwestern United States, Mexico, Puerto Rico, Portugal, Spain, and England. A former Spanish and art teacher, she has written articles for *Seasons for Writing*, a newsletter for writers, and has had published a short story in *Boys' Quest* Magazine. She was a humor, travel, food columnist for a bilingual Web site.

Letter to Our Readers

Enjoy this book?

You can make a difference.

As an independent publisher, Wings ePress, Inc. does not have the financial clout of the large New York publishers. We can't afford large magazine spreads or subway posters to tell people about our quality books.

But we do have something much more effective and powerful than ads. We have a large base of loyal readers.

Honest reviews help bring the attention of new readers to our books.

If you enjoyed this book, we would appreciate it if you would spend a few minutes posting a review on the site where you purchased this book or on the Wings ePress, Inc. webpages at: https://wingsepress. com/

Thank You

Visit Our Website

For The Full Inventory
Of Quality Books:

Wings ePress.Inc
https://wingsepress.com/

Quality trade paperbacks and downloads
in multiple formats,
in genres ranging from light romantic comedy
to general fiction and horror.
Wings has something for every reader's taste.
Visit the website, then bookmark it.
We add new titles each month!

Wings ePress Inc.
3000 N. Rock Road
Newton, KS 67114